FRIENDS BUT A POSSESSION

Just The Way It Was

To Luke Jordan

JC Woods

A Historical Novel By

T WOODS

AuthorHouse™ LLC
1663 Liberty Drive
Bloomington, IN 47403
www.authorhouse.com
Phone: 1-800-839-8640

Cover by: Troy C. Woods III

Published by AuthorHouse   02/17/2014

ISBN: 978-1-4918-5380-1 (sc)
ISBN: 978-1-4918-5379-5 (hc)
ISBN: 978-1-4918-5354-2 (e)

Library of Congress Control Number: 2014900915

Foreword

SLAP, GROAN; SLAP,GROAN; SLAP, GROAN! The slave, Big Man, was being beaten with "Black Annie", the long leather strap used by the Overseer to punish slaves. The Overseer had been ordered to punish Big Man by the plantation owner, John Inman.

Big Man was Buck Inman's personal slave. Man was three years old when he was given to Buck. Buck was one year old at the time. Now they were both young men. Although Buck tried to intercede, Big John, his father, was in complete control of the plantation. Buck had to make a decision. Did he want to remain on the family plantation where slavery was a way of life or did he want to leave? Since he abhorred the institution of slavery, he chose the latter. Big John would not allow Buck to take Big Man with him, so Buck left the plantation with just his clothes and the large inheritance that he had received from his grandparents.

Buck made his way west to the Mississippi River. Thru different circumstances, he found himself owning six thousand acres in the Mississippi-Yazoo Delta. He was enjoying life being a recluse in this wild unsettled area until he received a telegram at the closest town. His father had died. Buchanan Inman was now Master of five hundred slaves and the owner of an eight thousand acre cotton plantation back in South Carolina. His mother and two sisters needed him at home. He had to decide what to do!

This is the story of a young man that hated slavery, was opposed to secession, but ended up owning a plantation, five hundred slaves and fought in the war for the Confederacy. Although Buck still owned Big Man, they remained the closest of friends through it all. FRIENDS, BUT A POSSESSION; THATS JUST THE WAY IT WAS in the era they lived in!

ACKNOWLEDGEMENT

My wife Ann Inman Woods, who uncomplainingly
reviewed all of my rough drafts.

My sister Maxine Murrell,
who spent weeks reviewing and editing.

My son, Troy Crawford Woods III, who arranged the drafts
for publication and did the artwork for the cover.

My daughter, Lydia Woods Goodman, who edited
and corrected the final proof.

1

Early Life

The lake was the former riverbed of the mighty Mississippi River. It was formed when the River changed courses thousands of years ago. Nine miles long and a mile wide, its only connection to the river now was a narrow chute about 200 yards long. Standing like sentinels all around the lake were large cypress trees. Most of the taller ones had their tops destroyed by lightning. The Spanish moss growing from their limbs gave the trees an eerie appearance in the bright moonlight. The only sounds breaking the silence was the croaking of the bullfrogs and the occasional bellowing of a bull alligator resting between the huge cypress knees.

In the hot, sultry Delta night, a lone man sat on his horse gazing out on this majestic sight. To his knowledge, he was one of the first white men to set eyes on the beautiful lake that the Choctaw Indians had described to him several weeks earlier at their village located on several mounds.

Buchanan Inman was a young man of twenty-six years of age. Of medium height, he was heavily muscled yet had a slim appearance. The hot Mississippi sun had turned his natural dark complexion to a deep bronze and had caused his hair to become even lighter than its natural blond hue. Blue piercing eyes gazed out from under his hat. In South Carolina, his self-assured demeanor, handsome features and social position had made him one of the most sought after marriage prospects material. The young belles that traveled in his social circles considered him a prime candidate for a husband. They were thrilled if they could get his name on their dance cards

1

when attending the many balls that were given to entertain the young people in the privileged world where they grew up.

Now, viewing the beauty of the lake that the Indians simply called Yazoo, he reflected on the events that had brought him to this place: THE IMAGE OF A BLACK SLAVE TIED TO THE STAKE AND BEING WHIPPED WAS STILL VIVID IN HIS MIND. HE STILL COULD HEAR HIS GROANS!

Buchanan, or Buck, as he was called, was born in 1832 on a large sprawling plantation that was located near Inman, South Carolina. This village was named after his paternal grandfather. The Inmans were some of the first settlers to lay claim to this rich soil that produced bountiful cotton every year. Buck's father, John, had inherited the place and had added many acres. By the time Buck was born, the plantation comprised some 8,000 acres.

Buck's mother, the former Georgia Susanna Peacock, was wealthy in her own right. She had married John at the age of eighteen. Georgia was a lady that was remembered as the most beautiful girl in the area while growing up. When one looked at her, one could see where Buck had inherited his good looks. Still slim, she had the same blond hair as Buck and the same piercing eyes. The only contrast in their coloring was that her skin was more of an olive complexion. Her aristocratic carriage and pride of family could be traced back to her early ancestors. Most Southern aristocrats could recite their family linage for generations. Georgia was no exception, since she was extremely proud of her forebears. Georgia, or Mistress as she was called, was a direct descendant of the Peacocks of Jamestown. Her ancestors had slowly migrated inland to the area around Inman, South Carolina. She was a stickler for maintaining the customs and way of living that had been passed on to her from her parents. The house and grounds had to be immaculate. Every meal was a seated affair with the slaves dressed in black trousers, white shirts, and white gloves. Meals were served on fine china and beverages in the crystal glasses—all of which she had inherited from her parents and grandparents. The silverware was an inheritance from Big John's side of the family.

She was always fully dressed with her hair and makeup done to perfection. Her clothes, many of which were ordered from France, were of the latest style. She, as many Southern women, was proficient at the piano. These ladies were taught music and were expected to perform at any social occasion. The Mistress was extremely proud of her race, her place, and her grace. She had become a Christian as a teen-ager and regularly attended the Episcopal Church. Strangely, she saw no conflict between being one of the largest slaveholders in South Carolina and her commitment to Christ. In fact, she had insisted that a balcony be built in the local church so that the slaves could worship with the whites. The slaves just could not sit with their owners.

John Inman, on the other hand, made no pretense of following Christ. Oh, he regularly attended church with his wife and children, but when he left the church on Sunday, he left behind any thought of religion or Christianity. He was too self-sufficient to need the guidance of Christ in his daily life. In fact, he did not feel that he needed anyone or anything. As master of one of the largest plantations in the state and owner of 450 slaves, he was as self-sufficient as one could get. He stood six foot and weighted about 260 pounds. He had black hair and hazel eyes. He was broad-shouldered with the dark complexion for which all Inmans were known. He was quite a man!

The Inman place was the typical plantation of that era. The only thing that set it apart was its vastness. The main house, or the "Big House" as the slaves called it, had the customary Greek revival columns found on many plantations in the South. It had four large columns on the front, and four on each side, for a total of twelve. U-shaped porches wrapped the house upstairs and down. These ran the width of the back and were used as sleeping porches when the weather was extremely hot. Semi-attached to the structure was the kitchen where the meals were prepared by the plantation cooks.

A massive structure, it had eight bedrooms, two drawing rooms or parlors, entry hall, dining room, smoking room and a library. The library was Big John's pride. He boasted that he had the largest collection of books west of Charleston. He allowed no one to use the library without his express permission. Family portraits and tapestries decorated the walls of the mansion. Fine oriental rugs covered the floors.

With sixteen foot ceilings downstairs and twelve foot ceilings upstairs and a massive staircase rising between, the Inman Mansion represented all of the wealth and power of the family.

In the rear of the house was located the dairy room, smokehouse, blacksmith shop, barns and well as all the other structures needed for the operation of such a large plantation. Down a shady road to the rear of these structures were the slave quarters. They lined either side of this dirt road for approximately a mile. The houses in the quarters were of two types. One was a simple one room cabin with a large fireplace used for warmth and cooking. These cabins were home to families that were crowded together under one roof. Although not legally recognized by the state, many of the male and females heading up these families considered themselves married. They had performed the marriage ceremony called "jumping the broom". This union was recognized by the slaves and also by the Master.

The other type structures were buildings sixty feet long and twelve feet wide. This space was divided into five rooms. A long porch ran across both the front and back of these buildings. In these structures lived the unmarried slaves. Four or five single men shared a room. The single women also shared rooms. With about 450 slaves on the premises, the slave quarters had the feeling of a small village. The only other abodes for slaves on the place were the cabins reserved for the house slaves. The preferential treatment of this class of slaves allowed them to have cabins with two rooms.

Over to the side of the barn, stood a four room cottage that housed the overseer and his family. The overseer was charged with keeping the slaves under control and seeing that the orders of the master were carried out.

Another one room building on the plantation was the schoolhouse. Here, not only were the family children educated, but also the children from surrounding plantations. The teacher, usually a man, was an educated professional. This teacher was employed by Big John and given the respect that his position warranted. He was allowed to live and eat in the Big House just as though he were family. This educational system was an alternative to sending the children away to boarding school. There were no schools for slaves on the place, for as Big John always said, "You don't have to know how to read and write to chop and pick cotton!"

During this period, there were two types of slave holders. One type was the slave holder that owned just a few slaves-sometimes, just one. These owners had small farms or lived in town. It was not unusual for these owners to work side by side with their slaves. Quite often a relationship developed between them more like family or hired help instead of slave/master.

On the large plantations like Inman, these personal relationships did not develop often due to the large number of slaves in comparison to the number of whites on the place. These large plantations were an economic system where 10% of the Planters owned 90% of the slaves. In fact, most of the whites had no slaves at all. With land selling for $25.00 an acre or less, and the cost of slaves averaging $1000.00 each, the average white man could not afford to join the elite group of slave holders.

There were several categories of slaves on the plantations. The largest group was the field hands. They were responsible for the production of the crops and raising the livestock. Their schedule varied according to the seasons. They had to work long hard hours during the planting and harvesting season. They broke the ground, planted, weeded and harvested the crops. During this season, they worked from dawn to sun down, six days a week. Their only respite was Sunday and the days when it rained. Sunday was a free day to be spent resting, cooking, mending, washing cloths and socializing. Another class of slaves were the specialty slaves. In the social order they were a class above the field hands. These slaves provided the labor that kept the plantation running smoothly. This class was made up of carpenters, hostlers, yardmen, milkers, etc . . . Their daily jobs were not easy, but they were much preferred to the long hours in the fields.

The most sought after position by the slaves was being a house slave. These individuals provided the care that made the lives of the residents comparable to some of the royalty of Europe. There were cooks, maids, butlers, nursery workers, carriage drivers and even someone to keep wood in the fireplaces during the coldest of nights. Most of the whites had their own personal slave that was given to them at birth. The fact that the white child and slave grew up and played together made for a strange relationship. FRIENDS, BUT STILL A POSSESSION.

Another thing that was puzzling to an outsider was the relationship between the owners and the slaves. They didn't understand that most of the house slaves had been owned all of their lives by their masters, their masters' parents and sometimes their masters' grandparents. In some cases there were three or four generations of whites and three or four generations of slaves living and dying together on the plantation. By being confined daily to the big house, these slaves became attached to the whites and the whites to them. FRIENDS, BUT STILL A POSSESSION. Many a nursemaid felt comfortable scolding a young master even after he became grown. Because of their relationship, he would accept a chastisement from her, whereas if a field hand had said anything comparable, his anger would have been kindled and the slave punished for getting out of their place. So it went on for generations. The nurses' child would become the personal slave of the master's child and then the offspring of companion slave would become part of the Big House's staff. FRIENDS, BUT STILL A POSSESSION.

So it was with Big Man. He was the personal slave of Buchanan Inman. He had been given this name not because he was large, which he was, but because at an early age he had exhibited an unusual maturity for his age. The slaves would say, "Look at him, he acts like a big man!" So, he became Big Man Inman, taking on the last name of his owners as was customary. As an adult he lived up to his name. He was 6'6 and 280 pounds of muscle. He had a reddish color to his skin that set him apart from the other slaves. However, this was not unusual. The landowners did not make any preference as to where their slaves originated. They could have been from Africa, South America, the Caribbean, or from Native Americans. They didn't care. They just wanted them to be able to work. It was rumored that Big Man had the blood of a Tunica Indian chief running thru his veins. It was said that this chief had been captured by a Cherokee raiding party in Mississippi and brought back to Virginia to be sold into slavery. Big Man had been selected by the master to be Buck's personal slave. He was given to Buck on Buck's first birthday. Big Man was four.

Big Man was chosen for this position due mainly to the fact that Man's mother, Birdie was the cook for the Inman clan. A heavy set woman with a sunny disposition, she ruled the kitchen as if it were her domain. It was! She was in control and her assistants had better not forget it. She was renowned for her cooking. Everything was fattening. Her theory was "if it ain't fattening, it ain't no good". For breakfast, she prepared ham, bacon, eggs, biscuits and white milk gravy. Also available would be homemade jelly, molasses and local honey. The meal was complete when washed down with milk from the dairy or scalding boiled coffee.

As soon as the table was cleared and the dishes washed, Birdie and her assistants would start the dinner meal. On the plantation, one had breakfast, dinner and supper.

The family's favorite noon meal was fried chicken, green beans cooked with a slice of pork meat, mashed potatoes with gravy, fried okra, sweet corn, turnip greens and corn bread. The greens had to be covered in hot pepper sauce. Also served would be fresh tomatoes and cucumbers. The preferred beverage was Southern sweet tea. The tea was not mildly sweet, but really sweet! The secret to getting this taste was adding the sugar to the brewed tea while hot and then diluting with water. The favorite desserts were banana pudding and buttermilk pie. Birdie was also an expert at making pecan pies.

As could be expected, no family could be expected to eat all of this at one sitting. The leftovers were set aside to be eaten at supper. One of the perks in working at the Big House was the privilege of getting to share in these sumptuous meals. The other slaves, although fed substantially, were allowed to cook the poorer cuts of meat such as pig's feet, hog heads made into souse, back bones and other less desirable cuts. In season, they were allowed fresh vegetables. Another staple at the slaves' meals was hoe bread. This was cornbread placed on a flattened field hoe and then cooked on an open fire. Although their fare was not as choice as slaveholders, it was enough to allow them to work their long hours. Some owners took pride in how they fed and treated their slaves. Others treated their slaves well because of the investment that they represented. Just as malnourished mules could not be expected to work; neither could malnourished slaves. It was the overseers' responsibility to see that the slaves were kept in good condition so that they could perform the back breaking work that was required of them. TAKEN CARE OF, BUT STILL A POSSESSION.

Buck Inman grew up in this idyllic environment. His early days were filled mostly with playing with Big Man. They had the full run of the Big House, the out buildings and the grounds. They grew up wrestling and playing. They loved to sneak into the kitchen for left-over cake or pie when they thought Birdie wasn't watching. What they didn't realize was that Birdie saw them and was thrilled to see them as they sneaked in. "You boys better git out of hea before I takes a broom to you!" she would yell. They would scurry to the door to escape her mock wrath.

It never occurred to Buck and Big Man that there was any difference in their status in life. They were simply buddies and companions. Big Man, though just three years older than Buck, thought of himself as an older brother, mentor, and protector. Buck admired him and tried to do everything that Big Man did. Big Man was a friend and a companion . . .

BUT, STILL A POSSESSION.

As Buck became older, he started to notice a difference in his way of life and Big Man's. He noticed that while he was well dressed, Man's clothing was often patched. He noticed that on his eight birthday he had a large party and received many presents. On Man's birthday, he only received a small cake made by Birdie. He noticed that when he received his first pony, Man did not have one. Man had to be content leading Buck around on his new pony. He noticed that when he started school, Man was not allowed to attend. As Big John said, "You don't have to know how to read and write to be a slave." Strangely enough, this situation did not seem odd to Buck—nor anyone else on the plantation. The whites were the masters and the slaves were possessions required to serve. This was the way it had been, it was, and it would be!

2

Buck Leaves

As Buck matured, he began to be included in the group of planters that gathered in the smoking rooms of the grand plantation homes. Here, the older men liked to sit, smoke their cigars, sip their brandy and discuss local and national affairs. As Buck listened, the conversations always seemed to turn to the subject of slavery and the possibility of war.

They would ask, "Have you read that book, *Uncle Tom's Cabin*? Can you believe that she wrote that without ever having been on a plantation? She doesn't know what she is talking about. I don't treat my slaves like that. Hell, I paid too much for them to abuse them like she says. I hear congress is going to pass laws to make slavery illegal. That ain't going to happen. If they did that our whole economy would collapse."

Continuing the conversation, others would add, "Well, it ain't going to happen because if they did the Southern states would secede. You know that we joined the Union voluntarily and by God we can leave anytime we wish. If we secede you know that will lead to war."

"So what?"

"Well, you know the North has all of the factories and out numbers us ten to one. Man, that don't mean nothing. One southerner can whip any 20 Yankees.

"Ha! Ha!" Big John interjected. "You know that the issue is states' rights. When the states joined the Union, they made sure that they gave only specific powers to the Union. Legally, the Union can't tell us to do or not TO do anything."

"Well, they can if they send enough troops in."

"They aren't going to do that. They need us and they know that England will intercede on our behalf. England has to have our cotton for textile mills," replied Big John. So on and on the conversations would go as the timetable for war moved relentlessly on.

Returning from a social visit to Atlanta, Buck tied his horse in front of the Big House. Upon entering the massive entry hall, he heard wailing coming from the kitchen. Rushing into the kitchen, he found Birdie prostrate on the kitchen table. Her sobs were shaking her whole body. Buck could not imagine what had happened to cause this turmoil. He thought that maybe she had injured herself. "What in the world is the matter?" he asked.

"Oh, Mr. Buck!" she exclaimed. "They done took Big Man down to the quarters to be whupped with Black Annie."

"This can't be true, there must be some mistake," Buck said. Now, Buck knew that Big Man was not in good graces with Big John. Big John had caught him in the library reading. Over the years, Big Man had taught himself to read while working at the Big House. Not only was this illegal in many parts of the South, but Big John personally opposed any education of slaves. Also, no one used HIS library without his permission. But still, Buck could not imagine any circumstances that would lead to Big Man being whipped.

"Tell me what happened," he commanded.

Between her sobs, Birdie related the story the best she could. It seemed that Big John's friend, Senator Featherston, had stopped by for a visit. It became time for his guest to depart, so Big John sent Big Man to fetch the Senator's horse. Dutifully, Big Man complied. He then held the horse's head as the Senator prepared to mount. Now, the Senator was a short, fat man and it was quite a stretch for him to get his foot up in the stirrup and his hand on the saddle horn. It seemed in this instance that things did not go well for him. Just as he got one foot in the stirrup and reached for the saddle horn, the horse moved. Although Man held the horse's head, Senator missed the saddle horn with his hand and fell backwards. Being rotund, he looked as if he had rolled up on his back and his feet went up in the air. Although Man tried to contain his mirth, he could not help but smile. The problem was that the Senator was looking dead at him when this emotion flickered over his face. "What are you laughing at?" the Senator demanded.

"Nothing, Suh," Man replied.

The infuriated visitor turned to Big John and said, "What kind of slaves do you have? Do you allow them to laugh at your guest?"

Big John replied indignantly, "Of course not!"

"Well, if you are any kind of a white man at all you will have him punished severely and, in fact, I demand that you do so!" said the Senator. Big John, not wanting to be considered a "Nigra Lover", decided to take the easy way out. He ordered Man back to the quarters to be punished.

SLAP, GROAN, SLAP, GROAN. Buck could hear "Black Annie" being applied to Big Man as he rushed toward the quarters. There was a pole set in the ground near the center of the quarters just for such an occasion. Man was stripped to the waist and tied to the post. The overseer was sweating profusely as he labored to deliver the cruel blows to Man's back. "Black Annie" was the name that the slaves had given to the strap used for punishment. It was a quarter inch thick, four inches wide and six feet long. It had an eighteen inch handle so that the overseer could get both hands on it. With each blow, it raised a blister across the back. After several blows, the back would be raw and bleeding. Many a slave had collapsed and passed out under this dreaded punishment. The rest of the slaves were gathered around to watch. It was a rule on the plantation that if a slave was whipped—the other slaves had to watch. It was thought that this would be a deterrent to trouble from the other slaves.

"Wait!" Buck said, as he arrived on the scene. "What is going on here?"

"We are teaching this nigra that he can't disrespect white folks!" said Senator Featherston.

Buck turned to his father and said, "I know that you know that Man does not deserve to be punished. He has been practically raised in our house and he has never caused any problems. I am asking that you forget and put an end to this."

"No," said Big John. "He has affronted our guest and needs to be taught a lesson. As for you, it is time that you learned what running a plantation with hundreds of slaves is all about. Your mother has shielded you for far too long! I have sheltered you too much! You have to understand that these slaves are our property—not our friends. We can do to them as we will. We also cannot show any weakness. Weakness invites a slave uprising. If you are going to be running this place someday, you have to understand this."

Buck replied, "Well, if this is the way it is, I don't want any part of running this place. You know that I have never believed in slavery. So, I tell you what, you just keep Inman Plantation. All I want is Big Man. He can go with me as a free man. After all, you gave him to me as a child.

"No!" said Big John. "I will not have him set free, and you can't take him with you. I may have given him to you, but I never signed him over to you. Therefore, he is still legally belongs to me!"

Frustrated, Buck turned on his heel knowing that there was nothing that he could do. As he headed toward the Big House he could still hear the SLAP, SLAP of 'Big Annie'. As Buck stormed into the house, he was met by his mother.

"Buck, what in the world is wrong with you? I have never seen you so upset."

"Mother, Buck replied, "I have had enough of father and his way of running things. He is overbearing and cruel. I am leaving Inman Plantation forever. The only thing I am taking is my inheritance from my grandparents, my gun, and my horse. I don't expect or want anything from Big John. You know that I love you and my sisters, but I have to get away. I don't believe in slavery and I want no part of it. I will write you when I figure where I am going. Right now, I just don't know."

3

Traveling

Buck stood on the upper deck as the ship slowly moved downriver with the current of the mighty Mississippi River. He watched the swirls and whirlpools form and dissipate in the murky waters. He marveled at the power that this stream represented. The only thing that kept it from spreading out over the plantations on either side were the levees built by the plantation owners around their property. These earthen works had been laboriously built by the plantation slaves over the years. Without the levees, their homes and plantations would be inundated when the Spring floods up north sent their torrents of floodwater into this mighty river. He was able to see the great homes that had been built along the river. They came into view as the paddle wheeler slowly approached his destination, New Orleans.

"A magnificent view," said a young man as he walked up to the rail by Buck.

"Yes, I don't think I have ever seen such a river," Buck replied.

"That it is why the Indians called it the 'Father of Waters'," said the young man as he reached out his hand to Buck to introduce himself. "You know we can thank our Yankee cousins for the wealth that we have here. For years, they have sent their topsoil down the river to enrich the land that these plantations sit on. This is why we have the richest land in the world. My name is May. John May."

"Buchanan Inman or just plain Buck," Buck replied.

John May was tall, slim and good looking with dark curly hair. His aristocratic bearing and way of speaking told one immediately that he was a man of wealth, education, and breeding. The May family was one of the old families of New Orleans. They lived in the city where his father had offices but their land holdings stretched along the river road toward Baton Rouge. High-spirited and fun filled, John was a young man that everyone liked immediately. Buck was no exception. It seemed that an instant bond formed between the two young men.

As the boat edged into the docks of New Orleans, May inquired of Buck as to his plans. Buck did not go into a lot of detail about the situation back home, but simply stated that he was just traveling without any particular destination. He said that he had always heard about New Orleans and wanted to see it for himself.

" Well, my man, you are here and I am going to show you the sights. I was raised here and I know every nook and cranny of the French Quarters. I know all of the saloons, I know where the card games are being played, and I know where all the pretty girls make their appearances. We are going to have us a good ole time. I want you to come and stay at our house for as long as you wish."

"John May, you hardly know me and I do not want to be an imposition on your family," said Buck.

"Hey, you are not going to be an imposition on anyone. My parents are in England trying to spend some of their money, so we will have the house to ourselves with the exception of the house servants."

" Well, all right, if you are sure," Buck replied.

When the boat docked, the new friends set off in a rented carriage to the palatial mansion of the May's. On the way, John told Buck about his latest adventure. It seemed that John had been in a card game on the paddle wheeler. It had been a high stakes game and John had been the big winner. Not only had he won the pot of money, he had also won a six thousand acre Spanish land grant somewhere north of Natchez, Mississippi. Although he was exuberant about the money, he was really excited about his newly acquired land. "Buck, I'll tell you what. After we get tired of playing here in New Orleans, we'll board the paddle wheeler from here to Natchez. I've never been to Natchez, but I hear that it is wide open and full of fun. From there we will buy us a couple of horses and see if we can't find this wild land that I have acquired."

Always adventurous, Buck said, "Sounds good to me. I certainly don't have any other plans." They continued to make plans for their great adventure as they pulled into the driveway of the May mansion.

After refreshing themselves and cleaning up, John was eager to show his guest the French Quarters. He had the family carriage brought around and they set out for the old section of New Orleans. The French Quarter was the original city laid out by the early French on the highest strip of land along the Mississippi River. Its narrow streets were bordered by shops, townhouses, and government offices. It also had a number of hotels-many were impressive with large wrought iron balconies. There was a large square located in the middle of the Quarter. There was a magnificent hotel and restaurant standing on the southeast corner of the square. Balconies ran completely across the second and third floor. The rooms fronting these balconies had doors so that the hotel guests could step out and enjoy the revelry that was always going on in the city. The restaurant was famous for its French and Cajun cuisine. This was the favorite gathering place of the young aristocrats. They congregated here both from the city and from the surrounding plantations. They came to eat, drink, dance, see and be seen.

When Buck and John walked in, it seemed that everyone knew John. You could tell that he was well liked and popular—both with the young men and the young ladies. The escorts of these beautiful and fashionable young ladies could not help but notice how their dates were drawn to these two handsome young men. In fact, one young lady in particular seemed attracted to John. After Buck and John had taken a table, she continually glanced at him from behind her fan. John found this rather amusing and occasionally he would wink at her. After watching this flirting for some time, her companion became infuriated. A dark swarthy older man, he reeked of importance. When he could stand it no longer, he grabbed the young lady by the arm and said, "We are leaving."

The young lady shrugged his arm off and said, "You can leave; I am not ready." With this, she turned to walk away. It was more than her enraged escort could stand. He reached out, spun her around, and slapped her. There was a loud gasp from the people in the room and then . . . dead silence. The girl began to cry. This was all it took for John. He crossed the room and confronted the man. "Sir, gentlemen do not strike women. It seems that you just have to slap someone. Why don't you try slapping me?"

"Ah, my impetuous young friend, I will do more than slap you! I will challenge you to a duel if you are not too cowardly to accept." With this, he took his glove and struck John across the face. John glanced at the people staring and said, "I will be glad to accommodate you. You will find that I am a more worthy opponent than this young lady!"

In the South, no man could refuse a challenge to duel unless he wanted to be branded a coward without honor. Therefore, the arrangements were made. It was agreed that they would meet at daylight the next morning at the edge of the city under the dueling oaks. The weapons chosen were pistols. Since John didn't own any dueling pistols, the challenger said that he would be glad to furnish his matched pair. John asked Buck to be his second and the swarthy man picked one of his companions. If one had not known that one of the participants would die the next morning, one would have thought this was a business deal being worked out.

Immediately after the arrangements were finalized, the swarthy man grabbed the girl by the arm, motioned to his companions to follow, and stalked out. After the group left, one of John's friends said, "Do you know who you are dueling with?"

"No, and I don't care. I'll shoot the s.o.b. down like a dog! No one slaps me and calls me a coward."

"But John, that is the son of Baron Lafitte. It is rumored that he is the leader of the pirates that prey on the ships in the Gulf. He has had more duels than any man around New Orleans. He's gotta' be good or he wouldn't still be alive to challenge you."

John digested this information for a few minutes and said, "I don't care who he is. He looks old and fat to me. This will be the last duel he fights!"

The next morning dawned cool and clear. The birds at the dueling grounds greeted the daylight with a medley of tunes. There was no indication of the event that was about to take place. The carriages and riders started to arrive. The friends, the curious, and the participants slowly pulled in under the moss-draped oaks. The mist that was slowly rising up under the trees gave the place an eerie feeling. It was as if the spirits of the many men who had met their deaths there permeated the area. As all of the spectators lined up on the side, Buck and John stood quietly talking. "Buck," John said, "You know that I am pretty sure that I'll kill ole fatty. But, if things don't work out and he happens to kill me I have something for you." With that said, John reached in his pocket and pulled out a legal document. It was a quick claim deed to the Spanish Grant property that he had won.

Buck looked at it and said, "There is no way that I can accept this. Number one, you will win and number two, this should go to your family if you should fail."

John replied, "Look my family has more land and money than they can ever use. It would give me great pleasure knowing that the property would be yours." Then, John's countenance brightened and his bubbling personality returned. "Besides I am going to kill him dead as a hammer and you will have to deed it back to me!"

Buck replied, "Alright" as they shook hands.

Lafitte, upon his arrival, presented the matched dueling pistols to the somber man who was presiding over the match. Since the pistols were his, the referee allowed Lafitte to select the first pistol. John then took the other. The gentleman in charge gave them their instructions. Lafitte exuded confidence. Buck thought that this was confidence from his experience at winning so many duels. John was trying to cover his nervousness—but nervous he was. He had never seen a duel, much less participated in one. Per their instructions, the duelists stood back to back. They started their ten mandatory steps as the referee loudly counted, "One, two, three, four, five, six, seven, eight, nine, ten!" Each man turned to fire. It seemed that John might have been a little quicker. However, as they pulled the triggers simultaneously, John took one step back and fell to the ground-dead from a shot that had hit him right between the eyes. Buck rushed to him but there was no life there. Lafitte and his entourage quickly gathered the pistols, entered their carriage, climbed on their horses and made a hasty retreat. If only Buck could have heard Lafitte's remark to his companion, "Stupid young fool! It never crossed his mind to check and see if the firing pin on his pistol had been filed down so that it wouldn't fire!"

"Works every time," said his companion with a laugh.

Knowing that someone was not going to survive the duel, the funeral home had made arrangements to have a hearse at the scene. As John's other friends loaded John's body into the hearse, Buck pondered as to what to do next. He had never contemplated that John might actually be killed. Since this was the first death that he had witnessed, it affected him more than he would have expected. As he tried to compose himself, he decided that it was his duty to carry the news of John's death to John's family.

Since John's parents were in Europe, the only person at the May place was Maudie. She was the slave in charge of the home. Buck slowly related to her what had happened. "My baby, my baby!" she screamed as she sank to the floor. Her portly body shook uncontrollably as she sobbed. Maudie had been with the May family all of her life as had her parents and grandparents before her. She felt as much as part of the family as anyone. She took pride in the fact that her name was Maudie May. John had been entrusted to her care as an infant. With no children of her own, she took great pride in this care-free boy as he grew up. His death broke her heart. After Maudie composed herself, Buck sought her advice as to what he should do. She suggested that he inform John's grandparents since there was no way to immediately contact the parents. She gave Buck directions to their home in the French Quarters.

Buck approached the elder May's house with some trepidation. How was he going to explain to the grandparents his role in the events of the morning? The elder May's house was a luxurious townhouse on the outskirts of the Quarter. As Buck opened the gate and rang the bell, he was greeted by a stately black man dressed in a black suit. His starched white shirt, black bow tie, and white hair gave him an imposing demeanor. After Buck informed him of his mission, he was invited to sit while the servant went to fetch his master.

The aristocratic elder Mays entered the room and Buck introduced himself. After exchanging pleasantries, Buck reluctantly told them of the duel. He told them that he hated to bring this bad news but he didn't know who else to turn to. The elderly couple took the news exceptionally hard. John had always been the apple of their eye. The grandmother went faint and had to be helped to her chair. Although it affected the grandfather as much, he took pride in keeping his emotions under control. He suggested that the servant assist the grandmother to her room while he and Buck talked.

Mr. May told Buck that he did not fault him for his involvement in John's death. He knew his grandson. John was going to do what he wanted and no one was going to influence him. Being aware of John's playboy ways, he had always feared that something might happen to him. Feeling somewhat better, Buck brought up the subject of the Spanish Land Grant. Although legally the land belonged to him, he didn't think that ethically he should accept it. He told Mr. May the details of how and why John had willed this property to him. Buck told him that he had never thought that the duel would turn out the way that it had. He told Mr. May that he would feel much better if he signed the property over to John's estate.

"No!" Mr. May exclaimed. "If John wanted you to have the land, have it you shall. I can speak for myself and I have no doubt that I can speak for the rest of our family. This land means nothing to us. You shall keep it in remembrance of John. I thank you for your friendship to him during his last days. You two young men must have developed a wonderful relationship. If there is anything else that we can do for you, please let me know."

"Sir," Buck said, "I humbly consent to keeping the land. There is one favor that I would ask. Would you please direct me to someone that sells horses and tack?"

Mr. May replied, "I won't hear of you buying a horse. I insist that you have John's horse, saddle, and bridle."

Buck offered to pay but Mr. May would not hear of it. "You will be doing us a favor. The horse would just be a reminder of John. I am sure he would be pleased for you to have him." With that, Buck graciously accepted the gift. Thanking Mr. May profusely, Buck took his leave.

The next morning, Buck was up bright and early. He had slept fitfully during the night. He was ready to leave New Orleans and put his bad memories behind. Mr. May had made arrangements for Buck to pick up John's horse at the stable. After breakfast, Buck hired a coach to carry him to the horse. Arriving at the stable, he was met by the head hostler. An elderly white man, the hostler had been in charge of the May's animals for years. He took Buck back and introduced him to John's horse, Prince. A tall Tennessee Walker, the stallion was a beautiful Palomino with a flowing white mane and tail. The hostler said, "You can't find a better horse than this. He is well-mannered, and has the smoothest gait around. You can ride him all day and not be tired."

"I am glad," said Buck. "I have quite a ways to go." As Buck saddled up, he inquired from the elderly man the best way to get to the land grant that he had inherited.

"I have lived around here all of my life and I can tell you the best way that there is if you are traveling on land. Take the Military Road to Natchez. There, you will take the Natchez Trace north towards Nashville. It's an old Indian trail. It is tough to travel. Some folks call it the Devil's Backbone. You have to be mighty careful. There are bandits all up and down it. They prey on the flat boaters from up river as they walk back home. The bandits know that they all have money because they have just been paid for their produce."

Having taken his leave of New Orleans, Buck took the well traveled Military Road towards Natchez. As he rode, he became more and more pleased with Prince. The big stallion had the smooth gliding gait peculiar to his breed. Nodding his head with the cadence of his feet, the stallion covered mile after mile effortlessly. As this was a main thoroughfare hewn out of the wilderness by the French, Buck overtook and met a variety of travelers. The closer he got to Natchez, the more his interest was piqued about this city. He had been told in New Orleans that Natchez was one of the richest cities in the United States. He particularly wanted to see the huge ancestral mound of the Natchez Indians. He had never seen a mound that covered eight acres. He could not fathom how the Natchez could build such a mound with no equipment. He wished that he could inquire about this from the Indians. However, he knew that this was impossible as the French had practically wiped out the whole tribe some years earlier. As he rode along, he could not help but wonder what this country looked like before the Europeans arrived.

Arriving in Natchez, Buck found a place to board his horse, and walked to the Eola Hotel. Buck could hardly believe the size of the establishment, much less the lavishness of it. Upon registering, Buck was escorted to an upstairs room.

He was brought buckets of hot water and a stack of towels by the owner's slaves. Buck scrubbed several days of grime off. He then decided to see the town. He went downstairs and inquired from the clerk as to a good place to eat. The clerk said, "RED JACKS under the hill." "Under the hill?" Buck questioned.

"Yes. Natchez under the hill. This is an area where all of the flatboat men hang out along with all of the river folks. You can find plenty of gamblers there, too. You will have to be careful to stay out of trouble but if you really want a taste of Natchez, RED JACKS is the place to go. Good food, card games, Tennessee bourbon, women and plenty of fights. If you want to be entertained that's the place for you."

"How do I get there?" Buck asked.

The clerk replied, "Walk down to the end of the street, turn right and head toward the river. You can't miss it. Oh yeah, be sure and carry your pistol. You never know; you might need it."

As Buck took a right turn and started down the hill toward the river, he could hear boisterous laughter, yelling, cursing, and an occasional gunshot emanating from the direction of the river. As he made his way down the bluff in the dusk of the evening, he made out a large throng of men. In the middle, two men were going at each other with their fists. The younger of the men was short and stocky with big muscular arms. He had long greasy black hair. You could tell that he had worn his clothes so long that they almost adhered to his body. His clothes were just as greasy and soiled as the man himself. Buck had no doubt that this must be one of the flatboat men from up in Kentucky, Tennessee, or Ohio.

The flatboat men were tough frontiersmen who loaded their produce on to their homemade boats and floated their produce down one of the tributaries that emptied into the mighty Mississippi. After floating down to Natchez they sold their goods and dismembered their boats. They sold the planks for what they could get. They would then walk back up the Trace to Nashville and then to their homes. Always before their trek, they enjoyed visiting the saloons along the banks of the Mississippi. After being confined to their boats for weeks, they relished a chance to drink, visit with other flatboat men and FIGHT. Most of these men took pride in how tough they were and liked to prove it if someone trespassed on their honor. Like most men of the South, they couldn't take even the smallest insult. A perceived insult resulted in an instant challenge.

The flatboat man's opponent was a tall rangy man with flaming red hair. A man of about forty, he was covered with tattoos and scars. Buck could tell that fellow had lived a rough life. He looked kind of like a horse that had been ridden hard and put up wet.

Just as Buck approached, the redhead swung a long loping right that struck the flatboat man on his left ear. The force of the blow sent the young man staggering down the bank toward the paddle wheelers. He fell to his face, cold as a hammer. His companions picked him up and dragged him off. Strangely, not too many people paid this episode any attention. There were so many fights, cuttings and shootings in this area that they had become inoculated to the occasions.

As Buck turned to leave, the redhead turned around quickly. In doing so, he bumped straight into Buck. The big man stopped and looked straight at Buck with a piercing gaze. Buck stepped back and said, "Excuse me. Could you direct me to RED JACKS? I understand that they have the best food in these parts." The redhead's mood changed as if from night to day. A large smile came across his face. He clapped Buck on his back.

"Young fellow, you are here, and I agree that we have the best food around because I own the place. You will have to excuse the ruckus out here. Don't pay it no mind. I have to introduce myself to these young bucks from up the river. They have to find out that old Red can still whup anything in these parts. I don't mind their fighting and cutting up, but they can't do it inside my place. I'm tired of making repairs after one of their ruckuses. I told them to take their quarrel outside, but this one wanted to take me on. Anyway, come on in. I'll prove to you that we have the best vittles in Natchez. Nothing fancy, you know, but the best!" Putting his arm around Buck, he guided him into the tavern.

As Red and Buck enjoyed their meal of fried river catfish and trimmings, their conversation turned to the question of the location of Buck's newly acquired property. After listening to Buck's description of the place, Red told him that the place he was looking for was north of Vicksburg. Vicksburg was a small town located at the junction of a tributary and the Mississippi. It was about sixty miles north of Natchez. Red said that Buck could take a paddle wheeler from Natchez to Vicksburg and then proceed north to his land grant. Buck said that he thought that he would prefer riding his horse. He didn't want to sell him since he was a gift and secondly he believed that he would enjoy seeing the countryside.

Red said, "Buck, you are not going to believe that country up there. It is as flat as this table. The only way I know how to get there by horse is to take the Trace about sixty or seventy miles. This will bring you to a trading post owned by a Frenchman. His place is

26

called Lefluers Bluff. His father, Louie Lefluer, named it that before he moved north up the Trace. When you get there, he can direct you further. He is married to one of the Choctaw chief's nieces, so he pretty well knows all of the territory up there."

Buck thanked Red kindly for his meal and hospitality. He paid him and made his way back up the bluff to his hotel. He decided to go to bed early so that he could get an early start the next day. After sleeping restlessly during the night, Buck arose the next morning excited about the adventure that he was setting off on. His first order of business after breakfast was to purchase the necessary supplies for his journey. He bought just the basic staples that he could fit into the saddlebags strapped behind his saddle. He intended to shoot enough wild game to supplement these goods. He made sure that he had enough ammunition for hunting and enough to protect himself if necessary.

Buck returned to the hotel to settle his bill before leaving. The innkeeper inquired as to where he was going. Buck repeated to him Red's instructions. The innkeeper said, "Young man, you had better be very careful. The further north you go, the more dangerous the Trace gets. You have to watch out for varmints. The human varmints are worse than the animals. There are robbers all along the way. The Mason gang is the worst. I would suggest that you join up with some other travelers. Strength in numbers, you know. In fact, I know a group that is heading out in the morning. Why don't you wait and I will introduce you to them? Maybe you can travel with them."

Buck thought a moment and replied, "I think I will take your advice. One thing about it is if I don't like their company, I can always leave."

As they discussed this, a short stocky man in his late forties strode through the front door. Although past his youth, he was still a viral, handsome man. From his erect carriage and confident bearing,

Buck quickly sized him up as someone of a military background. He reeked of importance.

The innkeeper said, "This is the gentleman that I wanted you to meet." As the older man approached, Buck became aware of the young woman that accompanied him. She was tall, slim, with long auburn hair. The riding clothes that she was attired in accented a perfect figure. Buck thought to himself, this has got to be one of the prettiest girls that I have ever seen. Buck's concentration was broken by the innkeeper when he said, "Mr. Buchanan Inman, I would like to introduce Captain Glen McIntyre. Captain McIntyre was one of our heroes during the defense of New Orleans. As a young lad, he helped turn back the English during the war of 1812".

He turned to the Captain and said, "Buck, here, was looking for someone to travel with up the Trace. I told him your party was preparing to leave in the morning and that you would probably be glad to have an extra man along."

The Captain gave Buck a long look of appraisal. Satisfied that this was a young man who would be an asset on a trip such as this, he said, "All right young man, you may accompany us, but I will tell you up front, this is my party and I give the orders. You will have to go by our rules and our schedule. I must get to Nashville as soon as possible."

"I don't have a problem with that," Buck said. "I am going to turn off the Trace about sixty or seventy miles north and head west toward the Mississippi River. Until then, I would be appreciative of you and your daughter's company."

"My daughter, my arse!" exclaimed McIntyre. He drew himself to his full height and said, "This is my wife and don't you ever forget it!" Taken by surprise, Buck glanced at the young lady who was smiling and greeted his gaze with a coy wink. Buck thought, "Uh oh, I had better be careful here."

"No problem, Captain. You have my compliments on having such a beautiful wife," Buck said, trying to ease the tension.

The Captain relaxed and haughtily said, "We will be leaving at daybreak. If you wish to accompany us, meet us at the north end of town." Turning on his heel, he stalked off with his young wife in tow. Just as they exited the room, the young lady furtively looked back and gave Buck a quick smile and another quick wink.

The next morning, Buck was up at daybreak to meet the Captain and his wife in the lobby. Buck had Prince brought up and the couple entered their carriage. The carriage was driven by a middle-aged slave dressed to the teeth. Being in a hurry, they proceeded to the area where the Captain's party was waiting. At this location was a wagon loaded with food, camping, and cooking equipment. It was driven by a young slave dressed in homespun garments. Also in the group were two backwoods men on horses that been employed by the Captain to accompany his group back to Nashville. They had come down the river on a flatboat and were glad to be able to ride back to the mountains of Tennessee. Leading the group as they pulled out was Jake, a tall, slim, grizzled former soldier, who had served with the Captain at the 'Battle of New Orleans'. Buck was instructed to ride by him.

The group quickly made ready and took leave of Natchez just as the sun was appearing over the trees. They quickly arrived on the Trace and headed northeast. They made excellent time since this part of the Trace was wide, relatively smooth, and well-traveled.

After traveling all day, the group arrived at the first of many stands along the Trace. Since it was dusk, they decided to spend the night there. The innkeeper greeted them and invited the group to eat with them and spend the night. Mrs. McIntyre sniffed and rolled her eyes when they were told that the menu included bear, coon, and squirrel. The innkeeper then proudly showed the Captain and Mrs. McIntyre the extra room tacked onto the side. "You can sleep here in complete privacy," he stated. The room was furnished with one straight-back chair and one bed. It had a soiled cotton mattress held up by ropes running back and forth across the frame. Mrs. McIntyre spun around abruptly and stalked out with the Captain following. "I had rather sleep in a barn than a filthy place like this," she said.

"My Dear, you don't have to spend the night or eat here. This is the reason we brought the tent and our own food," the Captain replied, soothingly. He then ordered the men to prepare the camp site under the large trees.

Buck hobbled his horse and spread out his bedroll. He then was invited to dine with the others. After eating, he said, "Thank you for the meal. I am a little tired. I think I will turn in."

"That's a good idea. We had all better get some rest. I want to get an early start in the morning. I plan on making Lefluers Bluff by nightfall," said the Captain.

"What is Lefluer's Bluff?" asked Buck.

The Captain replied, "It is a stand located on the Pearl River north of here. It is owned by the son of Louis Lefluer. The father married into the Choctaw Indian Chief's family. He had had a trading post on the Pearl for many years before he moved north to put in a stand called 'French Camp'."

Buck said, "I would like to meet this son of Louis. Maybe he can tell me something about the location of my land west of him."

"I am sure he can. He trades with all of the Indians in the area," said the Captain.

"Well alright, I will see you folks in the morning," said Buck as he prepared to turn in for the night.

The clouds moved in and the rain began to fall as the group prepared to move out the next morning. Buck and the other riders hunkered down in their slickers and prepared for the uncomfortable ride. The McIntyres were much more comfortable in their carriage. The Trace was muddy, but passable. There were no major streams to ford so they were able to slowly make their way north.

By dusk, they finally arrived at their destination. Lefluer's stand or trading post was located on a bluff overlooking the Pearl River. It was larger than most of the stands along the Trace since it served as a residence, inn, and trading post.

Louis Lefluer's son came out to greet them as they arrived. "Bon Jour," greeted Lefluer, as the bedraggled group dismounted. "Come in to the tavern and let me fix you a drink. I guarantee what I have will make you fill better and perk you up." Taking him up on the offer, the group followed him inside. They were glad to get in out of the weather. Inside, they were greeted by an attractive Indian lady. Louis introduced her as his wife. Speaking perfect English, she also made them welcome. After drying out and several shots of Kentucky Bourbon, everyone felt much better. Since it was getting dark, Lefluer asked if they wished to eat at the inn. Everyone readily agreed. After a sumptuous meal, the weary group was thinking about sleep. Everyone prepared to make camp with the exception of the Captain and his lady. After inspecting the room that was offered by Lefluer, Mrs. McIntyre decided that, while it was not the best of accommodations, it was far better than the previous stand and certainly better than sleeping in the tent. Being tired, everyone but Buck left to retire for the night. Buck was too excited to sleep. He wanted to question Louis about the directions of his property.

After everyone else turned in, he finally got a chance to question the Frenchman. Lefluer found Buck's account of how he came to own the land on the lake very interesting. Lefluer said, "I have not traveled there myself but I have several natives from that area that come here to trade with me. They are from my wife's tribe and very

31

peaceful. They describe their area as almost completely flat and swampy. I can tell you that game is abundant because they bring me many furs to trade. The other thing is that they are mound builders. I understand that some mounds are used for burial and others are lived on by the chiefs. If it floods there like they say, I would think that a mound would be quite a handy thing to have. Now, in the morning I can point out the right trail and direction, but after that, you are on your own."

Rising early the next morning, Buck saddled Prince and prepared to leave. After buying some provisions from the Frenchman, Buck thanked Captain McIntyre for allowing him to travel with his group. He then took Mrs. McIntyre's hand and told her how much he had enjoyed her company. Giving his hand a little extra squeeze, she bid him goodbye. After shaking hands with the other men, Buck turned Prince northwest.

The trail to which Lefluer had directed him was broad and well traveled. Buck even met a few trappers and Indians as he rode west. Buck thought, "This won't be so bad after all!" After riding all day, Buck came upon his first river crossing. He was pleased to find a small ferry pulled up to the bank. He was greeted by a tall, lanky, middle-aged man with bulging arm muscles. Buck could tell that the ferryman had spent years pulling the ferry back and forth across the river. "You wanting to cross?" queried the ferryman.

"I sure do," replied Buck. "What's the name of this river anyway?"

The ferryman answered, "The Big Black. She pretty much runs northwest all the way across the middle of the state. Do you want to cross now or wait until in the morning?"

"I think that I will cross now and camp on the tall hill on the other side if it's alright with you," answered Buck.

"Long as you got the money it don't make me no never mind. Well, here are your charges. Let's get moving." After Buck and Prince were aboard, the ferryman grasped the rope and slowly pulled the ferry to the other side. After thanking the man, Buck mounted and headed to higher ground.

After spending the night on the tall hill overlooking the Big Black River bottom, Buck was mounted and moving by daylight. Again, he was surprised at how well the path seemed to be. He kept his eyes open but he did not encounter another living soul. After spending another night in the woods, he continued riding until he came upon a tall hill with a clearing on top. From this vantage point, he could see what looked like a vast swamp stretching as far as he could see. "Man," he thought, "this must be the great bottom lands that Lefluer told me about."

Buck started guiding Prince down the long winding trail towards the bottom. It was too steep and long to go straight down. Taking his time, Buck finally reached the bottom. Even then he couldn't see very far. His vision couldn't penetrate the dense vegetation. The path went between massive trees. Oaks, hackberry, pecan and elms crowded each other. In between them were huge clumps of cane. Some cane had grown to over twenty feet in height. Even though this terrain was interesting, Buck could not help but be a little anxious about what might be around the next bend. He decided that this would be a good time to unholster his rifle. Being on edge, he slowly urged Prince forward. Then to his surprise, he thought he could hear children playing. He emerged into a clearing on the banks of a wide river. There he came upon a rude cabin and barn. He also realized there were two little girls playing under the trees. He had come upon the dwelling of another ferryman. As he approached, he was met by a heavy—set man with a long dirty beard. Standing in the door of the cabin was the man's wife. Unkempt, with missing teeth and stringy hair, she looked much older than her years.

"Good morning," Buck spoke. "Howdy," the man replied. Buck said, "I am looking for directions. I am trying to locate some property of mine. It is located on a large lake next to the Mississippi River. I think it is northwest of here but I don't know how far. Can you tell me what this river is and if you know of such a lake?"

"Well," the ferryman replied, "this river here is what the Indians call the Yazoo. It runs all the way to the Mississippi River. I ain't never seen it but the Indians tell me that there is a large lake west of here. They also call it Yazoo-Lake Yazoo. I been hauling folks across this river for about five years, but I ain't never traveled more than ten miles up the trail. Ain't nothing up there but varmints and a few Choctaw Indian villages. Me and mine are pretty well satisfied hanging around here."

"When can you take me across the river?"Buck asked.

"Most anytime. But there ain't no use of being in a hurry. Why don't you stay a spell and eat with us? We'un's don't get much company," the man replied.

Looking around at the accommodations, Buck thought better of the idea. Politely refusing the offer, Buck bargained for the ferryman to take him and Prince across the flooding Yazoo. Arriving at the other side without incident, Buck paid the man and thanked him. "Be keerful. Keep your eyes peeled. There are some mighty big bears and panthers in them woods. Plus, you gotta keep a lookout for them big gators when you cross them swamps. Some of them gits up to twelve or fourteen feet long," the ferryman offered. Waving goodbye, Buck turned Prince into the dense forest.

Following the trail through the dense vegetation and winding around the huge clumps of cane, Buck headed further into the unknown. He could imagine that he was being watched by wild eyes as he traveled westward. Every once in a while he could hear the swishing of the tall grass as some critter moved quickly out of his way. Since he didn't know what was out there, he kept his rifle ready.

One of the things he didn't have to wonder about was the mosquitoes. Nothing like the little mosquitoes he had grown up with, these were huge! Big and black, they were more the size of the common housefly. They quickly swarmed all over Buck and Prince. Buck desperately tried to fend them off by putting on a long sleeve shirt and tying another around his head. He even had to slip on his gloves. This gave him some relief but Prince was soon covered. They seemed to concentrate mostly on the horse's neck. Prince got some relief on his hindquarters by swishing his long tail. Soon, Prince's neck started turning red with blood as the mosquitoes continued their attack. Buck stopped, got out a blanket, and tied it around Prince's head and neck to try and give him some relief. The mosquitoes could still get at his nose and eyes—but this helped immensely. Buck thought, "Why would anyone want to live in a place like this? I sure hope my place is not like this. If it is, someone else can have it!"

The trail that Buck followed twisted and turned as it followed the banks of the bayous and avoided the sloughs. Buck was extremely glad that bears, Indians, or both had gone before him and blazed a trail. There was no way that he could find his way on his own. Although he didn't have a clue where he was, at least he knew he was going somewhere. To follow the trail, Buck eventually had to let Prince wade some of the streams and the muddy water of the sloughs. Fortunately, most of the streams and sloughs were fairly shallow. With a little encouragement, Prince crossed without any incidents. Buck thought how blessed he was to have Prince to take him across. He also appreciated the fact that someone or something had selected the best places to cross as they travelled the trail.

Buck decided that he would push on without stopping to get out of the area as fast as he could. Later that evening, the vegetation seemed to clear out somewhat, and Buck was able to see some clearings along the trail. As he entered the clearing, as if by magic, the mosquitoes disappeared. It seemed that they preferred the dark dampness of the swamp. Buck was able to stop and take off his extra shirt and blanket off of Prince.

As Buck rode from one clearing to another, the tall grass came up to his stirrups. He couldn't help but think of what a cotton crop this rich soil would grow. Now, he fully realized the labor that had gone into turning the wild land of the Carolinas' into the great plantations that were there now. He also realized that this transition would not have been possible without the use of slaves.

As Buck glanced toward the horizon, he could see a large stream. On the other side of the stream were several mounds of dirt. From this distance, he could not make out exactly what they were. It seemed that the path crossed the bayou and continued in the mounds' direction. When Buck approached the bayou, he discovered that it was not too wide and was fairly shallow. He determined that the water was going to be about belly deep on Prince. Urging Prince on, Buck eased into the water. All of a sudden, he heard noises all along the banks. Startled, he realized that the noise was caused by hundreds of turtles sliding into the water. They were coming off of the logs and banks where they had been sunning. Buck's attention was then drawn to the slick spots along the bank where the grass had been worn thin by something sliding down the bank into the water. As Buck was trying to guess what caused these, he saw a huge log floating off to his right. As he looked at it, it seemed to be floating in his direction. All of a sudden, he realized that there were small waves coming out from either side of the object as it picked up speed. Prince and Buck realized at the same time that the floating log had turned into a twelve foot long alligator. It did not take much prodding from Buck to get Prince moving swiftly to the other side. Just as Prince scrambled up the bank, Buck turned to see the gator right behind them. She was opening and closing her huge mouth as she came toward them. As they cleared the bank, Buck was glad to see the 'gator slowly swim back in the direction in which she had come. All he could see were her eyes above the water. Buck found out later that gators are usually not aggressive. If you will leave them alone, they will leave you alone. The exception is a mother gator protecting her nest. That is what Buck had stumbled upon. Now, he understood what caused the slick spots along the banks. They were caused by the alligators that infested this particular bayou. These were their paths in and out of the water.

Stopping a few minutes to rest Prince and to calm his own racing heart, Buck turned his attention to the huge mounds of dirt in the distance. He could make out about five in various sizes. Moving ahead, he continued on the path towards them. As he got closer, he could see smoke rising and movement around them. Buck realized that living on and around the mounds was a tribe of Indians, maybe the ones that came to the trading post to trade with the Frenchman. Not knowing what kind of reception to expect, Buck was a little more than apprehensive.

His fear soon disappeared as the whole tribe came out to meet him. It was a small tribe of about fifty people, including women and children. They were not part of the Choctaw nation that dominated this part of the state. Instead, they were a branch of the Yazoo tribe that co-existed with the Choctaws. Speaking some English, they invited Buck to step down from Prince. Buck accepted and tied the stallion before entering the village.

The village was made up of rude huts located around the mounds. As he entered, Buck noticed that there was a larger hut on top of the largest mound. Coming down the path from the top was a gray haired man with an air of importance. Dressed in a combination of furs, feathers, and English clothes, he was quite imposing. Buck could tell that he was the leader of the tribe. He invited Buck to join him around the camp fire.

The Indian chief was just as curious about Buck as Buck was about him. In broken English, he questioned Buck about where he came from, how he managed to arrive at the village, and where he was going. After giving the chief an abbreviated version of his travels, Buck then started asking questions of his own. He questioned the Chief as to what tribe this was. The Chief informed Buck that they were part of the Yazoo. The larger tribe of the Yazoos lived on the Yazoo River close to the Mississippi River. This was the Yazoo River that Buck had crossed days before. The Chief explained that at one time the Yazoo had been a very large tribe, although not nearly as large as the Choctaws, which they had lived peaceably, but larger than they were now. He explained to Buck that over the years many of their tribe were captured by Cherokee raiding parties from Tennessee and Georgia. These raiders took their captives back to the coastal states where they promptly sold them to the slave traders. The slave traders then sold them to the southern planters. The planters did not care whether the slaves were Africans, Indians or mixed. They just knew that they had to have labor to work the vast cotton plantations. He told Buck that his people had moved to this isolated area to escape the Cherokee raids.

Buck then broached the subject of the location of his land. He told the Chief all he knew about the location. He showed him the crude map that he had which showed the location of the large lake next to the Mississippi. The Chief told Buck that his people often traveled to the lake to fish. The area was a paradise for hunting and fishing. He told Buck that if he followed the trail that it was about a two day ride there. The Chief also told Buck that he would pass a small Choctaw Indian village before he got to the lake. He said they called this lake, 'Yazoo'.

Excited but tired, Buck thought about the mosquitoes and where he was going to sleep. The Chief told him that he was welcome to eat and spend the night with the tribe. Buck accepted, but he was still thinking about those huge mosquitoes. As dusk settled in, the women of the tribe began preparing a meal of venison, hominy, and flat bread. The men gathered up stacks of dry and green wood. The green wood that burned on top of the dry wood would create a thick smoke. The Indians located these stacks all around the village. Buck at first thought they were doing this to scare off the wild animals. However, the Chief explained that they were doing this to ward off the swarms of blood thirsty mosquitoes.

Relieved, Buck began to prepare for sleep. First, he brought Prince in and tied him within the circle. He hoped this would provide some respite from the mosquitoes. Buck then joined the Indians for a meal and later spread out his bedroll for a fitful night sleep. Although the smoke helped, he still swatted the blood suckers all night.

Rising early the next morning Buck was anxious to be on the way. He bid his host goodbye, saddled up Prince, and was on the way toward the lake by sun up.

For the first couple of miles, Buck made good time. He let the big stallion settle into a smooth canter. This easy riding did not last. After two miles, the trail led into another swamp. Again, the large canes closed in on the trail. Large trees appeared again. Birds flew up in every direction as they were disturbed by Buck and Prince. It was both damp and muggy. Buck dreaded meeting the huge mosquitoes again. He lucked out. There was a brisk breeze blowing from the west right in their faces. It was strong enough to keep the pests away. Buck had to slow Prince down into the flat-foot walk that the Tennessee Walkers are famous for. This slower gait allowed Buck to watch for water moccasins and rattlers along the trail. They moved steadily westward until they came upon another river. This river was fairly deep and wide. Buck was pleased that it wasn't at flood stage. As he approached the bank, he was grateful that the ones before him had picked out the shallowest spot to cross. Keeping his eyes open for alligators, Buck eased Prince out into the water. He was apprehensive because he was concerned that Prince might step off into a deep hole at anytime. Again, he was fortunate. Going straight across to the trail on the other side, Prince was able to keep his feet on the ground. Now, Buck knew why the Indians had picked this place to cross. With the river water dripping off of them, Buck and Prince followed the trail west.

After traveling until about dusk, Buck came out of the swamp. He entered another large clearing and was able to see some more mounds in the distance. He assumed that this would be the location of the Choctaw Indian tribe about which he had been told. He soon realized that he had been spotted; it seemed as if the whole tribe had come out to see this stranger. The men came first, followed by the women and children. The men were led by the Great Mingo, their Chief. Speaking perfect English, he welcomed Buck to his village. Buck immediately noticed that these Indians looked different from the Yazoo that he had just left. The men and women were shorter with rounder faces. Although not tall, the men were compact, broad, and heavily muscled. Buck was glad that he had been advised that the Choctaws were peaceful. As Buck was being led into the camp, he noticed all of the young children peeking out at him from behind their mothers. Perhaps they had never seen a white man before.

Arriving in the village, Buck observed that each family had individual log cabins. They were located all around the mounds. Each family had already started a smoking fire to ward off the mosquitoes during the night. Buck then realized why everyone smelled of smoke. The Chief's cabin was located on the highest mound. The Chief invited Buck to the center of the village. Tying up Prince, Buck followed him. The other elders joined them.

As everyone else had been, the Chief was curious as to where Buck had come from and where he was going. Although tired of telling his story, Buck told the group about himself and where he was going. The group knew the exact location of the lake that Buck was seeking. It was located another hard day's ride further west. They told him to just follow the trail west and that it would end at the lake. Once there, he would have to try and determine where his property was. The group then turned their attention to the fish that the women were cooking. Buck was invited to eat with them and to then spend the night. Hungry, he readily accepted. He also figured that their smoke would keep the insects away during the night.

After the meal, Buck questioned the Chief about the tribe. The Chief told Buck that they had not always lived in the area. They had once been part of a large tribe near their ancestral home. They had lived peacefully there for generations. They had been able to adapt when the whites started pushing into their territory. They had tried to live peaceably with the whites by adopting some of their ways. They had accepted their religion, learned their language, and even intermarried. They also were their allies in wars. The Chief showed Buck the scar on his shoulder where he had been shot during the battle of New Orleans. As a young brave, he and other young braves had joined up with Andrew Jackson to help protect the coast. Later he told Buck that things began to change. More and more whites started settling on their land. The tribe gradually retreated and allowed the settlers to stay. After a few years of uneasy existence, everything changed dramatically. The whites, desiring the Choctaw land, implored Jackson, who had become President, to get control of this land for them.

President Jackson and the leaders in Congress came up with a plan to relocate all of the Indian nations to Oklahoma. By bribes and life-time pensions, the whites got many of the Chiefs to go along with the plan. "Did the Chiefs go along because of greed or did they go along because they thought they had no choice because of the whites' large armies?" asked Buck. The Chief did not know. He suspected that the Indian leaders had various reasons for signing the treaties with the whites. Since being forced out was inevitable, he surmised that probably they made as good a deal as they could for the tribes while benefiting personally. When it became time to begin the long walk to Oklahoma, some of the signers of the treaties went; others were allowed to stay. The Indians that did not want to go were rounded up by the army and forced to leave their ancestral land. Some small bands escaped the clutches of the soldiers and fled to less populated areas. One of these bands was the group that was sharing their hospitality with Buck. They had fled here to the swamp, hoping that they could elude the solders. They had been right. They were not a large enough group for the officials to worry about. The Chief told Buck that they had lived peacefully here for several years. The only contact that they had with whites was when they went to Lefluer's Bluff to trade and get supplies. Some of the women and children had never been exposed to whites. Buck thought, "These officials and army officers probably attended church and called themselves Christians. What a way to treat their former allies! Greed! Greed!"

Rising early after a fitful sleep, Buck was anxious to be on his way. He thanked the tribe and saddled up Prince. He walked him down to the small steam created by the spring that flowed out from between two of the mounds. After Prince drank his fill, Buck filled his canteen, mounted up, and once again headed west. After riding for about ten hours with a few stops, Buck began to wonder if the Indians had known which lake he was asking about. By this time of the year in Mississippi, the sun was beating down unmercifully. Both he and Prince were sweating profusely. Although both were tired, they pushed on west. Just as the sun set and darkness settled in, Buck suddenly rode out of a thicket onto the banks of the prettiest lake he had ever seen. After pausing, Buck decided it was time to find a place to spend the night. After looking at his crude map, Buck decided his land must be south. Following a dim trail along the bank of the lake, Buck picked his way south. There was almost no sound as Prince padded along on top of the cypress needles that covered the trail.

4

The Run Away's
Meet Buck

Suddenly, as Buck rode out of the bushes into a clearing, he came face to face with two young Nigras. Reacting quickly, Buck pulled out his pistol and leveled it at them. Just as surprised, the two Nigras fell to their knees and raised their hands. "Please Suh, don't shoot. We don't mean no harm."

After gaining his composure and settling Prince down, Buck took a good look at who was in front of him.-two of the most ragged young Nigras he had ever seen. "Stand up. I'm not going to shoot you," Buck said as he holstered his pistol. "Who are you and what in the world are ya'll doing out here?"

Nervously, the young men stood up. The oldest, a young man of about nineteen, answered, "We is just out looking for some stray cows for our master." The younger just kept staring at the ground.

"And just where does your master live?" Buck asked. Not knowing where Buck came from, the older replied, "On the trail that leaves the lake and runs toward where the sun rises every morning."

"That's mighty strange. I just came over that trail and I didn't see a living soul, much less a plantation," Buck replied. "Look, I am not going to hurt ya'll. I really don't care where you came from or where you are going. You don't have to lie to me. Ya'll are about the worst looking fellows I have ever seen. Your clothes are in rags, you don't have on any shoes, and your hair is as nappy as cotton. You look like

43

you haven't eaten a good meal in a while. I am getting ready to make camp and cook my supper. If ya'll want to join me, you can."

Getting over their fear, the older boy replied, "Thank you, Suh. We would be obliged. We ain't et anything but fish and wild critters in a while."

"Well, there isn't anything wrong with a little wild game every once in a while. In fact, I wouldn't mind having a young rabbit myself," Buck said. Shyly, the young Nigra extended the hand that he had been holding behind his back. In it was a plump young rabbit! "Well fellows, it looks like we are going to have us a mighty fine meal tonight," Buck said. "When we get thru eating, you can tell me the truth about yourselves. I expect ya'll can tell me more about this area than I can find out by myself in months."

As the young Nigras relaxed around the camp with full bellies, they felt comfortable enough to tell their story. They were born and raised in Tennessee, but sold at an auction before they were teens. Their buyer was a planter from Arkansas. They were shackled to other slaves and made to walk the long trip from Memphis to the Delta of Arkansas. After arriving at the owner's small plantation they were given the names John and Jim. Even though they were young, they were immediately pressed into the workforce by the owner. It was a life of drudgery and work. As the property of a small slaveholder, they were expected to not only work the fields but take care of the livestock. Minding the cattle was about the only job that they enjoyed. At certain times of the year, they were given the duty of taking the small herd down by the big river to graze. This was a wonderful respite from the back-breaking labor of the fields. Here, as the cattle grazed, they were free to watch the various kinds of boats passing by. They were especially enthralled with the big paddle wheelers. They could see the men and women passengers walking on the decks dressed in their finery.

"Where you think dem folks are going?" Jim asked John.

"Boy, you knows I don't know. I don't even know were we is. They must be going somewhere mighty nice the way they is dressed," replied John.

"Does you think we will ever be able to ride on one of dem big boats?" Jim asked.

"Boy, you must be crazy. Me and you is slaves. We ain't never going anywhere, much less ride one of them boats. You gotta be white and free to travel like that," said John.

Jim asked, "Ain't there some way we can be free? Can't we run away or something? I sho don't want to live the rest of my life working on this ole plantation."

John replied, "If we run away, dem slave catchers will get us and bring us back. Then ole Master will whup us and we will just be back working on the plantation again."

Later that night as the boys were preparing for bed, John said to Jim, "Let's go outside." When the boys got outdoors, John said, "I been thinking. You know how the big river makes a curve right where we graze dem cows? Well, what if we got a big ole log to hold onto and got in that river? I betch'a the current would float right over to the other side. And you know that we ain't never seen anybody on the other side of the river. We would be free and nobody would know where we was."

Jim replied, "I be afraid. You knows we can't swim. We would end up on the bottom of the river."

"I rather die trying to escape than live the rest of my life on this ole plantation," replied John.

As the days and weeks passed, the young Nigras formulated their plan. First, they had to locate a log. The log had to be of sufficient size to float both of them. But, it also had to be small enough that they could wrap their arms around it and maintain a good hold. Since there were quite a few fallen trees on the edge of the bank, it wasn't hard to find a log that met their needs. They selected a cypress that was dry but not rotten. They rolled it down by the bank so that they could easily push it in the water.

As the days passed by, they were able to save up food, clothing and other supplies. When it was their turn to graze the cattle, they hid all of their supplies in the hollow of a large tree that grew on the bank of the river. As time passed, the boys became more and more anxious to escape-especially Jim. "We got to wait 'til the river goes down and that current slows before we try to make it across," cautioned John.

The time arrived. It was mid-summer, hot and dry. The slaves were watching the cattle down by the river bank. The river was low and the current was slow due to the lack of rain upriver. John and Jim had decided this was the night that they would attempt their escape. As the sun went down and dusk settled in, the boys furtively gathered their supplies from the hollow of the old tree. About all they had was a change of clothes, some rope, a few matches and what tins of food that they had been able to steal over the previous months. Their prize possession was a long machete-like knife that Jim had been able to steal from the blacksmith's shop. They took all of the supplies and divided them in half. The supplies were then placed in two old sacks that they had obtained. John would carry one sack and Jim would carry the other. John tied the knife around his waist, and they were ready.

They quickly rolled the log they had saved down to the edge of the river. There, they tied their sacks around the log. "I sho is scared," Jim said.

John yelled, "Shut up, Nigga! We ain't got time for that. We done started and we gonna keep going!" They grabbed hold of the log and eased it into the river. At first it seemed as if the log was just going to float slowly along. Then suddenly the current caught it. The log spun around and headed down river backwards. The boys were holding on for dear life. "Help!" Jim hollered. There was nothing that John could do but hold on too. "Don't let go!" John yelled. Then, just as suddenly as the log had spun backwards, it spun around forward. At least the boys could see where they were going. As they floated toward the middle of the river, the current slowed but continued to carry them across to the other side. This was as they had hoped. Although they were heading toward the other bank, the current was carrying them past the spot they had hoped to land. John began kicking. "Kick Jim. We gotta make this log go to the bank." With a lot of effort they were able to slowly turn the log towards the other side.

Just as they were about to give out, the current shot them toward a sandbar that extended out into the river. Here, the river slowed down and they were able to paddle the log to the edge of the sandbar. Exhausted, they sprawled out on the bank. Luckily, the log bobbed along side of them. Gathering their strength, they were able to untie their sacks and drag them onto the bank. The boys decided that they had better head for the woods that lined the bank before anyone saw them.

Running down the sandbank toward the trees, they realized why the current had carried them to this spot. Here between the trees was a chute full of water that led off through the woods. The chute was about fifty feet wide and looked deep. The sandbar jutted out on the downriver side. John and Jim had no choice but to follow the bank of the chute into the deep woods.

The boys were scared to death of what might lie ahead, but they were even more afraid of getting caught. They had seen what happened to run—away slaves when they were caught. They headed into the woods carrying, their sacks. The large trees made a canopy over them which shut out the small amount of daylight left. It was pitch black!

"I ain't going any further! One of dem pathers might be up in there! I don't want a be et!" said Jim.

"You knows we can't stay out here on the bank. Someone on one of dem riverboats might spot us. I tell you what. We'll just go over and camp behind dem bushes under that big tree. I don't think anyone will spot us there," replied John.

The boys got out of their wet clothes and hung them on some bushes to dry. After getting on dry clothes, their spirits were much improved. They had a quick bite to eat and then prepared for sleep. They wrapped up in the quilts they had packed and tried to go to sleep. They were glad that they had thought to bring the quilts. The quilts helped ward off the blood-thirsty mosquitoes that came out in droves as the sun went down. Better to be hot than to be bitten all over.! With the buzzing of the mosquitoes as well as the strange noises emanating from the woods, John and Jim slept fitfully.

"WE IS FREE, WE IS FREE, PRAISE DE LORD, WE IS FREE!" exclaimed Jim the next morning as he danced around the campsite.

"Shut up, nigar. Can't you see that I am trying to sleep? You know I didn't get any rest last night!" yelled John.

"You got the rest of yo life to sleep. This is the first day you been free in yo life! Get up!" replied Jim.

Wide awake now, the two young men surveyed their surroundings. Looking out on the river, they could not see any river traffic. They were surprised that they could not see their plantation across the other side. The river had carried them much further before spitting them out than they had thought. They tried drinking water out of the chute but it had too much muddy river water in it. John then spotted a faint trail along the bank of the chute. "Come on, Jim. Let's follow this trail and see if we can find some water worth drinking.

"I 'bout soon to starve to death before I drinks any of dat ole river water. I be too scared. We don't know what kind of critters are in dem woods." replied Jim.

"You come on. You ain't gotta be afraid. You see this big old knife I got? Ain't nothing messing with us nigras!"

The trail beaten out by black bears was easy to follow. After several miles, the water in the chute began to clear up but was still too muddy to drink. The boys moved swiftly along, still ecstatic over their freedom. Around mid-morning, they came to a spot where the chute narrowed. Here, a huge cypress tree had fallen in the past. With its limbs having rotted off, it made a perfect bridge across the chute. The young men could see that the trail went across it and picked up again on the other side. Having no other choice, they walked the long log and continued on the other side. As they moved along, they could hear the rustling of vegetation as various wild critters moved out of their way. They moved ahead being confident that they could follow the trail back to the river if necessary. After a quick break for lunch, they continued on with Jim singing at the top of his lungs, "WE IS FREE, WE IS FREE, PRAISE DE LORD, WE IS FREE!"

"Shut up, nigar. You is so loud dat they can probably hear you plum back to the plantation. I 'spect ole master is looking for us right now. I don't 'spect they will ever believe we done crossed that big ole river! We just gotta be careful that we don't run up on some white folks on this side!"said John.

Since the Mississippi River was low, the chute began to get shallower and narrower. The boys were about to give up and turn around when the trail led them out of the canes into a large clearing. Here, the chute trickled into the largest lake they had ever seen. They had no idea where they were. Instead of turning back, they decided to continue their exploration around the lake. The walking was still fairly easy since the trail continued. As they walked, they could hear the turtles slide off of the logs into the lake. Wildfowl lifted themselves out of the water, squawking as they settled further away from the bank. Huge cypress trees lined the bank with their knees sticking up all around the trunks. John and Jim had never seen a place like this.

Forgetting their thirst, they pushed rapidly on. Still a little afraid, Jim let John go first. With the disturbed birds flying from the trees over their heads, there was no such thing as traveling quietly. The miles passed effortlessly by. They did notice that other trails joined the large trail as they continued on.

It was getting close to dusk when suddenly they walked out into a huge clearing. They didn't know it, but they were on the highest point around the lake. Looking about one hundred yards east of the lake, they could see a herd of deer grazing. Moving in the direction of the deer, they soon discovered why the herd had chosen this spot. There was a large artesian spring. It had enough force to squirt up into the air before creating a pool of water. The pool then created a stream as the water flowed east into the woods. John and Jim ran quickly to the water. They stuck their heads into the pool of cold clear water. They then drank their fill. It was apparent now why so many animal trails were leading this way.

Sitting there with their bellies distended with water, the run-a-ways collected their thoughts. They decided that this was the perfect place for them to hide out. John said, "We got everything we need. We got rope and string. We knows how to make traps and snares for the rabbits and birds. We got a few fishing hooks. We can find turtle eggs. We ought a be able to set a snare for one of the them deer as they go along the trail. I ain't ever done it but I bets I can figure it out. Jim, we got everything!"

"Not everything," Jim replied. "I sho wishes we had asked some of dem girls to come with us. Especially Sassy!"

"Nigar, you knows dem girls would have never made it across that river. All of us would have drowned. Anyway, Sassy was crazy bout me—not you!"

Taking the tops off of the molasses buckets, they took out some food for supper. They prepared to go to sleep. Going back towards the lake, they found a nice level spot. John took the large knife and cut bundles of grass. Jim spread the grass for a mattress. They spread one quilt over the pile and took the other one for cover. Still scared, they slept back to back with John keeping a firm grip on his knife.

The sun shining in their faces woke them up the next morning. Getting up and stretching, they had never felt better. After a small breakfast, they decided to go exploring by the lake. Once they got down there, it was no time before both boys were buck naked and wading out into the lake. They were surprised at how shallow the lake was along the bank. They had to go out about a hundred feet before the water came up to their chest. It also surprised them that there were small springs along the bottom. Every once in a while, they could feel cold water coming up between their toes.

As the days turned into weeks, the boys settled into their new freedom. For the first time, they could get up when they wanted to, go to bed when they wanted to, eat when they wanted to, and do whatever else they desired. Here to fore they had always been at someone's beck and call. Jim continued to sing, "FREE, FREE, FREE."

Their biggest concern everyday was filling their bellies. They found that the lake was teeming with fish. Although it contained many species, their favorite was the catfish. They made fishing poles out of cane that grew abundantly in the woods. After tying a string with a stolen hook to the cane, they baited the hook with the earthworms or grubs that they dug up. Then they would stick the poles into the bank, letting the end extend as far out as possible and then wait. Their wait was usually short. The catfish would bite almost as soon as the bait hit the water. With their diets augmented with turtle meat, turtle eggs, and snared rabbit, John and Jim thought they were in heaven. They even found wild plums growing at the edge of the clearing.

After snaring a rabbit late one evening, the boys headed north up the lake to look for turtle eggs. Just as they came out of a stand of thick cane, they came face to face with a white man riding a big palomino stallion. It was Buck Inman!

"How far is it to your campground?" Buck queried.

"It ain't but bout two miles down the lake," John replied.

"Well, I could sure use some cool spring water," Buck said. "Why don't we go down there and I will spend the night? I suspect the spring is on my property. With that, they gathered up all of their supplies and headed down the lake bank trail.

The sun had set but there was a full moon out. Buck thought that the reflection of the moon on the lake was one of the prettiest sights he had ever seen. The moon was so bright that it illuminated their way, and they made good time. When they exited the woods onto the clearing, Jim exclaimed, "Here we is!"

Buck thought, "What a beautiful spot." He couldn't wait to see it in the daylight.

Buck drank his fill of the cold spring water and then washed some of the days dust off of him. Worn out and tired, he was ready for some sleep. He picked himself out a spot right on the lake bank. It was just about 20 yards from the boys' campsite. He bid John and

Jim good night. Jim replied, "Good night and don't let the bed bugs bite!" Buck laughed and led Prince to the lake's edge.

After tethering the stallion, Buck spread out his bedroll and prepared to go to sleep. He then stopped and thought, "Something isn't right." He then realized what was different. NO MOSQUITOES! The perpetual west wind was blowing them back to the woods. He could see why the boys were able to sleep with no 'skitter' nets. What a pleasure to be able to stretch out under the moon and not have to worry about having to swat the insects all night!

After a good night's sleep, Buck woke up refreshed. He decided to take a quick swim before breakfast. Stripping down, he dived out into the lake. Like the boys had been, he was surprised at how cool the water was. As he waded around on the sandy bottom, he too felt the cool currents coming from the springs on the bottom of the lake. He thought, "I believe I have found a spot to live out the rest of my days."

After getting dressed and eating, he decided it was time to wake John and Jim up. He had a proposition to talk over with them. After letting them become fully awake, he laid out his thoughts.

"As I told you before, I never have been or am I now in favor of slavery. In fact, my stand on slavery is one of the reasons I left home. I just don't believe it is right for one man to own another. Therefore, I am willing to make a deal with you. All of us are going to require shelter by the time winter sets in. If you will help me build a cabin for myself, I will help you build one for yourselves here on my place. If we work hard, we should be able to complete both of them before winter."

The boys listened dumbfounded. They couldn't believe that this was a white man that didn't believe in slavery. They had never been given a choice in what they were to do. They had never had a white man sit down and talk to them. John replied, "We sho don't mind working. We been working hard all of our lives. You just tells us what to do and we'll do it. We been wondering how we was going to make it through the winter."

Buck told them, "I don't want to build my or your cabin here on this spot. I want to save this place for the larger house that I am planning on building some day. We will build both cabins a little further down the lake. We will still be fairly close to the spring and we will still catch a breeze off the lake. I sure wish I knew somewhere to get more supplies and building materials. I guess I am about the only white man within miles and miles of this place."

"Naw Suh, you ain't," replied Jim. "What do you mean?" asked Buck. The boys told Buck that on occasions hunting parties made up of white men, slaves, and dogs came through this area hunting for the black bears. The boys told Buck that they always hid when a party came through, but that one time they had decided to follow the group to see where they came from. The hunting party went to the south end of the lake and then turned west toward the river. They then followed a bear trail to a clearing on the banks of the mighty Mississippi. From a distance, the boys could see a collection of buildings that made up a small village. They could see slaves working the fields. They could see white men, women, and children going about their daily tasks. They saw that the residents had all types of livestock in their pastures. All in all, it reminded them too much of the place that they had escaped from in Arkansas. John told Jim, "We best get out'ta here. We sho don't want'a git caught by dem folks. We be back in slavery!" With that, John and Jim had made a quick retreat back to their hiding place.

Buck asked, "Just how far is this place?"

John replied, "We don't rightly know. It took us all day to get back, and we ran a lot of the way because we were skeered. It's a powerful good piece!"

5

Leota

Although excited, Buck decided to wait until the next morning to begin his trip to the settlement. He wanted to leave as early as possible in the morning. He hoped to beat the Mississippi heat that came with the morning sun. While the boys were swimming, he made preparations. He checked his weapons, groomed Prince, and packed his saddle bags. He also thought it best to hide some of his money there at his camp. He spotted a tree that had a hollow that was over his head. Buck took some of his funds and put them in his saddle bags. He then placed the leather pouch containing the rest of his money in the hollow.

Before retiring for the night, he told the boys his plan. He shared some of his supplies with them and told them that he would probably be gone for several days. The next morning, Buck arose before the break of dawn. He quickly saddled Prince and prepared to leave. He glanced down to where the boys were sleeping. He could see that they were deep in sleep. Mounting, he turned the big stallion south down toward the lake. After having rested a few days, Prince was raring to go. Buck said to him, "You might not be stepping quite so high after this day's trip." Moving out in the moonlight, Buck could hear all kind of wild critters move away in the darkness. He wondered what he was disturbing.

After riding for miles, Buck came to the south end of the lake. The water became more and more shallow. The lake was turning into a swamp. The huge cypress not only grew on the lake bank but lived out in the water. They were so thick that Buck's gaze could not penetrate the swamp. He could only imagine the large alligators that must live out there. Buck kept his eyes open as he continued south. Again, he was proud of the trail that had been beaten out by the wild animals. The going was not nearly as hard as he thought it was going to be.

Buck then came to a small stream. This was the outlet from the lake. Since it was mid-summer, the lake was down and the stream was quite shallow. Prince had no trouble carrying Buck safely to the other side. The trail now took a southwest direction. Pushing on, Buck followed the trail through the large trees and tall canes. The screeching of birds announced his passing. By mid-afternoon the trail widened and became more pronounced. Buck began to see hoof prints in the dirt. He felt like he must be getting close to civilization.

It was early afternoon when Buck rode out of the woods. He stopped to survey the scene. In front of him lay the mighty Mississippi. It was hard for Buck to believe that this was the same river that he had gazed out on from the deck of the riverboat in New Orleans. He also observed that the village the boys had described was more like a small town. He could make out several stores, a church, a livery stable and quite a few homes. He was surprised at how large and fine some of the houses were. He also noted that what the boys described as fields were really large gardens on the grounds near each house. He was surprised that the town was laid out with straight streets-almost as if the lots had been surveyed. Urging Prince into a canter, Buck headed for the town.

As he walked Prince down the dusty main street, Buck noticed all the attention that he was attracting. Not only was he a stranger, but he presented a bedraggled appearance. Weeks on the trail under the hot Mississippi sun had baked his skin and turned it a chocolate hue. His hair had grown down past his shoulders. He had grown a full beard. His clothes, though clean, looked dull and worn. For the first time in quite a while, Buck became conscious of his appearance. He said to Prince, "This is the first time that my horse looks better than me." As he proceeded toward the middle of the town, he spotted a sign advertising baths, haircuts and shaves. Buck stopped, dismounted, and tied Prince to the hitching post. He then entered the establishment where he was greeted by a short wizened elderly Chinese man. As Buck prepared for his bath, he took full notice of his clothes. He decided that he would need new clothes after his bath. He asked the Chinese man, called Jue, where he could buy new clothes. Jue directed him down the street to the local mercantile store.

When Buck walked into the store, he was surprised at the selection of fine men's wear. He thought, "There must be quite a few well off people around here!" The proprietor greeted him and observed his appearance. When Buck asked to see some clothes, the owner directed him to the section that displayed all of the work clothes. Smiling, Buck asked if he could see the better men's wear. Disdainfully, the proprietor escorted Buck to the gentleman's department. It wasn't until Buck started selecting several sets of complete wardrobes that the owner became interested. He was surprised at Buck's taste. After stacking up his new purchases, Buck then turned back to the work clothes. He bought enough to clothe not only himself, but enough to also clothe John and Jim. The owner was watching all of this in amazement. He was completely shocked when Buck pulled out a pouch of gold coins and asked how much he owed. After paying, Buck picked out a change of clothes and asked if he could pick up the rest of his purchases later. "Yes Sir! Yes Sir!" the proprietor replied.

Buck then returned to the barbershop. Jue had heated water and had laid out clean towels and bath cloths. After his bath, Buck asked to have his hair cut and his beard shaved. Jue was glad to comply. Buck put on his new clothes and boots. He told Jue to throw away his old ones. Jue was surprised at the change in appearance. Buck looked in the mirror and commented to himself, "I believe I look a little more like Buchanan Inman of the Inman Place, South Carolina." After paying Jue, he asked if the town had a land office. Jue gladly directed him up the street. Buck was again conscious of the stares as he walked up the plank sidewalk. Again, he smiled when the owner of the clothing store stepped out and half-bowed as he passed by.

When he entered the land office, he was greeted by an aristocratic looking gentleman. He introduced himself as George Knox, the land agent for the United States. He explained to Buck that he had been assigned the duty of parceling out the land in the area after the signing of the Treaty of Doak's Stand. It was under this treaty that the Choctaws had ceded all of the land up and down the river to the federal government. He told Buck that it had taken some time but all of the acquired land had been surveyed. There was a local surveyor that lived in town and worked for the government. This was the reason for the perfectly laid out town.

Buck then commented on how surprised he was that there were so many nice homes in the town. Mr. Knox replied, "If you think these are fine, you should see the large plantation homes that have been built up and down the river. They put these town houses to shame. You have to realize that the settlers in this area are not your ordinary settlers. Almost all are wealthy. Some are speculators who have bought up huge tracts of land, hoping to make a profit later. Others are wealthy planters from the old cotton states. Their land was getting worn out, so they sold out and brought their families and slaves here where the land is some of the richest in the world. Others are the sons of wealthy planters back east. They have taken their inheritance and purchased land and slaves. They hope to be extremely wealthy in a few years. So now you understand that this area is being settled by the wealthy aristocrats from the old slave states. In fact, we are having settlers arriving from Kentucky and the Carolinas almost every month."

After hearing this, Buck decided that it was time to inquire about his property, or what he hoped was his property. He pulled out the old Spanish land grant with the land description. He also pulled out his map that showed the location of the grant. Mr. Knox found the documents interesting. He compared the description on Buck's documents to his large map of the area. He asked, "Where did you get this?"

Not going into all of the details, Buck told him how he happened to acquire these legal documents. After listening carefully, Mr. Knox said, "Young man, you are in luck. Just recently the United States government has decided to honor all of these old Spanish land grants. This makes your claim valid. You are also lucky that some speculator has not unknowingly purchased your land. If this had happened, you would have a large legal battle on your hands. However, as things stand now, I can tell you that you own about six thousand acres of the best land around here. The land around Yazoo Lake is extremely rich. Of course, it is going to take a lot of man power to clear it and make it profitable for cotton. How many slaves do you own?"

Buck replied, "Well sir, I don't own any slaves. In fact, I don't really approve of slavery. I guess I will just have to do the best I can with my place by using hired labor." Taken back by Buck's reply, Mr. Knox curtly said, "You won't find much hired help around here and you might find that you won't fit in so well with the populace here. Most everyone here realizes that we have to have slavery to maintain our way of life. Without slave labor, none of these large plantations would be possible".

Buck said, "I understand plantation life. I was raised on one. If you will give me my recorded deed, I will be on my way. Mr. Knox handed Buck his deed and Buck turned and walked out the door. He was thinking, "All of these miles and I might as well be back home."

Buck walked back down the street and got Prince. He led him down the street to the livery stable. "Mighty fine horse," the liveryman said as he welcomed Buck.

"Yes sir, he's a good one. I want you to take especially good care of him. He has carried me a long way and deserves the best that you have to offer. I will pay for any extra trouble."

"Don't you worry," replied the liveryman. "I will treat him just like he was my own. He will be ready whenever you are ready to leave."

6

Miss Jane

Buck asked the livery owner if there was a place he could eat and if there was a place that he could spend the night. "Yes, Sir. There's the Southern Inn right around the corner. Its run by a lady everyone calls Miss Jane. You will find some mighty fine food there and a room to spend the night," replied the livery owner.

"Oh, by the way, tell me about the church that I passed on the way in. What denomination is it?" asked Buck.

"Ain't no denomination," the liveryman mumbled."We got Holy Rollers, Baptist, Methodist, Presbyterians and Episcopalians. In fact, I think we got a few Catholics. Just about everyone for miles around attends each Sunday. Some come because they are Christians, others come to socialize and the young folks come to court. You would be welcome if you want to come."

"Well, I just might the next time I am in town. I ought to fit in there somewhere," said Buck.

Buck left, walked down the street, and turned the corner toward the riverboat landing. On his left was the Southern Inn. As he walked in, he was greeted by Miss Jane herself. A rotund middle-aged woman, she was everyone's grandmother. She welcomed Buck and wanted to know all about him. She called her questions friendly; Buck called them nosey. He was tired of everyone wanting to know his life story. Divulging as little information as he could without appearing rude, Buck inquired about a meal and a room. Miss Jane said, "Bring your good looking self over here and have a seat. I will show you to your room after you eat. You are in luck. Back in the kitchen they are just finishing cooking tonight's meal. We are having fried chicken, peas, beans and fried corn." Miss Jane was not exaggerating. The food was delicious. It reminded Buck of the meals back home. After finishing his meal with Miss Jane's bread pudding, he leaned back and enjoyed the remains of his sweet tea. "Boy! I bet those girls were crazy about you back home. Did you leave anyone special?" Miss Jane asked. Embarrassed, Buck mumbled "No Ma'am".

Just as Buck was finishing his meal, other patrons started arriving. Tired of the curious stares cast his way since his arrival, Buck asked to be shown to his room. An old male slave grabbed his saddle bags and started to show him to his room. Buck said, "I can carry this myself." He was shown to a comfortable upstairs room with a view of the river. Buck was glad of the breeze coming off of the river. Tired from his long day, Buck decided to retire early. He quickly undressed and slid between the sheets. He had forgotten how good a bed with pillows felt. As he lay there relaxing, he thought about the town and the people he had met that day. The people that he met had actually been a lot like the folks back home. He decided that was probably because most of them had come from other southern states with the same culture that he was used to. By coming this far west, he had hoped to have put the slavery issue behind him. It seemed that it was not to be. Slavery was now a national issue! Not the events of the day or the noise from downstairs kept Buck from falling swiftly asleep.

7

A Place to Live

The next morning, Buck was eager to get back to camp. He had cabin building on his mind. He jumped out of bed and put on the new work clothes that he had bought. He asked Miss Jane if there was somewhere that he could leave his better clothes until he came back. He couldn't think of a place to store them back at camp. Pointing out a closet at the end of the hall, Miss Jane told him he could use it. "This way I know you will be coming back," she said, as she laughed.

Buck had spotted a hardware store as he arrived the day before and he headed in that direction. He went in and purchased enough supplies to last a few weeks. He also selected things that he thought he would need to build the cabins. His most important purchase was two double-bitted axes and a length of heavy rope. While the clerk was tallying up the bill, Buck went to the livery to get Prince. The liveryman had done a good job on the horse and Prince looked like the fine animal that he was. Buck thanked the liveryman and tipped him lavishly. He then saddled Prince and led him back to the hardware store. "You look mighty fine now Prince, but when we leave you are going to look like a pack horse," Buck said. When they headed out of town, that's exactly what Prince looked like. Buck had tied all of his purchases all over Prince. He was barely able to get in the saddle. Again, Buck felt the curious stares directed at him as he headed back to camp.

Anxious to get back to camp, Buck pushed Prince along. Feeling rested from his stay at the livery stable, the big stallion responded willingly. Buck had gotten a late start because of his shopping, but he still made it back to camp before it was too dark. He was welcomed profusely by the two run-a-ways. They couldn't wait to see what Buck had bought. The first two items Buck unpacked were two tarpaulins. No more sleeping in the rain. Next, he took out the clothes that he had purchased. The boys were surprised when he handed each of them several changes of clothes. They ran into the bushes and slipped on their new clothes. Although they were only work clothes, they were as proud of them as if they were tuxedos.

After eating a quick breakfast the next morning, they began cutting logs for the cabins. The boys cut the trees down and trimmed them up while Buck notched the logs. Buck was surprised at what good workers the boys were. They seemed to sense that it was important for the two cabins be built before the winter set in. By noon, there was quite an impressive amount of logs lying around. Buck had planned on using Prince to pull the logs to the site. But when it came time to actually hook him to the logs, Buck didn't have the heart. Prince was just too fine of an animal to be used as a work horse. He told the boys that he would have to go back to town the next morning to buy another horse.

The sun was just coming up when Buck eased Prince into his running walk gait. Buck thought, "I sure am glad I had second thoughts about using him as a work horse." Miles passed quickly and Buck was soon entering the little town of Leota. He rode straight to the livery stable. He was greeted by Tom, the owner. Buck quickly told him about the reason for his quick return. He needed a work horse. Tom told him that he had just what he needed. He told Buck that he had just traded for a nice gelding, his gear, and a wagon. Buck had not thought about a wagon but he could see where he could use one. Tom led Buck to the back where Charlie was stabled. Charlie was a large animal that probably weighed 1500 pounds. Buck could see that he had a little age on him but thought that he would do. He looked at the wagon. It also had some age on it but was sturdy enough. Buck asked Tom how much he wanted for the rig. Tom started with the usual horse trader's sales pitch. Buck stopped him, saying, "Look, I know you are an experienced trader. I know how to negotiate myself. Since I am in a hurry, why don't we skip all the haggling and you just give me your bottom price?"

Tom fell out laughing. "Boy, I like you. Looks like you are all business. Alright, I'll give you my lowest price." Satisfied with the amount, Buck paid, and Tom helped hook Charlie to the wagon. Buck then asked Tom to sell him some feed. Tom was glad to do so and loaded 20 sacks of feed onto the wagon.

Buck tied Prince to the back of the wagon and headed out of town. Again he was the center of attention as he drove down Main Street.

The trip back was not quite as fast as the one coming to town. Buck was quite pleased with Charlie. Although he was not fast, he willingly pulled the wagon toward the Lake. Since the way back was kind of rough, Buck was glad that he wasn't too fast.

When Buck arrived at his site, the boys had a surprise for him. They had worked all day cutting down trees and making logs. They had even learned how to notch the logs properly. They were excited to show Buck their day's work and even more excited to see the new horse and wagon. Buck untied Prince from the wagon and tied him to a tree. He then invited the boys to get in the wagon. It had just dawned on him that the boys had never ridden in a wagon. On the way back, he let them take turns driving. They bragged about how good drivers they were, but in reality, Charlie didn't need many instructions.

The next few days went by swiftly, as the three men labored from sun up to sun down. Using Charlie, they snaked the logs to the site of the boy's cabin. Buck showed them how to use skid poles and Charlie to roll the logs up one by one. After making a roof of cypress shakes, they filled the cracks between the logs with moss and mud.

Although all they had was a dirt floor, the boys thought this was a lot better than sleeping out in the open.

After finishing the first cabin, Buck turned his attention to his. He wanted to start with one large room with plans to add on as he had time. He was mainly concerned about winter approaching. He had built the boys' cabin back in the woods away from prying eyes. He also built his back from the lake. He was saving the high spot by the lake for his permanent home. With the help of the boys, Buck built a room fifteen feet by twenty feet. Using the same technique as he used in building the other cabin, it did not take them too long to make the second cabin weather tight. Buck also added a front porch. With netting at the windows, both cabins could get a breeze off of the lake. Buck decided that when he went to town again, he would purchase two stoves to heat and cook with.

Buck then turned his attention to a barn and corral for the horses. After building another small structure, Buck attached a lean-to roof for the horses and built a split rail fence. They were all tired but satisfied with what they had accomplished.

Buck woke the next morning after a good night sleep. He had been so busy that he had forgotten what day it was. After making some calculations, Buck determined that it was Saturday. He decided that this would be a good day to head to town. He thought that he could buy some furnishings for the cabins. He sure was tired of sleeping on the floor. It also occurred to him that it would also give him an opportunity to attend church. He could drive in, have a good meal at Miss Jane's, spend the night and then attend service on Sunday. He would have to take Charlie and the wagon. After making his plans, he told the boys. He also cautioned them to go to the woods if any strangers appeared. The boys hitched Charlie to the wagon while Buck was dressing. Buck then picked up his rifle, his bible, and headed for town.

It was the middle of the afternoon when Buck arrived in town. He went straight to Miss Jane's. "My, My!" Miss Jane exclaimed. "I thought you had forgotten about the clothes that you left here!"

"No Ma'am, I just haven't had any need for dress clothes for quite some time."

After getting his clothes out of the closet, Buck ordered a bath and headed up to his room. He had forgotten how good a hot bath felt. After dressing, Buck headed out to the barber shop. As Buck waited his turn, he could not help but notice how the rest of the patrons kept cutting their eyes his way. He tried to ignore them, but they got his attention when they started talking about the upcoming war.

"Did you read about what happened in Washington last week? Some of the Southern Senators actually had a fist fight with some of them Yankee Senators. They were arguing about secession. Our Senators told them that the Northerners could not tell us in the South what to do!" one man said. "

Well good for them! I wish I had been there to pass a few licks myself! Hey! We were a free state when we joined and we can go back to being independent any time that we want to," added another. Buck listened to all of this while keeping his mouth shut. He thought, "I have come this far but I am still listening to the same conversations like the ones back home."

The barber tried, as all barbers do, to pry into Buck's background and to find out what he was doing in town. Buck would have none of it. After being noncommittal, he paid and went for a walk around town. He checked on Charlie at the livery stable and headed back to the rooming house. The restaurant was full when he arrived. Taking a table in one corner, he had one of the best meals in a while. Then tired, he went upstairs to his room. It seemed a little strange to lie there with the window open and listen to all of the people walking about town. He was soon fast asleep.

He arose early the next morning and dressed for church. He put on the new suit and boots that he bought when he first came to town. It was a pleasure to be cleaned up and dressed up again. Picking up his Bible, he headed downstairs. There were already several people eating when he ordered. Miss Jane came by and embarrassed him by exclaiming in a loud voice about how good he looked. Buck hated it when people called attention to him. Buck finished eating and asked Miss Jane what time the church services started.

8

Church

Miss Jane told Buck that the services started about 10 o'clock, but that the preaching would start around eleven o'clock. The first hour would be mostly fellowshipping and singing. She explained that since most of the people attending lived quite some distance from town, this was a chance to be not only fed spiritually, but socially. She also explained that, as was the custom, there would be dinner on the grounds after service. Buck told her that he probably wouldn't stay for that since he wasn't taking any food and that he hardly knew anyone. "Well boy, you are sure welcome to come back here and eat with us ole backsliders that don't go to church!" Buck laughed and said he might just do that.

After walking slowly around town, Buck made his way to the church. Some people had already arrived and there was a steady stream of buggies, wagons, and horses pulling into the parking area. Buck could tell immediately that there was quite a gap in the wealth of the people attending. Some were attired in the latest fashion like Buck. Others' clothes were clean but a little threadbare. Buck was pleased that the social status did not seem to make a whole lot of difference. Everyone acted as if they were genuinely glad to see each other. Buck assumed that everyone got a little lonesome living out from town during the week.

While everyone was greeting each other and making their way into the church, Buck slipped in and sat on a back pew. The preacher, a long, lanky, elderly man called the service to order. He called upon the young song leader to come forward and lead the congregation in a song service. The young man responded by asking everyone to stand and join in the singing. Since there were no song books, he chose the songs that everyone knew by heart. Buck was able to join in because he had grown up singing these same songs back home. He was particularly glad to join in on "Beulah Land" and "Amazing Grace". These two had always been his favorites.

The sermon was entitled 'WAS JESUS' BLOOD ANY DIFFERENT FROM ANYONE ELSE'S'. Buck was surprised at the depth of the preacher's presentation. He had forgotten how good it felt to be in the house of the Lord and to worship Jesus. After the conclusion of the service, everyone was invited to stay for the meal. The preacher insisted that everyone stay whether they had brought food or not. "As usual, there will be more food than any of us can eat!" he exclaimed.

Still feeling a little uncomfortable, Buck tried to ease out the back so he could head to Miss Jane's. It was not to be. He hadn't noticed, but several of the unattached young ladies had spotted him standing in the back. As soon as the service was over, five of them made a straight line to him and introduced themselves. Buck found it amusing since they ranged in age from fourteen to twenty-five. After prying as much information from him as they could, they insisted that he stay and eat with them. By this time, some of the adults came over to introduce themselves. There was nothing Buck could do to get out of staying. In fact, it wasn't but a few moments until he was enjoying the food and the company. He too had been lonely.

After a pleasant night's rest at the Southern Inn, Buck went down to have breakfast. He asked Miss Jane if he could pick up his dress clothes when he left town. She told him that was no problem but teased him about where he was going to wear such fine clothes out on the lake.

Buck was in a hurry. He knew he had a lot to buy and that it would be a slow trip back home. He first went to the livery stable to pick up his horse and wagon. He was so glad that he had had the forethought to buy them. His next stop was the mercantile store. His welcome was a little different than the first one he received. This time, the proprietor fell all over himself making Buck welcome. You could almost see the dollar signs dancing in his eyes.

Buck started piling up everything he thought he might need. He selected a few more clothes for himself and the boys. He then asked about a bed, mattresses and bedding. The proprietor showed him an antique tester bed that he had bought from a family that had decided to return to Virginia. Buck commented, "Pretty nice for a log cabin but I will take it." He then purchased new cotton mattresses, sheets and blankets to go with it. He also picked out a wardrobe, a chair, and a dresser with drawers. "Not exactly what mother would have but it will have to do." Then, as an afterthought, he decided to buy the boys a couple of mattresses. Since they had never slept on mattresses, he didn't know if they would sleep on them or not. In the back of his mind, he kind of thought they would learn to prefer them to the floor. This also called for him to add more bedding to his pile of purchases. Buck also purchased the two cook stoves he had thought about. He was tired of cooking over the campfire. After this purchase, he decided he just about had a wagon load. The proprietor excitedly added up the bill. After Buck paid with gold coins, the owner and his help were glad to load everything onto the wagon.

Just as the loading was complete, Buck heard, "Mr. Inman! Mr. Inman!" Turning, Buck saw that it was the man from the telegraph officer calling him from across the street. As soon as Buck walked over, he said, "I sure am glad to see you. I have a telegraph here for you. I didn't know how I was going to get it to you. It looks very important." Buck thanked the postmaster and accepted the letter. He could see immediately that it was from home. He quickly opened it and read the following:

> *Your father has died. He had a massive heart attack. Since*
> *we couldn't reach you, we had to hold the funeral without*

you. Sorry. I hope this letter reaches you soon. Please come home at once. We NEED you! Love, mother.

Stunned, Buck stood there thinking. He had always thought of his father as invincible. He knew this was a life-changing moment for him. He knew that he was going to have to grow up in a hurry. He also knew that he had to leave for South Carolina immediately. Buck was glad that he had written his mother to tell her where he was located.

Hurrying back across the street, he told the merchant to finish loading the wagon with as much food and horse feed as he could possibly put on the wagon. He then rushed up the street to get the rest of his clothes. Stopping for a moment, he hurriedly sent his mother a telegram telling her he was on his way. By the time he got back to his wagon, everything was loaded. He paid the bill and was on his way back to the lake in a matter of minutes.

9

Return to Inman Place

Although Buck was in a hurry, he had to let Charlie take his time pulling the heavy wagon. This gave him plenty time to think and make plans. Still in shock, he tried to think of the quickest way to get back to Inman Place, S.C. He would have rather ridden Prince back home but he realized this would take too long. His other alternative would be to catch a riverboat at Leota Landing to New Orleans. There he could transfer to another ship heading to the coast of South Carolina. He could then purchase a horse and tack to complete his journey. The only other choice he had was to catch a paddle-wheeler north to Memphis, Tennessee. From there, he could go by rail to Atlanta and South Carolina. After pondering about what to do, he decided the best way home would be through New Orleans. He thought, "I will have to find out from Tom the boat schedules." Having decided on a plan, he pushed Charlie as fast as he could toward the lake.

It was mid afternoon when he arrived. As always, the boys were glad to see him. This time was different. They had never seen him so serious. He sat them down and explained about the letter that he had received. He told them what his plans were. Buck also told them that they were going to have to take care of the place and Charlie while he was gone. He didn't know how long he would be gone. The boys assured him that they could handle everything while he was gone. Buck hadn't realized how much John and Jim had matured during the time they had been with him. He felt comfortable leaving them in charge.

After the conversation was over, Buck and the boys immediately set about unloading the wagon. They unloaded Buck's belongings into his cabin first. Buck was in too much of a hurry to set everything up. He was satisfied to just get everything into the cabin. They then unloaded the boy's new clothes and mattresses. Buck was surprised at how proud they were of the mattresses. They flung themselves down on them as soon as they got them into their cabin. With a laugh, Buck said, "Come on now, we have got to get this feed unloaded!" After the wagon was empty, Buck asked the boys to put it and Charlie up. He also asked them to saddle up Prince while he went in to pack. He did not spend a lot of time on packing. He would be traveling light. He figured he could buy more clothes on the way if he needed them.

Dusk was settling in as Prince moved swiftly toward Leota. Buck was glad the days were still longer. He was hoping to reach town by dark. Coming into town, he headed straight to the livery stable on the edge of town. Tom was just closing up when Buck approached. Surprised, Tom asked what he was doing back in town. Buck told him his news. Concerned, Tom asked what he could do to help. He assured Buck that he could leave Prince as long as needed to. He then told him that he was in luck. There was a paddle-wheeler heading for New Orleans scheduled to dock the next morning. Pleased with this information, Buck headed for the Southern Inn to spend the night. In the morning, he would be on his way.

The paddle-wheeler backed slowly away from the dock into the mighty Mississippi. It then swung south towards New Orleans. The boat was heavily loaded with cotton bales and other passengers. Buck was glad that the muddy river current was fast. With only one stop scheduled at Vicksburg, maybe it would not take too long to reach the large city. Although it was a small boat, it made good time. They were soon stopping at Vicksburg. Buck had hoped to visit the town while they stopped, but the Captain told him there would not be enough time to get off. They were only going to stop long enough to pick up two passengers and they would be on their way. There was no room for any more produce. An elderly couple got on quickly and the boat resumed its trip South. Buck stood on the front deck and watched the wooded bank pass by. Occasionally there would be a clearing in the woods with a plantation facing the river. These plantations became closer together as the boat neared New Orleans. Buck thought about his friend John, who had been killed. What an adventure he had been on since that incident had occurred!

Upon reaching New Orleans, Buck disembarked. He quickly bought a ticket on a steam ship that made a regular run down the gulf coast, then around the tip of Florida, ending up at Charleston. Buck's ticket took him to Savannah. He had decided that it would be faster for him to get off at Savannah. There, he could catch the train that ran north. It passed within ten miles of Inman Place. Buck was sure that if he could get that close, he would have no problem getting friends to take him out to the plantation. With his plans made, Buck hired a carriage to carry him to the French Quarters. He checked in at the Hotel Monteleone on Royal Street. After a meal at Antoine's, he purchased Cuban cigars at a small shop. Lighting one, he took a stroll up Bourbon Street. The French Quarter was alive with people shopping and dining out. Buck had to be careful when crossing the street. The large carriages pulled by fine horses did not slow down for pedestrians. Buck thought, "What a difference from Leota!"

After stretching his legs, Buck returned to his room. He thought about visiting the May family but decided that he just wouldn't have time this trip. On the way back, he purchased a paper. It had been a while since he had caught up with the news. The first thing he noticed was that the editors were screaming for the Southern states to secede from the United States. They were giving the same reasons that Buck had heard for several years. The difference now was, instead of just talking about the possibility of secession; the people of the South were actually planning to do it!

Buck decided that he might as well go to bed and try to get a good night's sleep. He had to be up early the next morning to catch the steamer to Savannah. A good night's sleep was not to be. He was too tired and stressed. He could only manage a few hours sleep. He was up early the next morning, making his way to the dock. Since he was traveling light with only one bag, he decided that it would not be necessary to hire a carriage. Buck felt that he could make the walk through Jackson Square and on to the dock with no problem. He was soon in line to board the steamer with the rest of the passengers.

After a scenic but uneventful trip around the tip of Florida, Buck arrived at Savannah. He quickly disembarked and hired a carriage to carry him to the train depot. He hoped to catch a train that would get him close to home before dark. This was not to be. The best connection that he was able to get would have him arriving at Inman, SC, around ten p.m. As the train jerked to a start, Buck tried to catch a nap. This was unsuccessful due to the fact that the train stopped at all small and large towns. Buck now knew this would be a long trip.

Finally, the train pulled into the depot at Inman. Buck and a few other passengers got off. The town had basically closed up for the night. There was no one at the station and there was no one on the streets. Buck grabbed his bag and started up the street to the home of an acquaintance. Knocking on the door, he was greeted with, "Who is out there?" "Buck Inman!" was the reply. This brought the whole family to the front parlor to greet him. They were surprised but glad to see him. After a lot of catching up, Buck asked Robert, one of his childhood friends, if he could impose upon him to take him to Inman Plantation. Robert was only too glad to comply. While Buck and Robert visited a little more, one of the servants hooked up the carriage and brought it around to the front. Robert and Buck got in and started the trip to Inman on the road that Buck had traveled many, many times.

As they traveled, old memories came to Buck's mind. He recalled the happy times that he was allowed to come up this very road to town with his parents. He remembered riding his horse to town to date several different girls in town. But then the strongest memory of all came to him. It was so real that it nauseated him. "Slap, Slap" went the strap. In his mind, he could see Big Man tied to the post being whipped by the overseer. The reasons that he left began flooding back. Trying to shake off this mood, Buck started talking to Robert about the good times that they had had as boys.

As they turned onto the lane leading to the big house, everything was so familiar. Buck could smell the smoke coming from the smudge pots that were burning in the quarters to help keep the mosquitoes away. From there, he could here babies crying and dogs barking. He could hear the cattle lowing in the pastures. Horses were shuffling around the stalls in the barn. He could see the mansion looming tall in the moonlight. Home—but not home!

Buck thanked Robert and asked if he would like to come in. Robert replied, "Since it is almost midnight, I had better get back to town." With that, he gave a wave and headed back.

Holding his bag in one hand, Buck walked up on the wide front porch and pulled the chain that rang the bell. Immediately, the door was opened by his mother. She had been waiting for him to arrive but had gone to sleep in one of the parlor chairs. From his telegraph message, she had expected Buck earlier in the day. As Buck walked in, she didn't even look at him, but grabbed her baby boy around the neck and hugged and hugged him. He had put out of his mind how much he loved his mother; but all of a sudden, this strong emotion returned and he could fell tears welling up in his eyes.

After a long embrace, Buck said to his mother, "I am so sorry that I was not able to get here for the funeral. I just did not get the message in time. I would have liked to have been here in your time of need."

"I am sorry, too," his mother replied. "You know, it broke Big John's heart when you left. He never talked about it but I knew how much he regretted driving you away."

Changing the subject that they both found uncomfortable, she started talking about the funeral. "Oh Buck, you would have been so proud. We had one of the grandest funerals that has ever been had in South Carolina. I expect, including the slaves, we had almost a thousand people here. We had some of the most important people in the state in attendance. We even had the Governor and his family here. You know everyone loved Big John."

Buck too loved Big John. As a young boy, his father provided him with everything a young boy could desire. He took time to take Buck hunting and fishing. He also took him riding over the massive plantation as he inspected the crops. It wasn't until Buck got older that he realized that his father was attempting to mould him into another Big John. It just was not to be. Buck had too much of his mother in him. Although he loved his father, he slowly began to lose respect for him. As Buck reflected back, he realized that the subject that started pulling them apart was slavery. They simply could not agree.

As Buck imagined the elaborate funeral, he doubted that anyone questioned Big John's Christianity. In his mind, he could visualize the great crowd. He could almost hear the preacher reminding everyone what a great man Big John was. Everyone there would presume that since Big John had made a profession of faith as a youngster, been baptized, and attended church on occasion, he was automatically a Christian. Buck knew better!

His mother interrupted his thoughts. She told him that they had already read the will. As the only son, Buck had inherited the plantation and everything that went with it, including the slaves. His mother retained all of the household goods, silver, crystal and a great deal of cash. She was well fixed for life. Buck was then asked if he would be moving back home. Buck did not hesitate. He told his mother that he was going back to Mississippi. He was living a different life there. No pretense. No trying to keep up appearances. No politics. NO SLAVERY ON HIS PROPERTY!

Buck told his mother that he thought war was coming and that he was of the opinion that they should sell everything and leave South Carolina. He had heard the war drums beating in the state. He then said that it was getting late and that they would formulate a plan in the morning. He was adamant that keeping slaves was not going to be an option for him!

They did not know that in the next room Birdie was listening to every word. She had been waiting politely for Buck to greet his mother before she made her appearance. She still loved Buck as if he was hers. However, the conversation caused a knot to form in her stomach. SELL EVERYTHING! SELL EVERYTHING! That included the slaves. That included her. A FRIEND, BUT STILL A POSSESSION!

After agreeing to formulate plans, Mistress retired to her room and Buck made his way to his old room. It was basically just as he had left it. The room had not changed but Buck had. Home—but not at home.

Buck was awakened the next morning by loud voices outside his window. Startled, Buck jumped up and pulled on his trousers, a shirt and some slippers. When he walked out onto the upstairs balcony, he was amazed at the site. All of the slaves of Inman place were standing silently on the front lawn patiently waiting for Buck to wake up. The commotion was being caused by the overseer. He was confronting Big Man who was standing in front of the nearly 500 slaves.

"What is going on here?" Buck demanded to know.

"These nigras are not supposed to leave the quarters and come to the big house. I done told them that they better get themselves back where they belong. I guess they think that just because you are home, they can do what they want. Particularly this big buck nigra."

"Well, I am going to solve your problem. In case you were not informed, I am now the owner of Inman place. That means that you are standing on my property. As you know, I have never liked you. Therefore, I am going to give you and your family one hour to get off my property. You may pick out one wagon, two mules, a milk cow and one saddle horse. But I want you gone immediately. I will consult with my mother to see if you have any wages coming. If so, I will send them to you when I get dressed. Now, since your hour is starting, I suggest that you start packing!"

Dumbfounded and not wanting to confront the man that Buck had become, the overseer turned on his heel and headed back to his house to start packing.

When he left, Buck said to Big Man, "I am really glad to see you. What in the world are all of ya'll doing out here so early in the morning?" Big Man replied, "Mr. Buck, I sho am glad to see you. We didn't want to disturb you but we sho did want to beg you not to sell us with the place!" Buck smiled to himself and thought, "Just as always, there are no secrets at Inman Place."

Buck said, "Alright, I want everyone to go back to the quarters except you, Big Man. I want you to go to the kitchen and tell Birdie to make me and you one of her famous breakfasts. We can discuss this after I eat."

"Yes Suh, Mr. Buck! I'll go tell her!" FRIENDS, BUT STILL A POSSESSION!

Buck dressed quickly and headed to the kitchen. He was careful not to awaken his mother and sisters. When he walked in he found Big Man and Birdie in deep conversation. He greeted them, "Good morning, Birdie! Good morning, Big Man!" Birdie spun around and exclaimed, "We sho is glad to have you home."

"You is a sight for sore eyes," added Big Man. "You sho have growed up!"

Smiling, Buck said, "Where is that breakfast I have been missing?" Flustered, Birdie said, "It's almost ready, but Mr. Buck, you can't eat in the kitchen with us. You is the MASTER of Inman Place!" FRIENDS, BUT STILL A POSSESSION!

"I guess that if I am the Master of Inman Place I can eat anywhere I want to," Buck replied. "I haven't changed that much. Aren't you the one that use to change my diapers?"

Laughing, Birdie and Big Man relaxed and felt more at ease with their new master. She said, "You sho was a bad little ole boy. You always did what you wanted to and you ain't changed!"

After finishing his breakfast, Buck asked Big Man to sit at the table so that they could talk. "Why in the world were all of the slaves standing on the front lawn when I got up this morning?" he asked.

Birdie quickly turned around and said, "Ya'll got to excuse me. I best go see if Mistress and the girls are about ready for breakfast." She then quickly exited the kitchen. They all knew who had relayed Buck's conversation to the quarters.

Big Man said, "Mr. Buck, if you sell Inman Place what is going to come of us? You know that if we is sold we will be split up with families going every which aways. Some folks will never see their families again."

"I really wasn't planning on selling ya'll. I was actually planning on setting you free. You know I do not like the institution of slavery. I have always said that I do not believe that God ever intended for one man to own another. You will be free people when I leave for Mississippi," Buck responded.

81

"But Mr. Buck, free us to what? We ain't got nowhere to go. Most of us folks don't know nothing but working on Inman Place. We been here all of our lives just like our parents. Very few of us has ever been off the plantation. We wouldn't have no way to make a living or no place to live!" exclaimed Big Man.

Realizing that he had not thought this situation thru, Buck grew quiet for a moment. Then he said, "Well, if I can't sell you, and I can't free you here, I have only one other recourse. I will free everyone, but anyone who wants to go to Mississippi with me may do so. When we get there, I will devise some system where you will be free but work for me. I will try to come up with a plan where I will continue to take care of everyone but they will receive wages as free people. I don't know anything else to do. Slavery is like a tar baby; hard to get unstuck from!"

Big Man jumped up, "I don't know about everyone else but I is on my way to Mississippi!"

Birdie who had been listening in, burst into the room, "I don't know where Mississippi is, but I sho am going with you, Mr. Buck. I 'spect everyone else will want to go too. They sho ain't got nowhere else to go when you sell Inman Place!"

Buck said, "Ya'll talk it over with each other and with the rest of the hands. Explain that I would like to just set them free and let them go anywhere they want to but this can't happen in South Carolina. However, tell everyone that if they don't want to go with us, I will try to find a place for them on one of the neighboring plantations. I do know some owners who do not mistreat their slaves. We have plenty of time for everyone to make up their minds."

Getting up, Buck said, "Birdie, you go ahead and start fixing Mother's and the girls' breakfast. I am going to get them up. We have a lot of plans to make."

10

Leaving Inman Place

Mistress and Buck's two sisters were seated at the dining table when Buck entered. As always, Buck's mother was fully dressed with her hair and make-up done to perfection. Rachel, the oldest sister, was dark-haired and had dark skin like her father. A little on the plump side, she was still a pretty girl. Her mother was hoping that she would slim down as she got older. She was approaching 18 years old. Rebecca, or Becky as she liked to be called, was just the opposite of her sister. Whereas Rachel took everything seriously, Becky thought that life was a game not to be taken seriously. With long blond hair, blue eyes, and a slim figure, everyone said that she was the mirror image of her mother. She would be 15 years old on her next birthday. The two grabbed Buck and gave him a big hug. They had really missed their big brother.

"Buck. Sit down and have breakfast with us. We are just starting," Mistress said.

"I will sit with ya'll while you eat, but I have already had breakfast in the kitchen with Birdie and Big Man."

Appalled, Mistress said, "Surely you didn't do that! You are the master of Inman Place! You shouldn't be eating in the kitchen with the slaves! You are not ten years old again. You have a certain status that you must retain!"

Laughing, Buck replied, "You know that I don't think of Birdie and Big Man as slaves. Big Man is more like a brother and Birdie is like a second mother to me. I will tell ya'll what I told them. If I am now master of Inman Place, I guess I can eat anywhere I want to. Besides, that's not important now. We have got to make plans for the future. As I said last night, war is coming and coming soon. I believe it will start here in South Carolina. I am hoping that it won't reach down into western Mississippi. Anyway, I own six thousand acres next to the river in Mississippi. I like it there and I am hoping to ride out the War and not get involved. Now, this is my plan. I want to sell Inman Place. I am going to free all of the slaves and give them an option of going to Mississippi with me as paid laborers or they can stay here. The ones that don't want to go, I will find them a home on Mount Locust Plantation. Mr. Upchurch, the owner, has always been a decent man and I believe he will be fair to them. I believe he will take them, especially if I give them to him."

Continuing, Buck said, "Now, we have to make plans for you three. I stayed awake most of the night thinking about this. I came up with several options. Ya'll could go live in upstate New York near Aunt Margaret. Mother, with the money that you inherited from your parents and your part of this estate, you can pretty well do anything you want. You could buy some property close to Aunt Margaret and build you any kind of house you want. Or you could do like a lot of wealthy families from the south. Go to Europe on an extended vacation until the war is over. The final option would be for ya'll to come to Mississippi with me. If you want to come, I'll give up my log cabin and build one of the grandest houses on the river!"

Mistress and the girls sat there speechless as Buck laid out the options. After regaining her composure, Mistress said, "Now Buck, I don't mind visiting your Aunt Margaret but the Lord knows that I can't stand those cold winters up there. And I don't believe I could put up with those Yankees for the rest of my life. Besides, if the girls and I moved up there, they would probably end up marrying some Yankee boys! Wouldn't that be something, me with a bunch of Yankee grandchildren? No! That is not an option. I also don't consider going to Europe an option. No one knows how long the war might last. I sure don't want to be stuck with those royalty worshipping snobs looking down on me. The fact that I have ten times as much money as them would not keep them from snubbing me because we don't have any royal blood in our veins. No! I am not going to England or any other part of Europe except for a short visit."

"I guess that brings us back to Mississippi," Georgia continued. "I have only been there one time. Your father and I caught a paddle-wheeler from New Orleans to Natchez, Mississippi, in our younger days. I can see the city now, sitting up on top of the bluff as we pulled into the bank. I had never seen so many large, fine and beautiful homes. All of the ladies were sophisticated and the men were all gentlemen. They all bragged about the fact that there were more millionaires in Natchez than any other city in the country. I think I could be happy settling close to people like that."

Buck said, "Mother, I wouldn't want you to make a decision on any false assumptions. I agree with you that Natchez is one fine city, and the society there is fine. There is wealth everywhere. However, my place is not like that. I live about one hundred miles north of the city. There is only one city of any size close to me and that is Vicksburg. It is pretty nice but does not compare to Natchez. My place is about fifty miles from it. Most of the year, about the only way to get there is by paddle-wheeler. Where I am is almost like a frontier. People of all kind are moving in from everywhere. Most have class and wealth. The only thing that I don't like is that most of them are bringing their slaves with them. It just seems that I can't get away from slavery. All I can promise is that you will have the grandest home on the river—just as fine as any you saw in Natchez. We will put in all of the newest inventions. We will have running water, carbide lights in each room, and flushing toilets. I will start building it as soon as I get back to Mississippi. We will rent ya'll a place in Charleston until I can get enough built for us to move in. Then you can supervise the interior details. You can design the inside anyway you want."

Getting excited, Buck had already formulated a plan. He would sell Inman Place. He would form a wagon train of all the wagons, all of the stock, all of the slaves, and all of the household furnishing. He would start this on the way to Mississippi. It would be led by Big Man. He would then get his family settled in Charleston. After making these arrangements, he would be free to return home and start the building project. Strange. He was already thinking of his plantation as home. He was no longer the carefree young man that he had been just a year earlier. He was now the Master!

They all agreed that Mistress and the girls would talk it over and make a decision that day.

Buck left to go talk to the slaves. "Where is Big Man?" Buck asked Birdie as he walked into the kitchen.

"He jest stepped out on the back a few minutes ago to check on the chickens," she replied.

"Thank you," Buck said as he left the house to find Man. He didn't have to look far. Man was returning back up the path from the chicken yard area.

"Man, come over here and sit in the gazebo with me. We have a lot of plans to make."

After sitting, Buck started with his plans, "I want you and Birdie to move into the overseer's house. As of now, you are the overseer of Inman Place. I will make the decisions and you will see that they are carried out."

FRIEND, BUT STILL A POSSESSION.

Astounded, Man replied, "But Mr. Buck, ain't no nigra ever been an overseer of any plantations around here. I don't even know if them young bucks will even listen to me. You know they is all used to the white folks telling them what to do."

Smiling, Buck replied, "You know everyone on the plantation has always respected you. Me included. Besides, you need to look in the mirror. I don't think anyone is going to mess with a 6' 6", 280 lb. man! You will just have to get used to the idea of being in authority, because I have other plans for you. As you know, I am going to offer to free the slaves and allow the ones that want to go to Mississippi with me. This is not as easy as it sounds. I have several things that I have to get done before this can happen. First, I have got to get Mother and the girls settled in Charleston. Then, I have to sell Inman Place. When I got here, I had received several written offers from around the state from men who would like to purchase the place. So selling should not be that big of a problem. After I sell, I need to hurry back to Mississippi and start building the family a proper home. You will have to see the cabin I built. Its comfortable, but hardly a permanent home for my family. In fact, I want you and Birdie to live there when you get to my new place. Now, we get to the real problem-how to get nearly 500 bodies overland to their new home. I have been pondering on that problem. But, before we try to make plans on that, I want to talk to the slaves and see how many want to go with us."

Buck and Man got up and walked over to the massive plantation bell that had been rung for many occasions on the plantation. Ringing it started daily work. Ringing it stopped work in the evening. It rang when someone was born, it rang when someone died. It rang on joyous occasions and it rang on sad occasions. It was a way to communicate over the large plantation. Man reached over and grabbed the rope and started pulling. The large clapper began striking one side of the bell and then the other. The loud peal could be heard all over the plantation. All of the slaves realized that they were being summoned to the Big House for something important!

Buck said, "Remind me to take this bell with me when we leave."

It took a little while, but soon all of the slaves, from the young to the old, were standing in front of Buck and Man wondering what their fate was going to be. Buck was now the Master! Buck stepped up on the bed of an old wagon that had been left near the barn. He wanted to be sure that everyone could see and hear him.

He began his speech, "As you know, I have never approved of the institution of slavery. This is one of the reasons that I left Inman Place. I did not expect the sudden death of my father. I also did not expect him to leave all of his property to me. You, as slaves, became my property upon his death. This has put me in a strange position. I did not want anything to do with slavery but now I own about five hundred slaves. The other thing is that all of us here on Inman Place are like family. Most of you have been here for generations. You have served my family through the years and you have watched me grow up. When I was young, I played with a lot of you. Some of you older men took me rabbit hunting. What I am trying to say is that I have been trying to figure out what I can do for you. Man has convinced me that selling you is not an option. You would be scattered everywhere and your families would be split up. I told Man that I would just free you. I don't need the money. He asked, "Free you to what?" You would not have anywhere to go. Therefore, I have made a decision. Since I am determined not to be a slave holder, I AM GOING TO FREE YOU! However, if you wish, you can come to Mississippi with me. When you get there, I will provide you a place to live, food to eat and clothes to wear. I will also pay you for your labor. It won't be a whole lot because I will be furnishing your necessities, but you will have your own money, and will be free and can leave any time you want. Also, you need to realize that this is not going to be easy. The trip to my plantation will be long and hard. When you arrive, you will have to work hard. We will be clearing land and building barns and pastures. There are also cabins that must be built so that you will have a place to live. I will expect everyone to work hard. Also, I forgot to tell you that if any of you don't want to go with me, I have made arrangements for you to live with Mr. Upchurch. You will still be slaves, but he will be good to you.

Buck thought he was surprising the slaves with his announcement. In reality, they had already heard about the plans. The slave grapevine was still working well. Most of them had already decided to go to Mississippi. They were excited about being free and since most of them had never been off of the plantation they were looking forward to a new world and a new life. He was surprised when the slaves started clapping, dancing and saying, "Praise de Lord! We is free! We is free!"

"Mr. Buck, they had already made their mind up about what they was going to do. Almost everyone wants to go with you. They is a few old folks that want to go to Mr. Upchurch's. They think they is too old to make the trip," said Man.

After the commotion abated, Buck held his hands up and said, "Man tells me that almost everyone wants to go to Mississippi. That is fine with me. We will have a lot of work to do. We have to finish harvesting the crops. I will have to buy more wagons and a few more mules. You need to start putting up food for the trip. The wagon train will leave as quickly as possible, but it will still be several months before it can get on the road. In the meantime, you have a new overseer." The crowd grew silent. Who was overseer was very important to them. They only had contact with their master occasionally. They had to deal with the overseer every day!

"Your new overseer is Big Man!"

As Buck stepped down from the wagon to go back to the big house, he was approached by Uncle Bob. Uncle Bob was a small grey headed slave whose spryness belied his age. "Mr. Buck! I sho hope that you ain't put out with me because some of us old folks ain't making the trip with you. It ain't dat we don"t want to go, its jest dat we figure we is a little too old to be walking six hundred miles. Time we got there we, be wore out and no good to anybody."

Buck replied, "I certainly understand. It's going to be a mighty hard trip. Like I said, Mr. Upchurch has promised to take anyone that doesn't want to go to Mississippi. You used to run the dogs for him and my daddy when they were rabbit hunting. You know he will treat you well."

"Yas Suh, I knows that. We had some mighty fine times running ole rabbit. I is glad that you ain't mad at me." Then with a sly grin, Uncle Bob said, "I guess you already knows that I got me a woman over at Mr. Upchurch's place. I sho would miss her on some of dem cold winter nights."

"No, I hadn't heard about that. Can't say I am surprised. You always were volunteering to go to Mr. Upchurch's to help train his dogs. And just think, I was feeling sorry for you because you were too old to make the trip," replied Buck.

"I is a little old, Mr. Buck, but I ain't dead," Uncle Bob said with a grin as he started back to the quarters.

As Buck was returning to the big house, Big Man stepped up on the wagon. "I want ya'll to listen to me," he said to the slaves. "I didn't ask for the job as overseer. In fact I was as surprised as you were when Mr. Buck said I was going to be the new overseer. But this is the way it is. Ain't no slave ever had this job. I sho 'preciates the confidence Mr. Buck has in me. So I wants ya'll to know that I am going to be as nice to you as you will let me be. But you still have to do your work and your chores. Don't mistake niceness for weakness! You know I ain't weak! I plan on being the best overseer that any plantation around here has ever had. I expect you to help me. So let's get back to work. We got a lot to do before the wagon train leaves. In the meantime, I am going to be thinking about how to divide everyone up with a leader over each group. I wants to organize us something like in the Bible. You know the story about when the slaves left Egypt. Alright, everyone head on back to your jobs."

With that taken care of, Big Man headed back to the big house's kitchen to talk to his mother. They had to make plans to move into the overseer's house that was vacant.

The days seemed to fly by as Buck tried to complete the preparations to move everyone to Mississippi. His first order of business was to complete the sale of Inman Place. He was able to negotiate what he thought was a fair price for the acreage and the Big House. The buyer was pleased to acquire such a fine place with such a fine home on it. He planned to give the place to his daughter as a wedding present. Such was the wealth of that day. In the agreement, the buyer gave Buck ninety days to finish getting out the crops and to vacate the place. Buck thought that was a little quick, but on the other hand, he needed to get the wagon train on the road to Mississippi before the bad weather set in.

After taking care of the sale, he was able to turn his attention to getting his mother and sisters settled. Through an acquaintance, he was able to locate a fairly large house in Charleston. Though not palatial, it was nice enough for his family to stay in for several months. While Big Man supervised the plantation's operations, Buck loaded up several wagons with the contents of Inman Place. On the first trip he took, he carried all of the furniture and contents that his mother and sisters would need in their new house. With the wagons and slaves following, he drove the carriage containing his family to Charleston. It took him and the slaves several days to unload the wagons and place everything where his mother wanted. He finally said, "Mother, you are not staying here permanently! You know that I am going to have to move you again as soon as I get the new house built." His mother stood up straight and said in a firm voice, "Buchanan Inman! I don't care if I am only going to be here two weeks, I am not going to live like some squatter. You never know who might come to see us. This place may not be Inman Place, but it is going to look presentable!" Knowing he was fighting a losing battle, Buck said, "Yes Ma'am."

Buck made the trip back to Inman Place to load up everything left. It was strange to walk around the empty rooms where he had spent his life. Without the furnishings, the rooms seemed extra large and eerily quiet. Buck separated out the contents that were left into two groups. He left what he was going to take Mississippi on the first trip in the house. He took the remainder to the storage house in Charleston.

After he got everything unloaded, he told the slaves to remain with the wagon while he visited his family. Mistress assured him that she and the girls were comfortable. "Don't worry about us, we will be fine. You need to get back to the plantation to make preparations for the wagon train," Buck hated to leave, but he knew she was right. "I will stop back by to see ya'll when I come to catch the boat," he said.

While Buck was making the trip back and forth to Charleston, Big Man was busy trying to get the crop out and making preparations for the long trip west. There was a hum of excitement as the slaves put forth their best efforts to help out. Although technically they were free because Buck had given each a letter setting them free, they were in their mind still slaves. At this time, they could not comprehend what being free meant. It would take years and a new generation before they really knew what Buck had done for them.

When Buck got back to the plantation he finally had time to sit down with Big Man to discuss plans for the wagon train. They got Birdie to make them some coffee and they went to sit under the gazebo while they made plans. It was almost as if they had reverted back to their childhood when they were the best of friends.

"Big Man, I have made you overseer because I have complete confidence in you. You are probably going to have more responsibility than I have. I have to get back to my plantation to begin building a place for my family to live. I need to leave just as soon as possible. You will have to finish getting the crops out. Ya'll will have to put up food to take with you. Chicken coops and other pens will have to be built. As I said earlier, I am going to buy more horses and mules. I thought about buying some oxen but I think they are a little slow. You know we will have to use the stock to plow when you reach Mississippi. I have made arrangements for a lot of wagons. They are the large type just like the ones that the settlers are using to go further out west. I hope that we will be able to get all of the necessities on them and still have room for the older folks to ride. Everyone else will have to walk. Again, I will emphasize that ya'll need to leave as soon as possible. My plans are for you to make the trip before the really bad weather sets in," said Buck.

"Yes suh, Mr. Buck. Don't you worry. I will take care of everything for you. Everybody has been working real hard to get the cotton crop out. I guess you want me to take it to the gin as we gets it picked," said Big Man.

"That will be fine. I know you know what you are doing. You have been doing it almost all of your life."

" I also been making plans while you was gone. I thought I would divide everyone up into seven groups, and put some of the men in charge of each group. You know, sorta like the disciples appointed men to help them out in the Bible. I thought I would appoint some to take care of the livestock. Others, I would give the duty of getting firewood every night. I'll put some of the women in charge of seeing after the chickens and the other fowls. Mama Birdie will be in charge of all of the cooking. I am hoping that we can kill some game along the way so that we can stretch out the food that we will be carrying. I 'spect you might better get us plenty of barrels to carry drinking water. I don't know how far it might be between watering places," said Big Man.

"I can see that you have really been making plans. They sound good to me. We both know that we don't know what might happen on the road. You probably need to use one of the wagons to haul all of the tools and the equipment out of the blacksmith shop. You are going to have to be prepared for all kind of break downs," said Buck.

"The other thing I thought about is what we gonna do if folks get sick on the road. You best lay in a supply of different medicines. Mama Birdie is a pretty good doctor. She can probably tell you what she needs," said Big Man.

Buck said, "That's a good idea. I sure hope not too many of the girls are pregnant. It will be mighty hard on them birthing on the road. Anyway, we will talk some more tomorrow. I am about worn out and I think I will go try to get some rest."

Buck had trouble going to sleep. He was tired, but he was also a little depressed. Except for the bedroom that he was using, the house was empty. It seemed strange to him to look out his bedroom door and see all of the large rooms sitting empty. No furniture. No pictures. No tapestries. No drapes. Just nothing! He kept thinking about the happy days he had spent growing up there. Those days were past, but his mind kept returning to those memories. He knew that he would soon be leaving Inman Place forever.

In the next two weeks, Buck had made all of the purchases that the wagon train would need. He made sure that Big Man had a fine Tennessee Walking horse to ride. He had drawn Big Man a map of the route that the wagons would take. The plan was for the wagon train to head east until it intersected the Jackson's military road between Florida and Nashville. He was to follow it northwest until he got close enough to the Natchez Trace to take it south toward Natchez. The wagon train would follow the Trace until it reached the cutoff to Canton, Mississippi. There, Buck would be waiting on them to guide them on the new trail that led across the Delta to Lake Yazoo. Buck and Man had planned and planned and calculated. They decided that the train could be on the road by the first of October. They allowed two months for it to reach the destination of Kosciusko. This would put Buck at Kosciusko on the first of December. If the wagon train had not made it there by that time, Buck would ride north up the Trace until they met up. Their greatest concern was the fact that Big Man had no way to communicate with Buck as he traveled. As Buck said, "I am just going to have to trust in you and the Good Lord."

After checking on his preparations one more time, Buck reluctantly prepared to leave for Charleston. He and Big Man called all of the former slaves together one more time. Buck told them how proud he was of them for the way they had been working. He encouraged them to obey Big Man's orders and the other leaders that Man had appointed.

With that, he turned his back to Inman Place and entered his surrey. He would never see this home again!

As the horses pulled the surrey rapidly toward Charleston, Buck knew he had to force himself to stop thinking about the wagon train and the former slaves. He knew that he needed to start planning for the tremendous amount of work in Mississippi that had to be done before the winter really set in.

When Buck arrived in Charleston, he was glad to see that his mother had been able hire a young white girl to look after the family's needs.

After greeting each other warmly, Mistress asked Buck if he was hungry. She said they were just getting ready to sit down for supper. Buck was starving, so he was glad to accept the invitation. After saying the blessing, Mistress had the young servant bring out the food. The main entree was one of Buck's favorites-chicken and dumplings! Buck was surprised to find out that they tasted just like the ones that Birdie made. Mistress said that they should taste like Birdie's since she made them just like Birdie taught her. Buck was surprised again. He didn't know that his mother could cook!

After spending another day and night, Buck kissed his mother and sisters goodbye and prepared to leave for the ship. He felt a little better about leaving them since his mother had been warmly received by her old friends in the area. He knew that if she needed anything, she had someone to turn to for help.

Buck had hired someone to drive him and his trunk to the ship. It was a hot, sunshiny July day when they arrived at the ship. There was a lot of activity as the cargo was being loaded and the passengers were already boarding. Buck grabbed his small trunk, threw it up on his shoulder, and strode up the gangplank. Soon after he was shown to his room, he felt the ship shudder as the wind caught her sails. They were on their way to New Orleans.

When Buck arrived in New Orleans, he barely had time to reach the paddle-wheeler *The Delta Queen* before it left going north. He stored his trunk in his room and went out on the deck just as the whistle blew, and the boat swung out into the river. He stood there thinking about all of the changes that had taken place in his life in the year since he had travelled the mighty Mississippi River. There was no way he could anticipate the changes what would take place in the next year.

After making several stops while going upriver, *The Delta Queen* finally pulled up to the dock at Leota. Excited to be back home, Buck grabbed his belongings and disembarked. It was mid morning and he was in a hurry to get home to the lake. He made his way to the livery stable where he was greeted by Tom, the livery man. Buck didn't realize how attached he had become to Prince until he heard him nicker. Tom said, "He knows you are back!" Tom commented that the big stallion had been no trouble. Buck could tell that his horse had been well taken care of. After letting Prince nuzzle his neck, Buck saddled up for the trip home. He put his belongings in the large saddlebags and gave the trunk to Tom. He thanked Tom profusely and paid him well. He asked Tom if anything had happened since he had been gone. Tom told him that nothing unusual had happened. The only news was that wealthy settlers were still pouring in and buying the rest of the land up and down the river. Since almost all of the river bank land was sold, many of the newcomers were trying to buy back off of the river. Word had gotten out as to how rich this alluvial soil was in this area. The land was rich but was covered with trees that had to be cleared. This would require a massive amount of labor. SLAVE LABOR!

As Buck rode out of town, he thought, "Here I have come this far west to get away from slavery, and it has already caught up with me. These folks are really in for a surprise when my wagon train arrives with five hundred nigras. I just wonder what they will think when they find out that I have freed them."

Reaching the edge of town, he eased Prince into his running walk gait and headed to the lake.

11

Preparing to Build

Stepping Prince up into a canter, Buck soon arrived at the lake. He was surprised at the appearance of his place. The underbrush and small trees had been cut back leaving only the large oaks and hackberries standing in the clearing. They made a cool canopy over the area. The lot had been extended with a new rail fence. All of his equipment was stacked up neatly in the barn. There was also a large woodpile with enough wood to last the winter. As he rode around inspecting, he wondered where John and Jim were now. All of a sudden, Prince pricked up his ears and squealed as only a stallion could. He was answered by a low nicker. Buck wheeled him around. There were the boys coming up the lane on Charlie. It was a toss-up as to who was the proudest to see each other—Prince and Charlie or Buck and the boys. Buck hadn't realized how much he had become attached to the young nigras.

Dismounting, Buck and boys began asking each other questions. Buck wanted to know if they had had plenty to eat while he was gone. Jim pulled his shirt up and stuck out his stomach and said,"Do it look like we been going hongry?" Buck laughed and said, "I guess not, you both have got fat." Buck complimented them on how nice the place looked. He could tell that they had been working hard. He could tell they were so proud. "Yas suh, we sho been working hard. We didn't want you to come back and run us off for not doing nuthing while you was gone," John said.

"I did just as much as John," Jim chimed in. "I was the one that trapped and killed that big ole bar."

Startled, Buck said, "What bear?" "De one that was etting up de garden. That's his hide stretched out on the side of the barn. He sho was some good eating." Glancing at the barn, Buck could see the big hide stretched out. "Where in the world did you learn how to skin a bear and save the hide?" Buck asked.

John answered, "We used to help ole master back on de ole plantation we wuz on. He use to hunt and kill bars all de time. We had to help skin em and save the hides."

"I guess that I don't have to worry about you fellas anymore. You can take care of yourselves. As for as running you off, that's not going to happen. You can stay here as long as you want. In fact, I am going to need you real bad. My family is coming to live with me. I have to get my Big House built. Also, I have a wagon train coming with wagons, livestock, supplies and about five hundred nigras. We've got to get started building them a place. I will try to hire some more help. I am even willing to pay ya'll for your work. I know you know how to build cabins now. If you want to stay, I have plenty of work for you to do."

"Whooie," John said. "You means there's going to be five hundred black folks coming to live here? We sho is got a lot of work to do."

" Is de any young black girls coming along?" asked Jim with a grin. "Shut up, nigga. All you think about is girls! We be trying to talk serious business here," said his brother.

Buck told the boys that he was going to rest up a couple of days, and then he would have to leave to make arrangements for materials, supplies and a lot more labor. He asked if they had seen anyone coming around his place while he was gone. They told him that they had not seen anyone on his side of the lake. They had seen some white folks walking along the bank on the other side. They thought they were just hunting. Buck told them to stay out of sight if anyone came up while he was making his arrangements.

The next morning, the boys saddled Prince and Buck set out for town. It was Sunday and he felt a need to attend church. He also had another motive. He hoped that some of the planters there could recommend an architect to help him with his house construction.

Church was starting when he arrived. He slipped in and sat on the back pew. He felt like this was a sanctuary that insulated him from the world. He spent the next hour worshipping and communing with God. It seemed that the service put everything back into perspective. His problems did not seem so heavy anymore.

After the services, everyone greeted him and offered him condolences. They had heard about the death of his father. They told him that in a couple of weeks everything would return to normal. If they only knew! It was at this time that Linda, the eighteen—year—old daughter of Gee Harden asked Buck where he was going to eat lunch. Mr. Harden owned one of the larger plantations north of Leota. On it, he had built the largest house north of Vicksburg. Buck told Linda that he had not made plans but that he would probably eat at the Southern Inn.

Mr. Harden said, "Young man, that is where we were planning on eating. It would be an honor if you would join us."

"If it won't be an imposition, I will gladly accept the invitation. If you are ready to go, I will meet you there," answered Buck. Mr. and Mrs. Harden and Linda entered their carriage and made their way to the Inn. Buck followed on Prince.

When they entered the Inn, they were greeted by Miss Jane. She embarrassed Buck by saying loudly, "Well, Buck Inman, where have you been keeping your good looking self? I thought you had done followed some cute girl off to Natchez or New Orleans! Buck realized that she had not heard about the death of his father. Smoothing the situation over, he said, "Miss Jane, if I was going to

100

run off with anyone, it would be you!" Everyone in the inn laughed as Miss Jane showed the group a table.

After exchanging pleasantries, Buck turned the conversation to the question that he wanted to ask Mr. Harden. He told Mr. Harden that he had sold Inman Place and that he would be moving his family to his property on the lake. "I will have to build a house there on the lake. I was hoping you could recommend someone to help me with the plans and with the construction," he said.

Being experienced at building, Mr. Harden asked Buck what size house he was planning on building. Buck replied, "I don't want to appear to be bragging, but I wish to build one of the largest and finest houses north of Natchez. If it was just me, I would probably be satisfied with a large cabin, but like I said, my mother is coming. I have promised her and my sisters the best." Mr. Harden raised an eyebrow and kind of smiled. He had only seen Buck at church, but he had heard that he lived in a cabin out on the lake with no slaves. He thought he was a nice young man that lucked up on getting the land on the lake. He thought that he probably had little money. He had no idea what Buck had received from the sale of Inman Place or how much money he had inherited from his grandparents.

"Buck, do you realize how much a house like you are describing will cost? It will be very expensive." It was Buck's turn to smile. "Mr. Harden, again I don't want to appear to be bragging, but the cost will not be a problem."

Somewhat taken aback, Mr. Harden said, "The only man I would recommend would be SAMUEL SLOAN of Philadelphia. He has been responsible for many of the fine mansions in Natchez."

"Do you know how I might contact Mr. Sloan?" Buck asked. "Mr. Harden replied, "You are in luck. I was visiting in Vicksburg last week and I had the opportunity to meet Mr. Sloan. He is in Vicksburg supervising the building of a mansion on top of the bluff. It looks like the construction is about half completed. I don't think you will have any trouble contacting him if you go to Vicksburg."

Buck said, "I really appreciate this information. I don't wish to appear rude, but if you will excuse me, I will go to make arrangements to catch *The Delta King* to Vicksburg in the morning. I believe it is returning to New Orleans tomorrow."

"You are correct, Buck. The boat should be docking here first thing in the morning. You can be on your way by eight o'clock."

Buck arose and thanked them. Linda told him to wave to her as he passed her home. She said she would be on the bank looking for the boat.

Buck took a room with Miss Jane for another night. She took him to the closet where he kept his "town clothes". He picked out the best he had to wear on the trip to Vicksburg. He certainly did not want Mr. Sloan to brush him off as a dreamer with no money. He then walked down to talk to Tom. Tom promised that he would take good care of Prince while Buck was gone. He said Prince thought he owned the place anyway.

The next morning found Buck impatiently waiting for the departure of *The Delta King*. He had paid his fare and was anxious to get started. Then there was the sound of the steam whistle. The paddle-wheeler backed slowly out into the river. Reversing the paddle wheel, the large boat headed downstream. They were on their way.

As the boat picked up speed, the passengers did one of the favorite customs in the south. They asked each other, "Who do you know and who are your kin?" Buck found out more than he really wanted to know. It seemed that everyone there was kin to somebody that the others knew or at least knew the same people. Almost everyone was headed for New Orleans. The others were getting off at the smaller towns along the way.

Buck had almost forgotten that he had promised to wave to Linda. From her description of her home, he thought he would recognize it. Sure enough, they soon approached a large house set in a live oak grove. There were large magnolias growing all around the house. By all of the flowers growing, Buck could tell that Mrs. Harden loved her flower garden. Maybe she and Mistress could become friends. As they passed by, sure enough, Linda was standing on the bank waving her handkerchief. What a pretty sight Buck thought as he waved back. Many of the other passengers had joined Buck on the deck, and they were waving, too.

It was hard to believe that war was coming and this life style would be no more!

The large paddle-wheeler made good time running south with the current. As they passed the intersection of the Yazoo and the Mississippi Rivers, Buck caught his first glimpse of Vicksburg. He could make out the old court house that sat on one of the highest bluffs. As they drew closer, the magnificent mansions came into view. Here again was evidence of the wealth of the South during this period. *The Delta King* docked and Buck strode down the ramp to shore. The dock was teeming with workers loading bales of cotton and the boarding of passengers. Buck made his way through the sweating slaves, the overseers, the well dressed gentlemen and the high society ladies. Everything and everyone was heading south to Natchez and New Orleans.

Buck approached one gentleman that was waiting to board. "Sir, could you direct me to the mansion that Mr. Samuel Sloan is building? I understand it is located on one of the high points in the city."

"I sure can. In fact Mr. Sloan is building the home for my brother. It is called Inverness. They are about half way through with it. You will have no trouble finding it. Just walk up the hill past the courthouse and you will see it on your right. If you look carefully through the trees, you can see the top of it from here."

Buck wished the gentleman a pleasant trip and started up the steep bluff. The road led straight to the Courthouse. The Courthouse was the focal point of the city. As Buck made his way past the Courthouse, he heard a large commotion to his right. There was a large crowd gathered in front of a building that was located on the main road leading to the downtown. Buck decided to detour to see what was going on. It was a slave auction! The blacks were being led out of the building one by one. The auctioneer was bragging on each one like they were the best slaves to be had. He was trying to coax out every dollar that he could from the rich buyers. The slaves ranged from young to old. There were children, women and men. Some were fine specimens; others were skinny and malnourished. You could tell that the sellers had used every trick to make each one look as good as possible. Everyone had been bathed and somewhat clothed. They had been greased down with hog lard to make them shine. If any had any scars on their backs from being whipped, they were dressed so that the scars were not visible.

Most of the buyers were not fooled by these tactics. One by one each slave was inspected by the prospective buyers. The buyers looked at every part of their body and even examined their mouths. They felt their muscles and tried to determine their age. Some were looking to buy just one or two slaves to help them on their small farms. These would be the lucky slaves. Others were buying many slaves to man their large plantations. These slaves would replace the plantation slaves that had died during the past year or were needed to expand the plantation into the wilderness along the river.

The men and women slaves had to stand there and suffer these indignities. The young big bucks brought the best price. The larger ones would, not only be used to work, but would be used for breeding. The other highly sought after group were the young women. They would be expected to bring in a new crop of slaves for their new owners. The really nice looking young ones might be used by the new owner for his own purposes. The slaves were made to jump up and down. They were made to speak so that the buyers could see if they understood English.

The auctioneer and the owners were quick to point out if the slaves had any particular skills. If they had already been trained to cook, lay bricks, blacksmith or could do carpentry work, they were particularly valuable.

The slaves took this punching, prodding, and examinations in different ways. Some just slumped and stared off in the distance, resolved to their fate. One could tell from the body language of some of the younger ones that they were defiant. They had just been recently brought from Africa. It was only the shackles that were restraining them. The buyers knew that the strap would take care of this!

The whole scene nauseated Buck. He just could not get away from the institution of slavery. He thought, "If all of the fine gentlemen and women of the South could see this! I wonder how they could defend slavery. Most of them have never seen this side of the slave trade!" Buck wished that they could see the children standing around with their small arms in the child handcuffs. All of this was taking place in the shadow of the large church located up the street.

Knowing that there was nothing that he could do, Buck continued his trip up the bluff. After a short walk, he found himself at Inverness. He was impressed with the size of the mansion. It was a two storied structure with a long wing running down one side. At the back was the usual unattached kitchen. It had a cedar shake roof. The workmen had finished the exterior and were working on the interior.

There were two men conversing over some plans when Buck walked in. One was dressed in work clothes that were not dirty. The other was more formally dressed. Buck assumed that they were in charge.

"Could you direct me to Mr. Sloan?" Buck asked as he walked up. The men stopped talking and the better dressed man said, "I am Samuel Sloan. Give me a moment and I will be right with you." Buck said, "Certainly" and walked over to one side. When Mr. Sloan had finished giving instructions to his foreman, he turned his attention to Buck.

"What can I do for you, young man?" he asked in a deep voice. Buck introduced himself and told him the purpose of his visit. "I own property about fifty miles upriver and I am looking for an architect to construct a home for me. My mother and sisters are coming to live with me, and I need it built in a hurry. I was told that you were the best architect building homes in these parts."

"Thank you, young man. I appreciate the compliment." Taking note of Buck's youth, Mr. Sloan thought that there was no way that Buck could afford to build the type houses that he designed. He decided to politely get rid of him.

"Buck, again I appreciate your compliments. However, we have two problems. I don't think you realize how much a house such as this cost. Secondly, as you can see, I am pretty tied up here. It will take us several more months to complete this job."

Buck knew exactly what Mr. Sloan was thinking. He had been running into this every since he had inherited Inman Place. Everyone in South Carolina thought he was too young to handle big business. In Mississippi, no one realized the amount of his wealth. "Mr. Sloan, I will address the question of time first. I am willing to hire any amount of labor that you think you will need. Also, I have a wagon load of laborers leaving South Carolina heading this way around the first of October. When they arrive, we will have as much help as we need. I just want to get as much living space built as soon as possible so that I can move my family here. After I get them here, there will not be such a rush on the rest of the project. Now let's address the cost. I have promised my mother that I would build her the finest house in these parts. I intend to keep my promise. Cost is not a big factor; time is. To show you that I mean business, I will pay your usual price and I am willingly to pay a bonus of twenty thousand in gold. I will give you this bonus as soon as we sign the contract to build."

Taken aback, Mr. Sloan said, "Buck, you do mean business! Maybe we can work something out. Why don't we go down to the tavern by the river, get us a table, and talk this over. If you will give me a moment to give instructions to my foreman, I will have my surrey brought around."

Soon, they were on the way to the river. As they passed the Courthouse, Buck glanced down the street to where the slave auction was being held. It seemed to be over. The buyers that had purchased only one or two slaves for their personal use had taken possession and were leading them away. These slaves were the lucky ones—if it could be lucky to be a slave. The rest of the slaves had been bought to work the large plantations or clear the land of trees so that it could be farmed. They were being herded back into the barn to await transfer to their new homes. Buck averted his eyes hoping that he would never see another scene like this again.

After passing the courthouse, Mr. Sloan suggested that they ride around the town and look at the different mansions that had been built. He thought that this might give Buck an idea of the type of architect that he would prefer. Buck was impressed by the variations of style. His favorite was the mansion built up on the bluff that was a replica of a castle. It even had a moat and turrets. Mr. Sloan said that he also admired the structure, even though he had not designed it. After turning around at this point, they headed for the tavern to discuss the building of Buck's place.

12

The Wagon Train

The cotton had been picked and taken to the gin. The crop had been good and the weather perfect for harvesting. It was late September, so Big Man felt like he was ahead of schedule. He could now turn his attention to preparations for the long trip to Mississippi.

He had some of the workers shelling the corn as soon as it came out of the field. He wanted to take as much shelled corn as he possibly could for the livestock. Buck had made arrangements for dozens of barrels to be delivered to the plantation. They would be used to carry the corn. He also took bushels and bushels of corn to the grist mill. Corn meal would be a necessary staple to make cornbread on the trip. He was lucky that he did not have to spend any of the money that Buck had left him to pay for the grinding. The miller was glad to take part of the meal as payment for his services.

He had one group of slaves making coops for the fowls. They would have to drive the cows and pigs and extra mules. Another group was packing all of the canned and dried vegetables. They had already packed the meat in the barrels and covered it with salt. The days flew by as they hurried to get on the road before bad weather. They had to get the wagon wheels greased up and make extras in case of an accident. They attached barrels of water on each wagon in case there was no source of water on some days. Big Man didn't really know what to expect on this trip, so he was trying to prepare for any eventuality. He asked Birdie to get some of the women to pack as many medical supplies as they could lay their hands on. They also prepared for any new births that were bound to come while on the road. He was hoping that he could find grass along the way to augment the stock's food. He also hoped that they might be able to kill some wild game along the way to help out with the workers' food stocks. Regardless, he knew that they were going to mainly be dependent on the food that they carried with them. He certainly didn't want to have to try and buy food along the way from the white plantations. He didn't know how such a large number of Nigras would be received but he had a pretty good idea it wouldn't be favorable. He also didn't want to spend the money that Buck had left him unless it was an emergency. Some times as he laid awake making plans for the trip, he was amazed at how much confidence that Buck had placed in him, a former slave. He certainly did not want to let him down. Since everyone had been preparing for the trip ever since Buck left, it only took them about a week to finish their preparations.

It was a typical October morning when the wagons prepared to pull out. Although they were leaving early in the morning, the sun was already hot on their backs, and the humidity made it sweltering. No one seemed to mind the heat. They had worked in it all of their lives. Everyone was so excited to finally be on the way. Hardly any of them had known any life except inside the boundaries of Inman Plantation!

Buck had changed the route that the wagon train would take to Mississippi. He had visited with an older man nearby that had made the overland trip to Mississippi a number of times. He was able to help Buck come up with a new map and route. From his experiences guiding wagon trains west to the Mississippi, he could advise as to the best trails and roads to take. He told Buck where he would find grass and, more importantly, where the best river fords were located. He told Buck a wagon train such as his could not always go the straightest and quickest way. The wagon train would need to by—pass the largest towns and would need to cross the rivers at their shallowest points. He told Buck that they were lucky to be traveling this time of the year. The streams should be at their lowest points. Buck spent quite a bit of time going over the plans and map with Big Man. This was the best that they could do before Buck left.

Buck had made one other arrangement that made him very proud. He had asked one of his friends to be there when the train pulled out. This friend was to telegraph him with the news that Big Man was on his way. At least he would know when the entourage left.

That morning, the wagon train was lined up as planned. Big Man and five other mature men were astride their horses riding around making sure everything was ready to go. The first wagons in line were the four cook wagons. They held the food that was going to be so necessary for their survival. Each of these wagons had a driver with one of the cooks riding along side of him. After that, there came several wagons loaded with all of the left—over contents of the big house. Then, there were ten wagons loaded with all of the possessions of the former slaves. Each one did not have much, but when combined, it came to quite a load. Then there came the wagons loaded with all of the tools and equipment that had been used on the place. The axes, saws, hoes and plows would be very important when they reached their destination. The next wagons carried all of the shelled corn that had been sealed in barrels. Big Man was glad that the rats hadn't got to it. The next to last wagon contained all of the blacksmith equipment. The blacksmith drove this wagon. Big Man expected the smiths to be busy making repairs while they traveled. Finally, the last three wagons carried the tents that Buck had purchased. Not only would they be used on the road in bad weather, but they would have to provide shelter in Mississippi until the cabins were built.

Each wagon had water barrels and chicken coops tied to the sides and milk cows tied to the back. They did not bother to tie the calves. They knew that they would always follow their mother. Buck had sold almost all of the stock. He had kept only enough to provide food on the way. He knew he could always buy more when the former slaves reached his plantation. The herding of this stock was turned over to the teenage boys and girls. Although the herd was hard to guide at first, by the time they had walked several days, they were glad to just walk along with the caravan. In front of the herd walked the remaining former slaves. Big Man had tried to find a place on the wagons for the elderly to ride, but he had only so much room. Everyone else would be walking to Mississippi.

Buck's friend, Robert, had ridden out to the Inman Place to see how the preparations for the trip were coming along. Much to his surprise, the, train was almost ready to leave. He was greeted by Big Man who had ridden up on his horse.

"Good morning, Mr. Robert. You must'a got up about daylight to get out here this early," Big Man said.

"Yes. I wasn't sleeping well, l so I thought I would come out here to see how you were coming along. You surprised me. It looks like you just about have everything ready to roll," Robert replied. Big Man said,"Yas Suh, we been working mighty hard trying to get everything ready to go. We will be ready to pull out in about an hour. I hope to make at least ten miles today."

" It is a good thing I got up early and came on out here. I will telegraph Mr. Buck and tell him you are on your way. Is there anything else you want me to tell him?"

" Yas Suh. Tell him I figures we will get to our meeting place in about six weeks if there ain't a lot of trouble. Tell him I sho am doing my very best to carry out his plans. Tell him everybody has been working powerful hard."

Robert wished them good luck and turned to ride into town to send Buck the telegraph.

Big Man was now fully in charge, and they were on their way.

Big Man positioned two of his riders at the front of the train and let the other three bring up the rear. He would lead. He gave a signal and one of the former slaves started ringing the large plantation bell that they had attached to the back of one of the wagons. The bell would signal when they were to start and when they were to stop. It wasn't a lot different than when they were on the plantation.

After five claps of the bell, the wagon train slowly started moving. It was a sight to behold. The sound was immense. Drivers were yelling at the mules, urging them forward. The cows and calves were lowing and bawling. Disturbed by the noise, the chickens, ducks and geese started squawking. The dogs were running around yapping at everything. All of the former slaves were excited. This was the biggest adventure of their lives. Just to be off of the plantation would be something. They were laughing and yelling at each other. The babies were crying and the little children were running around everywhere. Big Man thought, "It's a good thing we aren't trying to slip off. Folks can hear us for miles."

As the train pulled out, Big Man made one last ride around the Big House and headed to the front of the wagon train. He would never see Inman Place again!

Big Man took his place at the front of the train and led it onto the main road and headed west. As the train gradually spread out, it was over a mile long. The assistants rode up and down the line making sure everything was alright. The former slaves did not have any trouble keeping up with the plodding mules. With the exception of the house slaves, they had spent all of their lives working the hot fields of Inman Place. Walking along slowly with their straw hats on was nothing for them. The house slaves had been assigned the duties of cooking so most of them were able to ride part of the way along with the elderly.

The young'uns were having a time guiding the loose stock along. They were frisky and had never had been herded before. Fortunately, there were enough teens to keep them heading in the right direction. The trailing riders had to help out every once in a while when one of the steers got loose.

By noon, they had covered about five miles and Big Man gave them a break. They pulled over to the side of the road to eat. Everyone had been told to prepare something to snack on at the noon stop. They had a snack of cold biscuits stuffed with cooked pork sausage. They washed this down with water from the barrels and they were on the way again. They had been promised a big meal that night if they made good time.

The afternoon was spent with everyone settling into a routine. Big Man did allow one adjustment. He moved all of the walkers to the front of the caravan. This got them out of the dust being stirred up by the mules and wagons. The rear riders dropped back a bit so that they were not riding in the dust.

By late afternoon, everyone was getting tired. The walkers were just shuffling along. No more laughing and joking. The dogs were content to just trot along. The calves had stopped running around and were walking behind their mothers. Big Man, not wanting to wear everyone out on the first day, called for the night stop. He figured that he had made his goal of covering ten miles the first day. He hoped to move up to fifteen miles a day once every one got acclimated.

Big Man had ridden ahead and found a clearing with a small creek running through it. He could tell by the wagon tracks that this was a popular place for travelers to camp out. As the wagon train pulled off of the road, the cook wagons separated from each other. These wagons were numbered one through four. All of the previous slaves and the riders had been assigned to a particular numbered wagon. Everyone, with the exception of the young people, split up and followed their cook wagon. They were told to drive the stock down to the creek where they could drink.

As the cooks prepared the meal, the drivers and some of the other men took their teams and the cows down to water, also. Others gathered firewood for the cooks. When the cows and calves had drunk their fill, the cows were quickly milked. Big Man was pleased with how quickly the campsite was set up.

With the stock tended to, almost everyone headed to the creek to wash the day's traveling dust off. By the time all of this had taken place, the evening meal was almost ready. Big Man was watering his horse and washing off when he heard a commotion down on the other side of the last campsite. He jumped on his horse and quickly road down to see what was going on. When he got there, he found almost all of the campers gathered in a circle watching two young bucks fight.

"Hit him, Jake! Whooie! What a lick! Don't give up, Tom. You can handle him! You bet'ta watch out, he gonna knock you crazy!" were some of the comments that Big Man heard as he rode up. He didn't stop. He forced his horse through the crowd and rode between the two fighting young men.

"What are you fighting about?" he asked.

"I caught that nappy-headed Jake fooling around with Fannie. Everybody knows that she is my girl. This is the second time that I caught him. I told him last time that if I caught him messing with Fannie again, I wuz going to whup his butt!" Tom said.

Big Man looked over at Fannie. He could tell that she was enjoying having two men fight over her immensely. She was a young girl of sixteen with a grown woman's body. Big Man could tell that she had been in the creek with her clothes on. Her wet skirt was clinging to her bottom. The material was thin and he had no trouble seeing the outline of her body. Her top was too small for her and now, being wet, could barely conceal her big breasts. Everyone thought that she wore the too small tops on purpose. All of the young bucks followed her around like male dogs follow a bitch in heat!

"Tom, she ain't your girl! She is everybody's girl! Now you and Jake stop this foolishness. I don't have time for this kind of stuff. I don't want you fighting every time the sap rises in ya'll. Ya'll go on down to the creek and wash off for supper," Big Man said.

He then turned his attention to Fannie. "Fannie, I want you to keep your dress tail down on this trip. Don't you be making these young bucks fight over you! I got enough trouble without some hot—tailed girl messing with the boys! Now, you get yourself back to your camp where your mother is. I'll be along in a minute to talk to her."

All the rest of the former slaves averted their eyes and returned to their camp site. No one wanted to mess with Big Man when he was tired and mad!

As Big Man turned his horse and started back to his campsite, he thought, "This is going to be one interesting trip!"

Everyone was so tired that they just fell out on the ground and went to sleep early. The next morning they ate breakfast, filled up their water barrels, hooked up the teams, herded up the loose stock and were on the road a little after day break. They wanted to get as far as they could before the hot southern sun started to bake them. Big Man had decided that it would be best to start early and take a long break after lunch when it was so hot. The lack of rain made for easy traveling, but they really needed some rain to relieve them from the heat.

They had been traveling about two hours and had just turned onto the Anderson road when they saw a cloud of dust coming toward them. It was five of the local Slave Patrol. The Slave Patrol was charged with making sure there were no unauthorized nigras on the road. These were also the ones that chased down any fugitive slaves that had escaped from the plantations. They were greatly feared by all slaves.

Their horses were lathered up when the Patrol stopped at the head of the wagon train. They were a fearsome looking group. Each had two guns strapped to their sides and rifles in their scabbards. Around some of the saddle horns was tied a coiled up rope. The others had whips tied to their saddles. Handcuffs were in the saddlebags. They were dusty and sweaty from the hard ride.

Big Man had ridden out to meet them. "What's going on here? Where you nigras going?" their leader asked as he glared at Big Man.

"We is going to Mississippi to join Mr. Buchanan Inman, Suh. We is from the Inman Plantation. I is got the papers that Mr. Buck gave me in case anyone stopped us." With this, Big Man reached in his saddle bag and handed the leader the papers giving everyone on the wagon train permission to leave the plantation. Buck had anticipated the train being stopped so he had carefully listed each former slave's name, age, and gender.

The leader of the patrol looked at the papers and his whole demeanor changed. He said, "I had heard that Buck had sold out and was starting over in Mississippi." The Inman name still carried a lot of influence in those parts. "Why don't I write ya'll a pass also? Just show it to anyone that stops ya'll and I don't think you will have any trouble."

The leader added the pass to Buck's papers and handed everything back to Big Man. He wished the wagon train luck and the patrol rode off in a cloud of dust just like they had arrived!

Big man rode over to where Birdie stood watching. "Oh man! that sho did scare me!" he said as he dismounted. " I was afraid they were going to make us turn around. I think we bet'ta take our break now and let my heart settle down!"

After the break, they started moving again. They settled into a regular routine: breakfast in the morning, on the road by daylight, a long lunch break. walk until dark, eat supper, go to sleep and get up and do it all over again.

The days turned into weeks as the miles passed by. They traveled in the heat and in the rain. They slogged thru the mud and walked on the hot dusty roads. They went up the hills and down the hills. They forded the streams. They tried to ignore the curious stares of people as they passed by. Big Man was accosted by local officials on occasion, but after showing his papers the train was allowed to pass on without any trouble.

The route took them past Anderson, SC, and took them southwest across the state line into Georgia. They made their way across Georgia, by—passing Atlanta. Each day, Big Man rode ahead and mapped out a route for them to take. He tried to go around the larger cities and towns.

After weeks on the road, they crossed into Alabama. They went around Anniston and headed toward Talladega. Buck had chosen this route for them so that they wouldn't have to go through Atlanta. After camping near Talladega, they headed southwest towards Tuscaloosa.

Here, they encountered a major river. As always, Big Man had ridden ahead to scout out the way. He was about ten miles out front when he came upon the Black Warrior River. It was a wide, fast moving stream coming down from north Alabama. As Big Man approached, he could see a ferry tied up to the bank. Further up the bank, he spotted a large log house where the ferry owner lived. He continued down to the river's edge where he found a post with a bell attached. There was a sign nailed to a tree that said, ' IF YOU WANT TO CROSS ON MY FERRY RING THE BELL'!

Big Man reached over and gave the bell a couple of hard pulls. In a few minutes, a large burly man dressed in overalls appeared. He was rough looking with long hair and an unkempt beard. He was armed with a shotgun. "Nigger, what are you doing here and what do you want? Are you a run-a-way?" he growled at Big Man. Big Man lowered his eyes and looked at the ground as he had learned to do when talking to a white man. "Mister, I don't mean no harm. I am leading a wagon train of folks to Mississippi. I have my papers right here." With this, Big Man reached into his saddlebags and handed the ferryman his papers. The man took them and looked at them intently. He said, "Looks good to me!" The ferryman couldn't read a lick! Satisfied, he handed the papers back to Big Man. "Ya'll wanting to use my ferry?" he asked.

"We sho do. I don't see no way we can cross this river by fording," Big Man replied.

"Well, Ya'll can't ride for nothing! Ya'll got any money?"

"Yas Suh! We can pay. How much is it going to cost?"

"Depends on what you want to take across and how many trips I have to make."

When Big Man told him the size of the wagon train, the ferryman's eyes lit up. He was already counting the money.

The ferryman did some calculations in his head and came up with a price. Big Man thought that it sounded a bit high but he had no choice. Big Man said, "I just barely got that much money but I got it. The other thing is, can we camp here a few days while we rest up and butcher some hogs and a steer?"

"Yea, that will be alright," the ferryman answered. Ya'll can camp up the river bank there. It is going to take several days to get all your stuff and everybody across anyway. Another thing though, you got to promise me that some of you men folks will help haul this ferry back and forth across this river. If I don't have some help, ya'll end up spending the winter here. Also, I want my money in advance. I ain't hauling everything across and have you nigras run off without paying me!"

Big Man replied, "How bout half when we get started and the other half when everything and everybody is across?" "Done," said the ferryman.""But I might want a mess of them hog back bones when you get through butchering them," he added with a grin.

"You sho can have some. We'll have aplenty. How 'bout I throw in some of them good cracklings my Ma makes?" Big Man said with a smile. "Hey! That'll be great. We ain't et no fresh meat in a while," replied the ferryman. Nothing like good food to make friends!

The wagon train pulled into the camp ground just before dark. They divided up into their assigned groups. While the drivers watered the stock, the others hit the river. They couldn't wait to cool off and wash several days of grime off their bodies. There was lots of whooping and hollering from the young folks as they tried to splash and duck each other.

Big Man had told everyone that they would be there several days. This would give them and the animals a chance to rest. The cooks at each wagon tried to outdo each other preparing the evening meal. This was the first time that they had had an opportunity to really cook. After the evening meal, with the dishes washed, the adults sat around and visited. Some of the men pulled out their corn cob pipes and smoked. A lot of the women mended their clothes while they talked. The young people returned to the river to play. Most of them could not swim. On the plantation, none of the slaves had had a chance to learn. They enjoyed paddling around in the shallows, anyway.

Big Man heard a big commotion down by the river. He got up and said to Birdie, "That's them boys fighting over Fannie again. She's probably got her clothes off by now. I best go see about them fo" somebody gits hurt!"

Before Big Man arrived at the place where all the racket was going on, he could hear voices.

"I done tole you not to be messing with Fannie!! She's my woman!"

"I wasn't messing with Fannie! Her top had washed off in the river and I wuz trying to help her get it back on!"

"You ain't fooling me! You wuz feeling of her titties. I saw you!"

Big Man recognized the voices at once. It was Jake and Tom going at it again over Fannie. He had gotten there before the fight started. He looked over at the edge of the crowd and there stood Fannie grinning. Her top was off and she was trying to halfway cover her big black shiny breasts with her hands. Big Man thought, "This gal ain't nothing but trouble. By the time we get to Mississippi she's going to be knocked up sho as the world."

"Tom and Jake git, on back to your camp! Fannie, you git on back to your mama and git some clothes on! I am too tired for this foolishness," Big Man said. Everyone went back to camp, and Big Man returned to his. He knew this was going to be an interesting trip with all of the young folks traveling together. It seemed like most of them had the hots for each other.

That night, there came a cloud burst. They were glad that they had set up their tents. The next morning arrived cool and clear. It felt a little like Fall was arriving. Everyone got up rested and feeling good. Since it was cool, Big Man decided that this would be a good day to start butchering the hogs. The older experienced men killed the hogs one by one by hitting them in the head with an axe. They then got water from the river and filled the big iron wash pots. Under these, they built fires. They waited until the water was scalding hot and then poured it in the big wooden trough they had built. They then placed the whole hog in so that the hot water could soften his bristles. After letting the carcass soak, they attached a single tree to the hog's back legs and hoisted the body up to a tree limb. The women took over then. They took sharp knives and scrapped all of the hair off. After this, they let the carcass down on a big table that they had constructed. Here, they proceeded to cut the hog into pieces. Hams, ribs, hocks, back bones, neck bones, bacon and the other parts were separated. Nothing was wasted. As they always said, they used everything but the squeal. The younger women took the intestines down to the river to wash. They would be used for casings to stuff the sausage in. They didn't waste the head or the feet. They boiled them in a big pot until tender. The meat was then stripped off and put in a big sack. They added a few herbs and spices to the mixture and hung it to a tree limb. As it hung there, the liquid would slowly drip through the cloth. By night, it would drain and congeal into hog head souse.

The next big chore was the making of the sausage. Again, the old experienced men and women were in charge. Birdie had memorized the recipe that they had always used back on the plantation.

After making and stuffing the sausage, they started on the pork skins. The hog's skin was cut up into small strips with the fat still on them. Some had more fat than others. Again, a hot fire was started under the big pots. A little lard was added and the skins were slowly added to the sizzling grease. As the skins fried, the fat melted off and turned into grease. This grease was treasured because it turned into lard. Lard was used to cook with. It made good biscuits. The lard was used to grease the wagon wheels and other equipment. Mixed with lye from the wood ashes, it made their soap. After each batch of fried skins were taken out, the grease was dipped out to save. A by-product of the frying were the small pieces of meat that came off the skins while they were cooking. These were the cracklings that Buck had promised the ferryman.

As the pork was being fried, Big Man walked up to the ferryman's house. The ferryman greeted him warmly. They had become buddies during Big Man's stay. "I got you a mess of back bones cut up, and we is starting to cook the pork skins. We going to have plenty of cracklings for you and your family. I promise that my mama can cook them things. They'll be ready by the time you get down there," Big Man said.

"I'll be right on down. Just let me git my boots on."

By the time Big Man returned to the camp ground, the aroma of the frying meat filled the air. All of the former slaves were eating the pork skins and cracklings as fast as they came out of the grease. The little kids particularly liked the cracklings.

The ferryman came down carrying a big wash pan. Big Man loaded him up with fresh backbones. He added a molasses bucket of fresh cracklings. "I tell you what, I am going back to the house and me and my family is going to eat up these cracklings. Then I am going to git my ole lady to boil up a mess of greens, boil up some of these backbones, and make a pan of cornbread. I am going to be full as a tick when I go to bed," said the ferryman.

"You better be full and rested up tomorrow. We be wanting to get started crossing this river early in the morning. How long do you think it'll take us?" asked Big Man.

"I 'spect it'll take at least two days to get everybody and everything across. It shouldn't be too bad since the river is a little low and slow this time of the year. If you had come through this spring when it was deep and fast we'd had a problem. Now don't you forget, half payment up front. I ain't going to even untie a rope on the ferry until I gits that money!" said the ferryman.

Big Man said, "Don't you worry, you'll get yo money in the morning. Just be down here by daybreak."

Well before daylight the next day, everyone was stirring. The fires were started for breakfast. Everyone thought that they were going to have their usual breakfast fare, corn fritters and molasses. This morning, Big Man had a surprise for them. He was allowing the cooks to fry up a mess of ham and bacon. This was an unknown treat for the freed slaves. They had never eaten this either. Back on the plantation, they were only fed the left over cuts of pork like neck bones, pig's feet and hog jowls. The better cuts of meat went to the big house.

After savoring their small share of meat and eating the corn fritters and molasses, they prepared to leave. The mules were hooked to wagons which had been re-loaded the night before. All of the new meat had been packed in the barrels and covered with salt. All of the tents and cooking utensils had been loaded on the wagons.

Just as it was barely daylight, the ferryman walked down. "Good morning. I see ya'll are about ready to roll," he said. Big Man replied, "More than ready. We is anxious to get across this river so we can head on to Mississippi."

"Don't you be forgetting the most important thing. You ain't going nowhere 'til I see them gold pieces!"

The night before, Big Man had gone to the false bottom of the cook wagon that Birdie was riding in. With Birdie standing watch, he carefully counted out the fare for the ferry crossing. He put half of it in one saddlebag and the other half in the other. He had slept with the bags entwined in his arm.

Again, the ferryman's eyes lit up as Big Man counted out the gold pieces. He was going to make more off this crossing than he would make all of the rest of the year. "Here's the first half! You'll get the rest when we are all across," Big Man said. Scooping up the gold, the ferryman said, "Some of ya'll be lining up while I run up to the house!"

Upon his return, the ferry was untied and the big burly nigras that Big Man had selected took their places on board. Some of the wagons were driven up on the ferry. A few of the freed slaves also boarded. Birdie and her wagon went first for obvious reasons. The ferryman and the big freed slaves started pulling on the rope. The ferry slowly started easing across to the other side. With a lot of yelling and slapping, they drove the wagons onto the opposite bank. There they prepared another campsite.

It would take two days and many trips to get everything and everyone across. Since the river was low and not too fast, the crossings were made with few incidents. The loose stock was the last thing to be taken across. Their feet had been hobbled, and there were enough men to drag them on board and hold them while the ferry was crossing.

With the crossing completed, Big Man reached into his saddle bag and handed the ferryman the rest of the fare. The ferryman said, "I ain't going to count this. It feels just as heavy as what you first gave me. Ya'll have good luck." He then slowly pulled himself back across the river.

It was a beautiful southern fall morning when the wagon train got on the road. The birds were singing and the squirrels barking. The dogs were running around in the woods and yelping. Everyone lined up in their respective places and headed west toward the Tombigbee River.

The ferryman had told Big Man about this river. It was quite a bit larger than the Black Warrior. Although wider, it was not as swift. The ferryman figured if the train had good luck, it could make it there in about three or four days. It was about sixty miles ahead.

Again, they plodded along with the same routine: eat breakfast, walk until noon, eat lunch, rest, walk all afternoon, stop and eat supper, go to sleep and start all over the next day.

They were seeing more people on the road now. It seemed that this was a popular route for anyone heading into the former Indian Territory. The Treaty of Dancing Rabbit Creek opened up all the land in Northeastern Mississippi to the white homesteaders. The Indians had been forced by President Jackson to give up their land and move to Oklahoma. Homesteaders had been pouring into the Choctaw territory for the past twenty years. Since the Federal Land office was located in Greensborough, Mississippi, the settlers crossed the Tombigbee at the town of Columbus, and made their way another fifty miles to the land office. Big Man had inquired of some of the other travelers on the fourth day as to the location of Columbus. They told him that he had about another ten miles to go. They said he would have to go through Columbus to get to the river crossing. The next morning, Big Man turned the train over to his assistants. He told them he should be back before lunch.

As Big Man rode along, he passed small wagon trains headed to the crossing. There were also single wagons, surreys, and buggies on the road. There were even a few people walking with packs on their backs. Everybody was heading west.

Just as Big Man approached town, he came upon an old slave driving his master's wagon. He told the old man what he was doing and asked him where the ferry crossing was. "The ferry's on the other side of town, but I don't 'spect you better be riding yo black butt down the main streets of town. All dem white folks going to want to know what a strange nigra is doing riding through de town! I 'spect it be best if yo train takes that old road yonder. It'll take ya'll around town and take ya'll to the ferry."

With this information, Big Man turned his horse onto the old road and by-passed the town. He soon came upon the ferry. He happened to catch the owner when he wasn't too busy. He showed him his papers and pass. Satisfied, the owner gave him a price to take everyone across the river. He said since he had such a large ferry, he could ferry everyone and everything across in a day. Big Man was surprised at the price. It was much less than what he had paid at the last crossing. His inclination was right. The redneck ferryman had overcharged him just as he had figured. His only consolation was that he had had no choice!

The ferry owner had told Big Man about a camping spot he owned. It was about two miles away. He said that they could spend the night there. He wanted the wagon train at the landing by daybreak. He felt like he could get everyone across before dark.

Big Man turned and met the train. He guided it to the campground that had been described. After everyone had gone to sleep, he again slipped to Birdie's wagon. With her standing guard, he carefully counted out the ferry fare and placed it in his saddlebags. He slept with the bags under his head.

The crossing the next day was fairly uneventful with the exception of one incident. One of the piglets managed to force his way under the bottom rail of the ferry and fell into the river. The last glimpse of it that anyone saw was it scrambling back up the bank on the other side. Someone said, "I guess he like Alabama more than Mississippi!" Another said, "Naw! dat ain't it. He done watched us eat dem other hogs. He don't want to be et!"

When the last ferry run was made and everyone was on the western side of the Tombigbee, supper was started. They were tired and hungry. They took care of the stock, ate and laid down to sleep. The next morning, they would be heading to the junction of the Natchez Trace. This leg of the trip would take about two days. The ferry owner had told Big Man that there were no major rivers between the train and the Trace.

The next day was miserable. A slow drizzle of a rain had set in. Although not a cold rain, it eventually made the road muddy. The freed slaves were just slogging along with their heads down. The wagon wheels were cutting deep grooves in the mud. The cows were pulling back on the wagons which made them harder to pull. There was no talking. They just plodded along.

Due to the conditions, Big Man made a decision to stop early. He found a spot and pulled off to the side of the road. The people riding on the wagons quickly crawled under them to get out of the rain. The others set up the tents. This was a welcome respite from the rain. After about a hour, the rain moved out. It became a very pleasant evening. The temperature fell and the smell of fall was in the air.

Big Man told Birdie, "We best be moving as fast as we can the rest of the trip. I sho believe we is going to have an early winter." Birdie replied, "I believes you is right. I am starting to feel it in my bones. Ole man winter is coming purty soon."

The next day dawned crisp and clear. They were on the road as early as possible. By mid—morning, the northern breeze had dried the road, and they were able to walk at their normal pace. The mules stepped briskly along. They were enjoying the cool air. The traffic picked up and Big Man could sense that they were approaching the Natchez Trace.

They intersected the trace close to Greensborough, Mississippi. The train turned left onto the Trace. Big Man put one of his assistants in charge and rode into town.

This was a growing little town. It was the county seat and the location of the federal land office. All of the settlers came to the town to apply for the land that the Indians had been forced to give up. There were so many strangers coming through that Big Man didn't attract much attention. A lot of the people on the streets thought that he was a Choctaw Indian that had managed to escape the forced march to Oklahoma.

He was searching for the telegraph office. Finding it at the end of the street, he dismounted and walked in. The telegraph operator was startled to look up and see this big black man standing there. He was like the other residents; he didn't know if he was a Nigra or a Choctaw.

Big Man presented his papers and asked the operator how far it was to French Camp and Kosciusko. The operator told him that it was about twenty five miles to French Camp and another twenty five to Kosciusko. Big Man then told him he wanted to send a message to Mr. Buchanan Inman at Leota, Mississippi. The message was:

NO BIG PROBLEMS. SHOULD GET TO KOSCIUSKO ABOUT NOVEMBER 1, 1859. WE WILL WAIT IF YOU ARE NOT THERE. Big Man.

The operator had rephrased some of the message to make it clearer.

After paying for the telegraph, Big Man mounted and rode hard to catch up with the wagon train. It always worried him when it was out of his sight.

After riding about five miles, Big Man caught up with the train. It was stopped on the side of the road. He could see his assistants talking to five rough white men in a wagon. The white men were rafters that sold their produce in Natchez and were returning to Tennessee. Just as he arrived, two of the white men got off of the wagon and was berating his men. He couldn't hear what they were saying, but he could tell that they were angry.

He rode up, dismounted and said, "What's going on here?" One of the rough looking men said, "I'll tell you what's the matter. These Nigras let their stock git out on the road when we wuz passing. They made our mules run away. We was lucky our wagon didn't turn over!"

"Big Man, we done told them we wuz sorry. We sho didn't mean for them cows to scare de mules. But you knows, sometimes dem cows got a mind of de own."

Big Man said to the whites," I'm sorry bout that. I know they didn't do it on purpose. We'll be sure the stock don't git in your way again."

The big white man said, "I don't give a damn about you being sorry. Them nappy-headed nigras liked to have give me a heart attack! I got a great mind to take this here whip to them slaves."

"Now wait a minute, we ain't going to have none of that!" Big Man said. "Everybody done said they wuz sorry. Ain't nothing else we can do. Ya'll best git back in that wagon and carry yo selves back to where ya'll come from!"

"Don't you black son-of-a-bitch sass me. I'll take this whip to you!" With that comment, the large white man drew back the butt of his whip and tried to strike Big Man. Big Man reached up and caught the man's arm in his hand. He slowly bent the arm backwards.

Feeling the power, the white man said, "you better let go, I don't want to have to hurt you!"

'Big Man just smiled and said, "Don't worry bout hurting me! Ain't going to happen! I am going to turn you loose and I want you to git yo lard butt back on dat wagon, and git out'a here." With that, Big Man let go of the arm.

The man said as he crawled back up on the wagon, "You damn Nigra, you bout broke my arm. Come on boys, we ain't got time to be fooling with these slaves. Let's git out of here before I have to hurt somebody."

As the wagon started off, Big Man yelled, "Yo fust mistake was thinking we wuz slaves! We is just as free as ya'll are, and we got the papers to prove it." The men on the wagon didn't look back as they high-tailed it up the Trace.

The wagon train moved along until they came to McCurtain Creek. They decided to camp there that night. The land there had not been homesteaded or bought. It still belonged to the government. Since it had never been cleared, there were large native pines everywhere. It was a great place to camp, and they pulled off by the creek. It was nice to camp by a stream. It allowed everyone to bathe and change into clean clothes.

After cooking and eating some of the beef they had put up, everyone was ready for sleep. Since they were walking so far every day, it took a lot of food to keep them going. It seemed like they were always hungry!

Big Man planned on reaching French Camp the next night.

As usual Big Man rode ahead to find a place for the wagon train to stop for the night. After riding south down the Trace, he came upon French Camp. Since it was early morning, there was not a lot of activity going on. He dismounted and walked into the tavern that Louis had built after leaving Lefluer's Bluff. There he found Louis Lefluer's youngest son and his wife having a late breakfast. After Louis' death, the son had taken over the stand. Having a big black man walk in did not bother Lefluer at all. Since his stand was located on the main thoroughfare, he had just about seen every kind of traveler passing through.

Big Man pulled out his papers and showed them to the Frenchman. He had found it was always best to show his papers and tell folks who he was and what he was doing before asking for permission to camp.

After reviewing the papers, Lefluer gave Man permission for the wagon train to camp down by the creek. He asked Man if they would be needing any provisions. Man thought and said, "We sho do. I'll pick up some in the morning." Man thought that he needed to buy something to repay Lefluer for his hospitality.

Lefluer asked, "Where will you be heading in the morning?" Big Man replied, "We be heading for Kosciusko. We is going to meet Mr. Buck there and he is going to guide us to de plantation." Big Man then returned to the train and led it to the campground.

After spending the night at French Camp and then another stand further south, the train was approaching Kosciusko. Traffic was picking up. They were being passed from behind by riders that were traveling faster than they were. They met other travelers heading north. Some were in wagons, some in carriages and some on foot.

Big Man was out front leading, when he spotted a lone rider approaching. He could not see who the rider was, but he sure did admire the horse. The Tennessee Walker was glided along at a smooth fast pace. His head was nodding in beat with his feet. As the rider drew closer, Big Man recognized him. He spurred his horse and set out at a gallop to meet him.

Buck saw Big Man coming and sped up to meet him. They both dismounted, and Buck clapped Big Man on the back.

"I see ya'll made it. Big Man, I am mighty proud of you. Ain't many folks, black or white, that could guide a wagon train this far with no more trouble than you had. I told you when I left that I had great confidence in you!"

"Well, Mr. Buck, I done de best that I could. We had a little trouble along the way but nuthing big. All yo folks been mighty good about walking and trying to git here. They going to be mighty glad to see you. We is all wanting to make it to yo new plantation."

13

Mount Hope

When Buck returned home from South Carolina, he found Mr. Sloan and his workers hard at work on his plantation that he had named Mount Hope. He had decided this was a good name for his place. After all, everyone that would be living there had great hope for the future. Activity was going on everywhere.

He was greeted first by John and Jim. They were excited to see him and could not wait to show Buck what they had accomplished while he was gone. They took him to a cabin that was almost complete. Using the techniques that Buck had taught them, they had done a good job. Buck was impressed at how quickly they had been able to build a cabin by themselves. This would be the third cabin on the plantation. He complimented the young men and went to find Mr. Sloan.

Mr. Sloan was in his shirt sleeves and sweating profusely in the hot September sun. He was excited by Buck's arrival and wanted to show him his progress. He showed Buck how the workers had dug the foundation trenches down to the water table which was about six feet below the surface. Here they had placed huge cypress logs that they had squared up to two foot by two foot by twenty foot beams. He explained to Buck that the beams would serve as footings for the weight bearing walls. The idea was that the beams could shift with the soil. By doing so, they would actually be floating and moving with the ground. This would prevent the brick walls from cracking.

Out to the side, they had constructed a huge lime pit to mix the mortar. There were piles of river sand that they had hauled in. They had also built a large brick kiln to dry the brick. Men were filling the brick forms that they had made so that the clay mixture could be dried by the sun before being placed in the kiln. There was a huge fire going around the kiln to bake the brick. It was a hot dirty job. The results were large red bricks that were being stacked and used as soon as they cooled. Mr. Sloan said that he was having a slight problem with the brick in the center. They were not getting quite as hard as the ones stacked on the outside. The outside bricks were getting more heat.

Mr. Sloan's technique was to build the floors as they built the walls. They had started by laying the bricks on the foundation beams. When the walls reached five feet above the ground, they started to add the floor. The five foot height was a precaution in case of flooding. The workers cut and fitted the floor joists to run from wall to wall. The ends of the beams rested on the walls. All of the exterior walls were two foot thick, and the interior walls were eighteen inches. Metal tees were attached to the end of the joists. These would extend out into the new brick being laid to make a better bonding. With everything in place, the bricklayers could continue building the walls. The joists and the tees would hold the walls firmly in place once the mortar dried.

This was the structure that Buck saw when he arrived home: footings, partial walls and floor joists. He congratulated Mr. Sloan on his progress. The workers had made great strides on the house while he was in South Carolina.

There were mansions being built all over Mississippi at this time. With the growing of the new Petit cotton strain and the invention of the cotton gin, there was an amazing amount of wealth being accumulated all over the state. Not only were the planters getting rich, but so were all of the related businesses such as the banks and shopkeepers. Everyone thought that this boom would last forever.

Little did they know that the ensuing war would destroy this new wealth and their way of life.

The craftsmen from the New England states had traveled south to take advantage of the building boom. It was fortunate that Mr. Sloan had many of them employed at his other building sites. He was able to move the bricklayers and carpenters back and forth from job to job.

Before Buck had left for South Carolina, he and Mr. Sloan had spent considerable time drawing and redrawing the plans for Mount Hope. Buck had some pretty firm ideas about how he wanted his house built. He wanted a three-storied house with fifteen foot porches running around the front and sides of the first floor. He then wanted balconies running around the sides of the second and third floors. He wanted massive Corinthian columns all the way around the front and sides to hold up these massive balconies and porch roofs.

He asked Mr. Sloan to design the mansion so that all of the floors had massive front doors that would open up to large entry halls. The first floor would have twelve foot ceilings with twenty by twenty rooms. Each could be reached by the entrance hall. There would be a total of eight rooms on this level including three bedrooms with their accompanying sitting rooms. The other two rooms would be the downstairs parlor and music room. Buck was preparing this area for his mother and sisters.

Right above the first floor would be another eight rooms. Here, the ceilings would be fourteen feet tall. There would be circular stairs on either side of the front doors curving up from the front porch to the second floor balcony. These would be used to reach the main entrance of the house. All guests would be expected to use these stairs to enter Mount Hope. On this level would be two connecting front parlors off one side of the entry hall. On the other side would be the massive dining area. This area could be partitioned by sliding pocket doors if necessary. Behind the front parlors would be Buck's quarters. He would also have a bedroom with a separate sitting area. There would be a library in the two rooms across the hall from him. These rooms could also be partitioned off with pocket doors if desired.

The third floor would be the ballroom. Buck could envision the dances that he and his sisters would give all through the years. This ceiling would also be fourteen feet tall.

Buck's other request was an observatory above the third floor. He not only wanted to look over his plantation, but he thought he would enjoy watching the traffic going up and down the mighty Mississippi River. From the ground to the very top of the copula, the structure would be some fifty feet tall.

Mr. Sloan suggested adding an Italianate flair by using arched windows. He also wanted to use large brackets under the roof all of the way around the house. On his drawings, he added massive bay windows on the front and sides of the house. He informed Buck of some of the conveniences that he had begun using in some of the other homes he was building. Things such as Jib windows/doors, cisterns fed by pipes coming off of the gutters around the roof, septic tanks, water closets in each room supplied by cypress water barrels on the roof. He thought they could harness the power of the artesian spring in the back by using a ram pump. It would have enough force to push the water up to the barrel on the roof. From the barrel, gravity could then feed the water down to the water closets. The kitchen would be supplied with water by a hand pump from one of the cisterns. The plans called for three septic tanks, two twelve foot deep cisterns, and sixteen fireplaces.

Buck and Mr. Sloan had not completed the plans for the two two-storied wings on the back of the house. Buck told Mr. Sloan to direct all of his energy toward finishing the front part of the house. He still wanted to get his family moved in as quickly as possible. They could add the additions later.

The building continued at a torrid pace. Buck used Mr. Sloan's connections to hire as many laborers and craftsmen as possible.

Although the sawmill on the place was providing all of the rough timber they required, Buck had to make arrangements for all of the mill work. He was fortunate that he was able to buy most of the millwork from the new mill in Vicksburg. However, the light fixtures, ceiling medallions and the more intricate woodwork would have to be shipped from Philadelphia, Pennsylvania. The Italian marble mantels for the fire places had to be ordered from Italy.

Two other conveniences would be built into the structure as it was being constructed. Pipes from the carbide plant out back would have to be run through the walls and floor as they went up. The plant would provide the gas that each chandelier burned. Also installed, as the structure went up, was a communication system. This consisted of wires being attached to small silver handles in each room. These wires ran to a cupboard in the kitchen where they were attached to small bells. By giving the handles a twist, each room occupant could ring their respective bell. The servants would know which room needed service.

With all of this going on, it became Buck's job to get all of the materials to the workers. He had to go to Vicksburg to give Mr. Sloan's window and door drawings to the mill. He made arrangements for them to be shipped to Leota as they were completed. Again, through Mr. Sloan's connections, he was able to contract and make shipping arrangements for all of the light fixtures, medallions, and mantles. As these purchases started arriving, he, John and Jim were kept busy hauling everything from Leota to Mount Hope in the wagon.

Buck soon realized that he could not haul all of the materials coming into town with Charlie and the small wagon. He loaded John and Jim on the wagon and headed to town. The first time that Buck took the young men to town with him they were terrified. Buck told them to stay on the wagons and to not talk to anyone. Buck would do all of the talking. After several trips, the young nigras relaxed and the town people became accustomed to seeing them with Buck. Everyone assumed that they were Buck's slaves.

When Buck pulled up to the livery stable, he was greeted warmly by Tom. He and Tom had become friends since Buck rented Tom's storage next to the livery stable. He made arrangements for Tom to haul the materials for Mount Hope from the landing to the storage room. Buck, John and Jim were picking up the materials there and hauling them on to the Big House.

Buck said, "Tom, are you ready to out trade me again?" Tom grinned and said, "What are you talking about? You know I always git beat every time I trade with you! What you going to beat me out of this time?"

"As you can see, I can't keep up with hauling the materials with this one wagon. Do you know anyone who has a much larger wagon that might be for sale?"

Tom scratched his head and said, "You know, I just might. Why don't ya'll start loading this wagon and let me see what I can do? I'll try to find a couple of horses while I am at it. Course you know, I got to make a little something!"

Buck replied, "I know about your little something. It always turns out to be a big something!"

Tom got on his old horse and took off out of town. Buck and the boys started loading the materials on hand. They were just about loaded when they spotted Tom coming back. He was riding in a large livery wagon, pulled by two of the largest mules that Buck had ever seen. Tom had tied his horse onto the back.

"I told you I might know of a wagon. I just thought of an old man that went out of the livery business several years ago because of his health. I thought he might be inclined to sell since these big mules was about to eat up all of his feed. Course you know, this rig didn't come cheap!"

"Yea, I know," said Buck sarcastically. "Just how much are you going to have to make your "little something"?" Tom gave Buck a price, and Buck put on a show of complaining about it being too much. The truth was that he got a kick out of trading with Tom. He really didn't mind Tom trying to make a little extra off of him. He just didn't want Tom to know it.

The mules stood perfectly still while the big wagon was being loaded. With both wagons full, Buck had to decide how he was going to get both wagons home. Since he wasn't familiar with the mules, he decided that he and Jim would ride in the big wagon. John would ride in the other wagon and drive Charlie. Since Charlie had made this trip so many times, Buck figured John could handle him.

As they started the trip back home, Buck said, "Thanks, Tom. I guess I will be seeing you regularly for some time. I'll have a lot of material and supplies coming in over the next few months. I'll try to make room in the storeroom as fast as I can."

"Buck, I guess you know you are causing quite a stir in these parts. Everyone is trying to guess what your house is going to look like and how large it is going to be. They are questioning Mr. Sloan when he is in town, but he is pretty tight lipped. They are also wondering where you are getting your money and if you are going to have enough to finish. I been kinda wondering the same thing myself."

"Tom, I guess you and everyone else will just have to wait and see. You can tell everybody that they will know pretty soon because we are going to build Mount Hope in record time. I promised my family that I would get them out here as quickly as possible. You and your men just keep on bringing the loads from the paddle wheeler, and we will take care of getting everything out to the place."

As they left town, Buck could feel the curious stares on his back. He was an enigma when he arrived and more so now.

They had no problems on the road home. Buck could tell that the big mules were used to pulling large loads. They gave him no trouble. Charlie followed along, content to follow the big wagon. John thought he was doing a great job of driving, but really, Charlie would have followed along if there had been no one on the wagon.

When they arrived at the plantation, they pulled around to the large storage building that Buck had had the workers construct. He went to check with Mr. Sloan as John, Jim, and some of the hired hands unloaded.

The next few weeks passed by in a blur. They settled into a routine. Every morning Buck and Mr. Sloan had breakfast together and conferred about the building. Mr. Sloan would give Buck a list of additional supplies that he needed. While they were doing this, John and Jim ate a quick breakfast and hooked up the animals to the wagons. By early morning they were on their way to Leota. Buck thought, "They might as well change my name to Gofer. Go for this and go for that!"

It was nice that he could now trust the driving to the young Nigras. They had matured and handled the teams with ease. Buck now let them put him off in the middle of town so that he could purchase the orders that he had been given by Mr. Sloan. They then continued on down to the livery stable and started loading. He also used this opportunity to check by the telegraph office. He thought that he was fortunate that Leota had an office. He was able to send purchase orders over the wires and receive transmissions about the shipping dates. This convenience saved him a lot of trips out of town.

By the end of October, 1858, the framing of the front rooms of the house was almost complete. The structure had reached about forty feet and could now be seen by the passengers of the paddle—wheelers going up and down the Mississippi River. The size of the structure being built caused so much local interest that the town people were continually riding out to see what was going on. Buck really didn't have time to fool with them, but he tried to be cordial. He knew that most of them thought he was going to run out of money before he got his home built.

At their breakfast meeting, Mr. Sloan told Buck that it was time to order the roof. He suggested a standing seam metal roof made out of a combination of tin and copper. He gave Buck the address of the Virginia mill that manufactured the roofing panels. Mr. Sloan was hoping to get the roof on the front part of the house before the winter rains set in. He figured that he would be ready to install it by the time it arrived. He also gave Buck a list and measurements of the wrought iron that would be used in the construction.

"Goodness, Mr. Sloan, you are really keeping me stretched out. I guess it's my fault for trying to build so fast. I'd better get on the road if I'm going to get all of this done."

When he and the young men reached Leota, he dismounted, and as usual, made his first stop at the telegraph office. The operator told him that he had the usual telegraphs, but he had also gotten one that was kind of unusual. Buck asked to read that one first. It was from Big Man! Big Man hoped to have the wagon train in Kosciusko by the first of November. "My goodness," Buck thought, "he didn't allow much time for me to meet him." Buck sat at the little table and hurriedly read all of his telegraphs. He replied to all of them and then sent off his orders for the roofing material and the wrought iron. The telegraph operator was happy to have Buck use the telegraph so often. He and many of the other merchants were making money off of Buck. It was a boon for Leota's economy when Buck started building.

After taking care of his telegraphs, Buck hurried down to the livery stable. He encouraged the boys and the hired hand to load as quickly as possible. He told Tom that he would be gone for about a week. He asked him to store all of the incoming freight in the big shed until he returned. Tom assured him that he would take care of everything.

With Charlie following, Buck drove the big mules as fast as he thought possible with the big loads. When he arrived at the plantation, he started the boys and some hired hands unloading. He told the boys that he would be gone for about a week and that he was trusting them to take care of the stock while he was away. They promised that that they would take good care of the animals. He asked John to get Prince saddled as quickly as possible. He also told them to sack up Prince a bag of grain to take along. He knew that he would be pushing the big stallion and he wanted him to be well fed. He then turned towards the house to find Mr. Sloan.

Upon finding Mr. Sloan, he explained to him where he was going. Mr. Sloan said, "I don't think we will have a problem with materials for at least a week or maybe longer. You don't worry about the house construction. I'll take care of everything while you are gone. I'll even watch them young nigras for you They are rascals but I like them."

"Good," Buck said and went to pack.

Buck threw a few cloths into his saddle bags and was soon ready to go. He went out and climbed up on Prince, told the boys goodbye, and was on his way.

He decided he would take the trail that ran north by the lake to Wayside plantation. From there, he figured he could head east on the new road that had just been beaten out by all of the settlers coming into the area. It was a pretty good road with bridges over the larger streams. Buck thought, "What a change since I arrived here!"

He followed the road east across the Delta. He could see that he had to get the wagon train to the plantation before the rains came. There was no doubt that the road would become impassable when winter arrived.

Buck figured he could cover the one hundred miles to Kosciusko in two days if he rode steady. He spent his first night at the little town of Tchula. This little town was in the Delta just before you entered the hill section of Mississippi. As was the custom of the day, Buck stopped at a large plantation home and asked the mistress of the plantation if he might spend the night in her barn. It was looking like rain and he figured he needed shelter. "You most certainly can not!" she replied. "I'll have my stable boys take care of your horse, and you will spend the night in one of our spare rooms. You will take supper with us, too. I know it is late and I bet you haven't had a thing to eat. Now get down off that horse and come on in. My husband will be back in a few minutes and ya'll can talk while you eat."

Buck started to protest, but thought better. This lady reminded him too much of his mother. He said, "Yes Ma'am" and dismounted. A young nigra appeared and took Prince to the barn. Buck followed the lady into her home. As they went in, the mistress reached for a silver bell that was on a table in the parlor. When she rang it, a short fat nigra women responded immediately. The Mistress turned to Buck and said, "This is Mae. She is our cook. You just tell her what you want and she will fix it for you." Buck thought to himself, " I guess that all plantation cooks are fat. They all must like to eat." He then said, "I don't want to be any trouble. Just anything will do."

The lady of the house introduced herself as Mrs. Barr and invited Buck to sit down at the large dining table. She told Mae to warm up the leftover chicken and biscuits and to bring a glass of cold milk. She also told Mae in which room Buck would be staying. She told her to be sure there was plenty of hot water. She told Buck where he could go and wash up before eating. Buck could tell that she was used to being in control. He decided he would just have to go along with the plan.

Just as he started eating, Mr. Barr returned home. When he spotted Buck, he stuck out his hand and introduced himself as Robert Barr. Buck told him who he was and told him where he was going. He told him that he hoped his spending the night would not be an imposition. Mr. Barr replied, "Hell no, boy. We don't get much company out here. It'll be a pleasure to talk with someone besides the overseer and nigras here on the place!" And talk he did. He covered the price of cotton, the new settlers coming in, the slave problems and the upcoming war. Buck was so tired that he had a hard time showing interest. He finally was able to excuse himself for bed. He told the Barrs that he would be leaving early the next day. He would just slip out when he woke up and be on his way. "I don't know what you call early, but we get up about four every morning. You just come by the kitchen, and I'll have you a snack to eat on your trip." Buck bid them goodnight and went to bed.

Because he had so much on his mind, he did not sleep well. He woke up about four-thirty, and dressed and was ready to travel. True to Mrs. Barr's word, the Barrs were already up and drinking coffee. Mrs. Barr had his breakfast sacked up. Buck told them he would eat it on his way. Mr. Barr told him that the hostler had already fed and saddled Prince. They invited him to come back anytime. Buck told them he would be coming back through in about four or five days with his wagon train. The night before, Mr. Barr had given him permission to stop overnight on his place when he came back through.

After riding about an hour, Buck reached the steep hills that bordered the Delta. As he climbed, everything changed. There were huge pine trees on either side of the road. The few farms along the way were small and the houses were small compared to the Delta homes. Buck made good time and was in the town of Lexington by lunch. He stopped there to stretch his leg, buy some lunch meat, and inquire about the distance to Kosciusko. He was soon on his way heading east.

He did not see the wagon train as he rode through Kosciusko. Since this town was a hub with several roads intersecting, Buck was afraid he might have missed the wagon train. There were several old men sitting on the porch of a small hotel. Buck asked them if they had seen a wagon train come through. They said they hadn't but pointed Buck in the direction of French Camp. It was getting late, and Buck was getting concerned. He felt immense relief when he rode around a curve and saw the wagon train stretched out for a mile. He and Big Man spotted each other at the same time.

With both Buck and Big Man galloping their horses, they soon met. When they both dismounted, Big Man grabbed Buck around the waist, picked him up and swung him around just as he used to do when they were boys. It was a strange relationship between these two men. Slave owner and slave! Now, boss and employee! But still after all of these years, FRIENDS!

They re-mounted and rode back to the train. Everyone had crowded together to get a glimpse of Mr. Buck. They yelled and clapped when he rode up. Buck thought, "I kinda feel like Moses leading the slaves out of Egypt."

Everyone was pressing around, trying to tell Buck of their experiences on the road. Since they were all talking at once, Buck could hardly understand what they were saying. Big Man soon intervened, "Ya'll need to back up now. Mr. Buck has been riding all day and I know he's wore out. Ya'll will git a chance to say somethin' to him tomorrow. Why don't ya'll pull off in that grove of trees yonder and set up camp? Ya'll better be resting up. We gonna be traveling hard the next few days. Now ya'll be sho to set up one of them new tents by Birdie's wagon for Mr. Buck." Buck was surprised as to how quick everyone responded to Big Man's orders. Big Man was in charge!

They had the camp set up in no time. Buck and Big Man walked down to Birdie's wagon and tent. Birdie was as glad to see Buck as

Big Man had been. He was still the little boy that she had carried around on her hip years ago. It was a relationship that only people in the South could understand.

While Birdie was preparing a meal, Big Man started telling Buck about his experiences on the road. Buck laughed and laughed when Big Man related what happened with the boys and Fannie. Man told Buck about the river crossings and told him how the first ferryman overcharged him. Buck told him that it was all right and that he probably could have done no better if he had been there. Big Man asked if Buck wanted him to get the remaining gold for him. Buck told him to just leave in the hiding place and he would get it when they reached the plantation.

Since everyone was tired, no one stayed up too late. Buck and Man sat by the fire for a little while and then turned in. When Buck entered his tent, he found a pan of hot water and towels. Birdie was still taking care of him.

As Buck lay in the tent, he started thinking about the next days of travel. He figured that with good luck he could reach the plantation in about a week. He was glad he had just ridden the route. He at least knew where he was going. He just hoped that he could get across the Delta before the winter rains set in. He knew that in the areas where the soil was gumbo(clay) the trail might become impassable after a big rain.

With these thoughts running through his mind, Buck was soon asleep.

The train made it's way around Kosciusko and turned west toward their destination. They spent two days traveling through the woods and up and down the hills. Since Buck was the only one that knew the way, he and Man rode in front.

The morning of the third day found them traversing down a long high hill. This led them to the Delta! The former slaves had never seen land so flat. As far as they could see, there were no hills, just flat land. A lot of the land was still covered in trees, but there were huge tracts that had been cleared. These big clearings were being used for pasture land and to grow cotton. Each of these cleared areas had a plantation home with the usual slave cabins. Buck knew that it had taken a lot of slave labor to clear the land of trees.

As the train moved past these plantations, a lot of times there would be slaves working in the fields besides the road. These slaves would yell at the wagon train, "Where you nappy-headed nigras from? Some of you women's is sho looking good!!" The ones on the train would yell back, "Ain't none of yo business where we from. Ya'll need to get yo scrawny butts back to work." This was all said in good fun and each party was laughing and smiling as they insulted each other.

After a day's travel, they approached Robert Barr's plantation. Buck and Man rode ahead to find out where Mr. Barr would allow them to camp. They met Mr. Barr coming up his driveway in his surrey. He told Buck that they could camp down in the clearing by the bayou. He said, "Ya'll better build some smudge fires to run off them mosquitoes. They are terrible this time of the year." He then asked Buck who he had with him. Buck replied, "This is Big Man. He led my wagon train all of the way from South Carolina. I am mighty proud of him." Mr. Barr said, "I reckon so. I wish I had a big buck nigra like him. I ain't got nobody to help me worth a hoot. Do you want to sell him?" Buck smiled and said, " I don't think so. We were raised together. He's almost like a brother to me." Mr. Barr said, "I understand. I was given a young slave when I was a boy back in Georgia. He was mighty good to me. It like to have killed me when he died. He was about fifteen when a horse threw him and he broke his neck. Anyway, enough of this talk. Mrs. Barr said for you to come and eat supper with us tonight. She has a surprise for you and you know that she won't take no for a answer."

Since it was getting late, Buck told Mr. Barr that as soon as he got cleaned up he would be on up to the big house.

Washed and with clean clothes on, Buck knocked on the front door of the big house. Mrs. Barr herself answered the door. "Oh Buck," she gushed, "come on in. I have someone I want you to meet. It just so happens that my niece from over at Riverdale plantation is visiting. She is a darling sweet girl and I think that ya'll will get along famously." Buck could feel it coming. Many an old woman had tried to fix him up with some of their kin. He took a deep breath and walked into the parlor.

His intuition was correct. When he walked in, he was introduced to the one of the ugliest girls he had ever seen. She was thin and stooped. Her long black hair was swooped across her forehead and almost hid her weak eyes peering out from under her bangs. She had a prominent nose, and protruding teeth. Buck thought, "Oh, my goodness! I believe I am becoming nauseous!"

Mrs. Barr was still talking, "We will have a lovely meal, and then you and Doreen can spend some time visiting in the parlor. I know you young folks will have a lot to talk about. In fact, you may be able to entice her to play the piano and sing for you. Ya'll will have a marvelous time!"

Buck replied, "Mrs. Barr, I am so sorry. I am just not feeling well. I don't believe that my stomach can tolerate any food at this time. Would you and Doreen accept my apologies? I feel that I must excuse myself and return to the wagon train."

"Oh Buck, I am so disappointed! I had so wanted you young people to get to know each other. Maybe you can come back for a visit another time."

"Yes, Ma'am. Maybe another time," Buck replied, as he beat a hasty retreat out the door.

When he got on his horse, he said to himself, "At least I didn't lie. The thought of spending the evening with Doreen was making me sick to my stomach. I know I couldn't have eaten a bite."

When he returned to camp, he found Big Man and Birdie sitting around the campfire. Everywhere he looked, he could see campfires. There was a pall of smoke all over the camp site. Everyone had placed some green limbs on the fire to create the smoke. They were doing their best to run off the large Delta mosquitoes.

"What you doing back so soon? I thought you wuz going to take supper with Mr. and Mrs. Barr," Birdie said.

"I had planned on it but I changed my mind. Mrs. Barr tried to fix me up with her niece. I believe that was just about the ugliest white girl I ever saw. I had to get out of there. I was starting to get sick to my stomach."

Big Man and Birdie fell out laughing. "I guess you don't like no ugly woman," Man said.

"You are right about that," Buck replied.

Birdie said, "I bet you done recovered enough to eat these chicken and dumplings that I cooked. They is still warm!"

Slowly, the wagon train snaked west toward the Mississippi River. The new road followed all of the ridges and the river banks. Most of the road had been created out of old bear and Indian trails. The new settlers had beaten back the vegetation along the road as they proceeded west to the new land. The flat land made the going fairly easy. The walkers had a hard time with the fine dust that was being stirred up by the wagons and mules. The soil in the Delta, for the most part, was sandy loam or clay (gumbo). The only respite from the dust came when they were lucky enough to have a rain shower. When this happened, it created another problem—mud. If they were unfortunate enough to be crossing the gumbo soil when it rained, they had to contend with the sticky soil. The clay would stick to the animals' hoofs, the wagon wheels, and everyone's feet. It made walking miserable.

After the first shower, Buck said to big Man, "You see now why I wanted to get across the Delta before the winter rains set in. This road will be almost impassable all winter."

"I sho do. I ain't never seen mud that sticks to you like this."

It seemed like the weather changed daily. It would be hot; it would be cool. There would be showers and then hot sunshine. Typical Mississippi weather in November.

After traveling for days, they made their last camp before reaching Mount Hope. Buck had Man gather everyone up after they ate supper. He wanted to talk to them. He told them that he had a surprise for them. When he told them that this would be their last night on the road and that they would arrive at their destination the next day, everyone whooped and hollered. Buck told them how proud he was of them for making the long trip without many complaints. He told them that they had better go to bed early and get a good night's rest because they would be leaving early the next morning. He told them that they could rest up after they arrived at the plantation.

It was a beautiful, fall morning when the train pulled out. The weather had turned cool and crisp. It seemed that not only were the former slaves excited, but that the animals were, too. The walkers and the animals had a spring in their steps as they started their last day on the road.

It was mid-afternoon when the train reached Wayside Plantation. They soon turned left on the river road that headed south toward the lake. Along the way, they met several different groups of people.

Some Buck knew and others he didn't. Soon the word would be out about Buck's wagon train and the 500 nigras that he was bringing in.

The road followed the Mississippi River bank until they came to the north end of the lake. Here they left the main road and headed for home, Mount Hope.

It was dusk when the wagon train reached the plantation. Mr. Sloan had already headed to Leota to eat. The hired hands who were sleeping in one of the finished rooms were outside cooking their supper. When John and Jim spotted the wagon, they ran out to meet it. They were anxious to tell Buck how well they had taken care of things while he was gone to meet Big Man.

When they got closer, they came to an abrupt halt. They could see the train stretching out over a mile. John said, "Would you look at that! I didn't know there wuz that many black folks in the world!"

Jim said, "Reckon how many girls they has got with them? I sho hope they has got some purty ones."

"Boy, that's all you think about! Girls!, Girls!"

"What you think I'm gonna think about? I ain't never had a girlfriend and you ain't neither!"

"Well, anyway! When you see them, try not to act like a fool."

What you mean, "Like a fool"?

"I mean don't be standing there looking like a fool with your eyeballs sticking out. Try to have some manners like me."

"You don't know no more about girls than I do, with yo grown-up self! I 'spect I be teaching you about dem girls fore it is over with!"

Their conversation was interrupted when Buck and Big Man rode up.

"John and Jim, I want you to meet my overseer, Big Man," Buck said. "He and I grew up together. His family has been with us for generations."

"Mr. Buck, you said he was big'un, but I didn't know he was gonna be this big. I 'spect he don't have any trouble with them Nigras."

"I better not have any trouble with you two either," Man said with a grin.

Jim said, "Ya'll got many young girls with you?"

"There he goes again. That's all he thinks and talks about," John said.

Big Man looked at Buck and said, "Just wait until he gits a look at Fanny. She'll drive him crazy when she starts swishing her tail around!" Buck laughed and said, "I expect she will be too much for both of them to handle."

By this time the wagon train had caught up. Buck directed them to a clearing down between the big house and the bayou. He told Big Man to set up a temporary camp for the night. They would start laying out a permanent one the next day.

14

Settling in on the Lake

When Mr. Sloan arrived at the plantation the next morning, he found a beehive of activity. His laborers were already at work. Buck and Big Man were directing the building of a permanent camp site down by the bayou. Some of the men were stringing more wire fences for the stock. Others were setting up all of the tents that they had. The women were involved in setting up the camp site. Some were cooking; others were washing. John and Jim had taken a wagon with several barrels on it to the lake. They had brought back water to the women. The water was put in the big cast iron pots that were set up over fires. After it was heated, the women were able to start a clothes wash.

There was so much to do. Temporary latrines had to be built. They had to build store houses for the remaining food. Cabins and barns had to be built. The fresh water barrels had to be replenished from the spring. All of this was being done with an eye toward Winter. It was on its way.

Buck introduced Big Man to Mr. Sloan. Birdie brought the three men cups of coffee and they sat down to discuss the tremendous job that was before them.

Mr. Sloan said, "Buck, you weren't joking when you said you were bringing in some labor. I had no idea you meant this many people. We just might get the front part of the house stood up and roofed by the time winter sets in. If we can do that, we will be home free. We can add the windows and plaster the walls even if it turns cold on us. We just need to be sure we have the front fireplaces functioning."

Buck said, "I have been thinking. I want to devote about fifty men to the building of the house. Everyone else can work on the permanent cabins. I am going to put Big Man in charge of the cabin building. He can put some men to work cutting trees. Others can snake the logs to the building sites. The rest can build the cabins and apartment buildings. Big Man, I want you to build the cabins far enough apart so that each family has enough acreage to have a garden, a cow and a pig pen. Make sure they have plenty of room. I want you to build the apartments like the ones we had on Inman Plantation. I want each single person to have one large room. They will have a front porch and a back porch. I want each apartment to have five rooms. As ya'll cut the trees for lumber you should be clearing the land as you go. This should give us plenty of room."

Big Man said, "Why don't we build a big wide road from the back of the Big House down to the bayou? Kinda like the one at the Inman Place, but a lot wider and longer. We could put all of the apartments on one side and the houses on the other."

"That's a good idea, but I don't think we can get all of the buildings on that road before we reach the bayou. I believe that, instead of stopping the road at the bayou, you will have to continue it down by the side of it. You can go as far as you need. After all, we have six thousand acres to work with. I want everyone to have plenty of room. You will just have to cut timber and clear the land as you go."

"Mr. Sloan, tell me how we can help you," Buck said.

Mr. Sloan told Buck that what he really needed was more physical labor. He said that his workers at the sawmill and brick kiln could not keep up with the demand. If Buck could keep the materials coming from the place and from the dock, his men would be free to construct. This would allow the house to go up much faster.

Buck agreed. He would take care of the materials. Big Man would supervise the building of the cabins, and Mr. Sloan would handle the actual construction. John and Jim would be given the responsibility of hauling from the dock.

They agreed to give everyone a day's rest and then start working the next day.

After lunch that day, Buck and Big Man called all of the former slaves to a meeting. Buck explained the plan to them. He also took the opportunity to explain his plan in their sharing in proceeds of the plantation. He told them that he did not have the details worked out, but he wanted them to be shareholders, not slaves. He agreed to take care of all of their needs until they could get the houses and barns built. Between the Fall and the next Spring, he would devise a plan to make everyone more independent.

He then suggested that everyone take the rest of the day off and rest. For the ones that might be interested, he pointed out that John and Jim knew a good shallow swimming hole down the lake.

All of the younger people and some of the older ones were excited to be able to get into the water. They followed John and Jim as they headed down to the lake. Soon, everyone was in the lake laughing and splashing.

This was the time that John and Jim spotted Fanny. She was out in the water waist deep with about a dozen of the young boys surrounding her. She was enjoying every minute. She had been under the water and her wet blouse was sticking to her big breasts. As she twisted and turned, they seemed to go up and down in the water. John and Jim stood there with their mouths open. Jim said, "Is you looking at what I is?" "I sho is!" John replied. "I'm fixing to head into the water for a closer look."

The young men headed out into the water where Fanny and the others were. All of the other boys just stood there and looked at them. Fanny, realizing that she had a new audience, continued to flirt and tease. She slung her hair back and forth, showering the youth with drops of water. Accidentally, one of her breasts fell out of her blouse. She pretended that she didn't notice. All of the young men did. They were pushing and shoving each other to get a better view. John and Jim were right in there with them. John thought that Jim was going to have a heart attack. After tormenting the boys for awhile, Fanny made her way to the bank. Her thin blouse and skirt stuck to her body as she prissed down the road back to the camp. The boys could tell she had nothing on underneath. Her big high hips rolled up and down with every step. All of the young men were beside themselves. They all wanted her, but just didn't know what to do about it! John and Jim were no exceptions.

After the day at the lake, Jim was smitten with Fanny. Everywhere Fanny went, there was Jim. If he wasn't working, he was following Fannie. Fannie pretended that she wasn't aware of him, but in truth, she was enjoying his adulation.

Jim finally got a chance to be alone with her. When Fannie went down to the chicken house to feed the chickens, Jim was right behind her.

Fannie said, "What you want, boy? Why you following me all de time?"

"I'm following yo cause I'm crazy bout you. I ain't never been around a girl before and especially one like you!"

"What yo saying? You mean to tell me as old as you is you ain't never had no woman?" laughed Fannie.

Embarrassed, Jim hung his head and replied, " Ain't my fault, I just ain't never had a chance!"

Fannie stared at him and said, " I 'spect I could teach you a thing or two bout women!"

"I sho hope you will! I'm ready!"

"You so ignorant. We can't do nothing here. Somebody might come by. You probably tell everybody anyways."

"I promise. If you will teach me about womens, I won't tell a soul. I won't even tell John!" Jim begged.

Always ready for a new conquest, Fannie replied, "I tells you what you do. Tonight when it gets dark you come around to the back of me and my mama's cabin. She be sleeping in the front room and I will be in the back. I'll prop up the window of my room so that you can crawl in. You just better not make no noise!

Excited, Jim said, "Don't you worry. I'll be quiet as a mouse. Won't nobody see me when I slips down behind yo cabin."

It was a dark night as Jim prepared to keep his rendezvous with Fannie. He washed himself off real good and brushed his hair. He then slipped away from everyone else and headed to Fannie's cabin. It was a dark night, so no one saw him. He eased around to the back of the cabin and sure enough, Fannie had done what she had promised. Her window was raised with a big stick holding it up. She was in the bed waiting on Jim. The cabin had been built up off of the ground in case of high water. Jim's chin came just about level with the bottom of the window. He would have to jump up, hook his elbows on the window sill, and pull himself up and over.

Jim made a little jump and hung his elbows over the sill. But in making that move, he accidentally knocked the prop out from under the window. The heavy window came crashing down and caught Jim behind the neck. There he hung. His toes were barely touching the ground. He couldn't push himself up. He couldn't use his hands to raise the window because he was holding on for dear life to keep from choking.

"Fannie, come git dis window off my neck. I bout to choke!" he whispered.

"You be making too much of a racket. You better git away from here!"

"I can't git away!" Jim said getting louder. "You better come help me!"

With Jim getting louder, Fannie became scared. "Mama! Mama!" she yelled. "Mamaaa! Mamaaa!"

Fannie's mother, who was a big old woman, came rushing into the room. She took everything in—Fannie laying in the bed with no clothes on., Jim hanging out the window opening with the window caught behind his head. She didn't say a word. She turned and walked out of the cabin and found a large switch off of a tree. Picking it up, she walked around to the back of the cabin and proceeded to wear Jim's butt out. There was nothing that Jim could do but hang there, holler, and take the whipping.

After getting tired of whipping Jim, she stopped and told him, "I best not catch you back at my cabin again!" With that, she raised the window. Jim hit the ground running. He didn't say a word. He high-tailed it back to his cabin as fast as he could.

When he came rushing into the cabin all out of breath, John wanted to know what was going on. Jim told him everything that had happened. John laughed and laughed. "I guess you did learn something about women tonight!" John said.

The next morning, Jim's butt was so sore he could hardly put his pants on. When he did get dressed, he headed down to the barn to feed the mules. The first person he met coming up the path was Fannie.

"Morning, Jim!"

"Don't you be morning me. You know what you got me into last night!"

"Well, it weren't my fault that you were kicking, hollering and making all that noise. I told you that you had to be quiet. You knowed that my mama was in the next room!"

"I knows that you got my butt whupped!" Jim said as he turned and walked away. It would be a week before he would speak to her again.

John and Jim had managed to build a few cabins of logs during the summer. These were quickly filled up with all of the household help, like Birdie and Fannie's mother. Everyone else had to live in tents until their cabin was built. Since they had a sawmill now, they no longer used logs. They used the sawed boards. They were easier to handle. This made the construction much faster. They were mainly interested in getting the walls, floors, doors and roof constructed. They could finish the interior and put the windows in later.

With all of the manpower that was available, construction went much faster on the cabins and the Big House. Buck's plan was to use all of the cypress and native pine trees in the construction. The rest of the softwood trees, along with the brush, were piled and burned. Buck was getting two things accomplished at once. He was getting lumber for the houses and clearing farm land at the same time. The large woodpile burned day and night.

With everyone becoming accustomed to their jobs, Buck now had time to turn his attention to the materials for the inside of the house. He made more frequent trips to Leota. On his first trip to town, he was anxious to check with Tom to see what new supplies had arrived. He rode Prince up to the livery stable and was greeted warmly by Tom. He was told by Tom that the warehouses were just about full of materials for Mount Hope, with more arriving every day. Buck assured Tom that they would start hauling the next day.

Buck left Prince in Tom's care and started to the telegraph office to see if he had any messages. On the way, he met Mr. Knox, the land agent. Mr. Knox said, "Young fellow, you sure do have everyone's curiosity stirred up around here. Is it true that you have just arrived with five hundred slaves from South Carolina? Where in the world did you get that many nigras?"

Buck started to tell Mr. Knox that they were free nigras, but decided against it. Everybody would find out soon enough. He really didn't like people being nosey about his business. He told Mr. Knox that, yes, he had that many workers at his plantation. He then excused himself, and continued on to the telegraph office. Along with the telegraphs from his suppliers, he had one from Mistress. She said that she and the girls were doing fine and for him not to worry about them.

After visiting the telegraph office, Buck decided to go to the Southern Inn for lunch. When he walked in, Miss Jane greeted him like a long lost son. She gave him a big hug and said loudly, "We sure have been missing you! Come on in and sit with me and catch me up with the news." The other diners spoke and nodded to Buck as he followed Miss Jane. Buck could feel their curious stares and hear their whispers as he sat down.

"Buck, everyone is talking about the house you are building out on the lake. They say it is so tall that the passengers on the river boats can see it as they go by. Why in the world would a young man like you with no family build such an enormous house?"

"I do have a family. A mother and two sisters. I am really building such a large house for them. I promised my mother if they would move to Mississippi, I would build her one of the grandest homes on the Mississippi River and that is what I am doing. Also, you never know, I might get married and have a dozen kids myself."

"Well, you'll have a big enough place for them! I am looking forward to meeting your family. Will they be coming soon?"

"Just as soon as I can get the front part of the house finished. Maybe early Spring."

Miss Jane said, "You are in for a treat. They are cooking chittlin's out back. We will be serving them for dinner. Fried and boiled. Which way do you like them?"

"Nether way! I thought I smelled something when I walked by. I can't get real excited about eating hog intestines no matter how they are cooked."

"I can't believe you don't like chittlin's. I know you smelled them out back. That's the reason I won't let them cook them inside. I don't know why you don't like them. I always have my help wash them out real good."

"I don't care how good they are washed!" Buck protested. "Every time I get a bite close to my mouth, I can smell them and I think about where they came from! I can barely tolerate the fried ones but I can't stomach the boiled ones. The truth is I really don't care for them no matter how they are cooked!"

"Ok!, Ok! How about some of my fried chicken. It will be ready in a few minutes," Jane offered.

Buck replied, "That will be better. I have been having a craving for your chicken for weeks. You fry some of the best."

Satisfied, Miss Jane turned the conversation back to Buck's plantation. She was still curious.

"Is it true that you have a thousand nigras working on your place?" she asked.

"No, I have two thousand," Buck replied. Miss Jane's eyes opened wide with surprise. Buck laughed and said, "Truthfully, I really don't have but five hundred."

Miss Jane said, "That's still a lot of folks. No wonder everyone is talking. You ride in here all dirty and unkempt on a dusty horse and now a year later, you have a six thousand acre plantation, five hundred slaves, and you are building the largest house in these parts. Buck Inman, you are a puzzle to everyone!"

With everyone busy at Mount Hope, time flew by. Buck was extremely busy. It was about all that he could do to keep the materials coming to Mr. Sloan and his crew. In addition to that, he had to feed over five hundred people every day! The provisions that they had brought from South Carolina were dwindling rapidly. Buck bought herds of cattle and hogs from the neighboring plantations. He bought as many chickens as he could find. He had to locate corn for the stock and for the people. He was grateful that the lake provided fish, turtles and alligators.

Everyone was working six days a week from sun up to sun down. They were able to rest on Sunday. The only other days that they took off were Thanksgiving and Christmas. They took a couple of days off on each holiday to celebrate and then went right back to work. Winter had arrived and everyone was trying to get out of the tents.

By the first of March, the front section of the big house was completed. They had closed off the back where the wings would be added. They would remove the temporary back walls when they were ready to start on the wings. Buck decided that by the time he actually moved his family, their quarters would be complete. All they lacked were the plaster moldings and medallions in each room. Mr. Sloan's men could do this, but Buck had hired artisans to faux paint the doors and woodwork. Buck wanted a more grainy look than the native cypress provided. This graining was done by using rags and feathers to imitate dark grained wood. This technique was used on all of the wood work with the exception of the library. Buck was real proud of the technique that the artists had used in there. One artist had shown Buck how he could stain the doors and wood work in there with a light color. He could dip his fingers in a darker paint and randomly touch the woodwork everywhere. The finished results looked like Birdseye Maple.

It was a breezy March day when Buck rode into town to telegraph his mother. He told her to start getting their things together. He told her that he expected to reach them in about a week. Everything depended on the connections he could make. He went back to Mount Hope to give final instructions to Mr. Sloan and Big Man. Satisfied that he had made the best preparations that he could, he left the next morning for Charleston.

15

The Family Moves to Mississippi

Arriving at his mother's home, he was met with a storm of activity. Mistress had hired extra help, and they were packing as fast they could. Mistress was supervising, hoping that nothing would get broken. Buck's sisters were just about finished packing their belongings.

Everything came to a screeching halt when Buck walked in. Mistress knew he was coming, but hadn't known the exact day he would arrive. His family grabbed Buck, hugged him and gave him a warm welcome. Buck thought, "This is the way a family is supposed to be!" He hadn't realized how much he had missed his FAMILY!

Buck was glad that his family was excited about moving to his plantation. His sisters peppered him with questions. It was then that he realized that he had forgotten about continuing their education. He would have to hire a teacher when they got back to Mount Hope.

Mistress had other questions. She wanted to know if the house was finished. Buck explained to her that the front section of the house where they would be living was complete. She wanted to know about the household help. Buck told her that they were all there and anxiously waiting her arrival. They would be glad to stop the grueling work that they were doing and get back in the Big House.

She then wanted to know about the window treatments, wall tapestries and rugs. These questions took Buck by surprise. He had been so busy building that he had not thought of decorating. He had to admit to her that he had not made any plans for the window treatments or tapestries. He told her that they had built louvered shutters for each room. These could be opened and closed. When closed, no one could see in.

Mistress said, "You are just like all men. You don't have a clue as to what makes a house a home. Don't worry. When I get there, I will put the finishing touches on the place. I presume that there is someone who can make draperies there. I know where we can order the tapestries. We may have to order more rugs to match the draperies I pick out. There should be a good selection in New Orleans." Buck quickly agreed with her. He told her that she could decorate any way she wanted. The girls asked him about their rooms and he told them the same thing, "Decorate any way you wish." He was just glad to get off of this subject!

In a few days, the crating of the furniture was finished and it was taken to the steamer. Mistress had decided to keep all of her silver with her. It had been packed in trunks and each person would keep a trunk with them in their stateroom. She had made moneybags that she and the girls could wear under their dresses. The women would be carrying all of the family's jewelry and some gold.

Early the next morning, the Inmans boarded the steamer and were on their way to New Orleans. Upon their arrival there, they would have to unload everything onto the paddle wheeler that would take them to Leota. Buck was dreading the transferring of the furniture. He hoped that nothing would be damaged!

When they arrived in New Orleans, Buck got them rooms for the night at the Bourbon Orleans Hotel. While the ladies rested, Buck returned to the dock to watch the furniture transferred. The Captain of the paddle-wheeler told Buck that he would be heading north early the next morning. Buck told him that his family would be on time. Visiting the May family would have to wait for another time.

When the paddle wheeler landed at Leota, Buck escorted his mother and sisters up the street to the Southern Inn. He had made arrangements for his family to stay there while he got all of the furniture transported to Mount Hope.

As always, Buck could feel the curious stares directed their way. He had picked up a couple of Sam's men to transport the trunks to the inn. They were trailing along behind. Mistress was not about to let the trunks get out of her sight. When they entered the inn, they were greeted by Miss Jane. After the introductions were made, Miss Jane said to Mrs. Inman, "I now know where Buck gets his good looks; you are as pretty as a picture! Your girls are pretty, too. These young blades are going to go crazy when they see them!" Mistress did not pay the compliment too much attention. Having been told all of her life how pretty she was, she had become used to these kinds of comments. She replied, "Thank you. I am getting a little up in years, but I agree that my girls are mighty pretty. They are getting to the age that I expect I will have to keep an eye on them."

The girls said, "Oh, Mother!"

Miss Jane then said, "I know ya'll are tired. Why don't I have someone show you to your rooms. I will have water brought in for your baths. After you are rested, I will have a meal prepared for you." She then turned to Buck and said, "Will you be needing a room?" Buck said, "No, I won't be needing a room. I am going to try to get at least one load out to the plantation tonight. However, I will be here to eat with ya'll. I have been bragging to Mother about how good your food is."

Puffing up, Miss Jane replied, "Ah Buck, you shouldn't have bragged on me like that. You know that I can't cook anything fancy." Turning to Mistress, she said, "I hope you won't be disappointed. All we cook is just country cooking but I promise there will be plenty of food." Mistress said, "Don't worry, I know that whatever you serve will be good. Buck has told me so much about your inn. Why don't we get out of your way and go freshen up." Miss Jane had one of her maids show the ladies to their room.

After sharing a meal, Buck returned to the livery stable. Sam and his employees were busy transporting the furniture crates to the storehouse. Buck told them to leave everything crated. He then picked out some of Mistress's bedroom furniture. He wanted to get his mother set up first.

After hiring one of Sam's wagons and a couple of his men, Buck had the wagon loaded. He mounted Prince and set out for the plantation.

Sam sure was glad that Buck had come to Leota. It was taking him almost full time to keep up with Buck's demands. It pleased him that Buck didn't mind paying for what he got. Buck just always made sure that he received what he had bargained for!

Using his own wagons and Sam's, Buck was able to move enough furniture to furnish the completed part of the house in four days. He tried to set the bedrooms up like he thought Mistress would want them, knowing all of the time that the furniture would have to be moved several times before she would be satisfied.

The day came when it was time for him to move his family to his plantation. With Big Man driving, Buck took the big carriage to Leota to pick the ladies up. He had John and Jim follow in the small wagon. This wagon would be used to haul the large trunks. The other people sleeping at Miss Jane's would never know what a treasure they had been sleeping near to.

After traveling the beaten out road that led from Leota to the plantation, they emerged from the woods and there she was, all three stories of her, MOUNT HOPE! The ladies could hardly believe their eyes. Buck had Big Man stop the carriage so that they could take everything in.

"Buck, what a magnificent home. I could not have visualized anything this magnificent!" Mistress said. Buck's sisters sat there stunned. Buck said, "I promised you and the girls the finest home on the river. You are looking at only half of it. The back two wings are still to be built." He then turned to his sisters and said, "Your rooms are built, you just have to decorate them. You each have a suite." Buck was trying not to act overly proud but he could not wait to show them the interior.

"Let's go show the ladies their quarters, Big Man!"

Mistress said teasingly, "Big Man, you sure have built a mighty fine house." Big Man replied, "Mistress, you knows I didn't build this big thing, but I'll tell you one thing, we all been working mighty hard on it!"

When the carriage pulled up in front of the home, all of the house servants were lined up to greet the family. The rest of the former slaves were standing a respectable distance back on the lawn. When the ladies were helped down, everyone started clapping and yelling greetings. Birdie was the first to reach Mistress. Beaming, she greeted Mistress warmly. "Just you wait till you see yo rooms," she said. "They gonna be something when you git thru decorating them. You is going to have the best of everything. You got a fireplace, a bathroom with running water and a toilet. You even got one of them handles that you turn so that us know to come. I sho am glad you finally made it here."

Buck didn't want to appear too proud, but he couldn't wait to show his family their new home. They entered, and Buck introduced his family to Mr. Sloan. After touring the three stories that were completed on the front, Mr. Sloan got out the plans and showed everyone the wings that were to be added. The girls were particularly interested in their suites.

Later, Mistress pulled Buck aside and said, "I am so proud of you! You are building one of the finest houses I have ever seen. I know we are going to be so happy here!"

The ladies had arrived at a wonderful time in Mississippi. Winter was turning into Spring. The cold winds of Winter had dissipated. They were replaced by a more balmy breeze coming up from the south off of the Gulf Of Mexico. The animals were shedding their long winter coats. Birds were building nests and the trees were putting out new leaves. The new leaves and the young green grass were changing the drab brown Delta into a beautiful green landscape dotted with the blooms of the wild fruit trees. It was a wonderful time to be alive!

It had been a rough winter for the freed slaves that had lived through the winter in tents. Now that working conditions had improved, the building moved rapidly along. Man had his crews building cabins, fences, and planting crops and gardens in the newly cleared land.

Buck was busy trying to finish Mount Hope. Mr. Sloan and his men started on the two wings. Mistress was busy furnishing and decorating the home.

Buck and his family decided to go to New Orleans to buy new wardrobes and shop for more furnishings for the home. They caught the paddle-wheeler at Leota and had a pleasant trip south to New Orleans. As they traveled, it became increasingly warmer. They enjoyed standing on the deck and watching the activity in the fields. Upon arriving in New Orleans, they checked into a hotel. Buck sent a message to Mr. May telling him that they were in town and that they would like to pay the May family a visit.

Shortly thereafter, there was a knock on the door. Mr. May had cut through the formalities and had come himself to greet the family. Buck introduced him to his family. Mistress said, "I feel like you are an old friend. Buck has told me so much about you." Mr. May replied, "Thank you. Now, as an old friend I want you to pack up and come stay with us. My wife will not hear of you staying in a hotel when we have all of our empty rooms." Buck said, "We wouldn't want to be an imposition." Mr. May replied, "An imposition? Buck, you know how much room we have. You also have met all of our house slaves. You will not put us out at all. We would welcome the company. It's been a while since we've had young folks in the house. Besides I want to hear all about your adventures since you rode off on that big Tennessee walking horse stud. Also, I know that John's parents will want to meet ya'll while you are here."

Seeing that Mr. May was not going to take no for an answer, they agreed to move from the hotel to the May home. Mr. May said that he would go home and return with the carriage and help to move them.

By the time that the family had repacked, Mr. May was back with the carriage and four of his slaves. The slaves loaded the wagon that they had brought with them while Mr. May escorted the Inmans to the carriage.

The family spent an enjoyable week visiting with both families of Mays. Buck told John's parents the details of their son's death. This was the only downside to the visit. The rest of the time, Buck kept them amused by telling them about his adventures since he had first left New Orleans. John's mother was a big help to the Inman ladies with their shopping. She knew just where to take them.

After the family returned from New Orleans, Buck, John, and Jim were kept busy transporting the large pieces of furniture that Mistress had purchased out to the Big house. Buck was scared to trust his help with the valuable pieces that had been bought. The thing that gave them the most trouble transporting was the Chickering and Son square grand piano. It took several good men to load it off of the boat onto the large wagon, and several to unload it at Mount Hope. This was Mistress's prized purchase. She and the girls had missed being able to play. She watched it carefully as it was unloaded and set up. She said, "At last I feel that some of our culture is returning."

The next few days were spent getting the furniture placed where the ladies wanted. The house had an added feature that was not included in their old house. Each room had large walk-in closets. Mistress and the girls could hardly wait to get their clothing hung in them. As they unpacked all of the trunks, Mistress placed all of her fine silver and china in the dining room. With the help of Big Man, she hung all of the family portraits and her fine oil paintings. Mount Hope was changing from a house to a home.

Weeks earlier, when Mr. Sloan and the laborers had gone to town, Buck created a hiding place for his gold in the side of the fireplace in his room. He accessed the side of the chimney by going into his closet and cutting a hole in the wall next to the chimney. He then removed bricks until he created a hiding place. He made a door with recessed hinges to fit the opening. He then hung one of his old coats over a peg above the door. By doing this, he completely obscured the opening. From that day forward, no one was allowed in his closet.

After Mr. Sloan and his laborers left and the girls went to bed, Buck showed his mother his hiding place. He told Mistress that he did not want anyone else knowing of its location, not even his sisters. He was afraid that in a moment of carelessness they might divulge the hiding place. His mother agreed. She promised to keep this between the two of them. They spent the next hour placing the gold and other valuables in the hiding spot.

The following Saturday morning, Buck invited his mother and sisters to the Sunday church services in Leota. He explained that the service might seem a little strange to them since it was an inter-denominational church. Since the congregation was having their monthly dinner on the grounds, Buck thought this would be a great opportunity to introduce his family to the community.

Sunday morning arrived and Buck had Big Man bring the carriage around. Big Man was dressed in his finest. The Inmans entered the carriage and headed for church. When they got there, church had begun. Big Man let them off at the front and went to tend to the horses. Every head turned when the Inmans entered the sanctuary. Mistress entered first on Buck's arm with the girls following. The way she was dressed and the way she carried herself, you would have thought she was the Queen. She was not putting on airs. This was her normal carriage. She had been raised with wealth and she was Mrs. John Inman, formally of Inman Plantation of South Carolina. Although many women in the congregation were of means, none could rival Mistress in her apparel and jewelry! The music stopped and some of the people were looking and whispering. Others, who were more polite, quickly cleared a pew for this entourage to sit. When they were seated the service started again. Mrs. John Inman had arrived at Leota.

16

Josephine Juliette Jourdain

Buck had decided to ride into town to check his correspondence at the telegraph office. He was a regular customer there. Afterwards, he walked down the street to eat at Miss Jane's. Everyone in town was still curious about him and his family, but they were starting to accept them. Money had a way of creating new "friends". It had become a week-end past time for everyone in the area to ride out to see the erection of the plantation home. The questions on everyone's mind was just how big was this house going to be, how Buck was able to feed all of these "slaves", and where in the world did he get so much money! Some admired the structure; others secretly hoped Buck would run out of money and have to stop. The latter didn't want anyone to get too far ahead of them. Jealousy!

After Miss Jane brought Buck up to date on all of the local gossip, he decided to walk down to the dock and see what *The Delta Queen* had brought him from New Orleans. Was he in for a surprise! It had brought him something alright! Stepping off of the boat was the most beautiful lady that Buck had ever seen. Buck guessed that she was about twenty years old. She was of medium height with a slim waist that didn't need a corset. Her long curly black hair hung way down her back! She had a light olive complexion with beautiful green eyes. Her dress and shoes would rival anything that Mistress and the girls owned. She stood there under her matching parasol looking confused. Everyone on the boat was standing by the rail watching her. Buck could see that she was about to cry.

Buck walked up to her and said, "May I be of assistance?" With her lip trembling, the young lady replied, "I don't want to be a bother, but I will put my pride aside and tell you that I really need help. You see, I have been put off the boat for lack of funds. I don't have enough money for passage up the river any further. Somewhere between my house and the boat in New Orleans, my money bag must have come untied. I guess it dropped to the ground. In all of the excitement of boarding, I just didn't notice. The Captain allowed me to continue on the boat while I looked for my money. I had enough to pay him passage this far. When my money ran out, he apologized and said that I would have to disembark at the next stop, Leota." With tears starting to run down her cheeks, she said, "I just don't know what to do. Do you know of any place that I might get employment?"

Watching the Delta Queen pull away from the dock, Buck said, "I don't know any place right at the moment, but, don't worry, we will figure out something. What type of work are you qualified for?" She replied, "Actually, I am a trained seamstress. I don't want to brag, but I made this outfit that I am wearing."

Touched by the plight of this young lady, Buck's mind was racing, trying to think of a way to help her. His first inclination was to get her a room at the Southern Inn for the night. He then realized this would only be a temporary solution. Where would she go and what could she do the next morning? Then an idea came to him.

"What would you think about coming home with me? We have a large house with plenty of room. My mother and two sisters live with me. I know they would enjoy another female's company. They would be glad to have you."

"Oh, I couldn't possibly surprise them like that. I do not wish to be an imposition on anyone. I do not wish charity. I just need to find a way to replenish my funds, and then I will be on my way."

"I admire your pride, but you don't have a lot of options. Besides it won't be charity. We have just returned from a shopping trip to New Orleans. My mother and sisters brought back bolts and bolts of the prettiest fabrics you can imagine. They bought the fabrics with the hope that they could find someone to make them new dresses. Since they have not been able to find a seamstress anywhere near here, I can assure you that they will be excited to see you. This will take care of your charity concerns. You can visit us and make dresses for everyone. When they pay you for your work, you will have enough money to continue your journey." It was if the sun had broken out from under a cloud. The young lady stopped crying, and her pretty face started beaming. She said, "I accept your kind offer with the understanding that I will work for my keep. If the ladies will allow me, I think I can design and make dresses like no one around here has seen. In fact I know that I can." By this time, Buck was smitten by this young lady's looks and character.

Buck and the young lady temporarily left her trunks sitting besides the dock. They walked down the road to Sam's. Buck wanted to borrow one of Sam's carriages. As they walked, Buck could feel the eyes of some of the Leota residents looking at him. He was always a curiosity. When they arrived at Sam's, Buck prepared to introduce the young lady. Sam was so enthralled by the lady's beauty that he wasn't paying attention to Buck. Buck then realized that he didn't even know the young lady's name.

Buck turned to her and said, "Please forgive me. I haven't introduced myself. I am Buchanan Inman. Most people call me Buck!"

The young lady said, "I guess I was making too much of a scene by the dock for any formalities. Forgive me. I am Josephine Juliette Jourdain. Most of my friends call me Julie."

After tying Prince to the back of the carriage and assisting Julie to her seat, Buck went back by the dock and picked up the trunks that they had left. They then drove through the middle of town and took the road to the lake. Now the town people were really curious!

As they were riding back, Buck could contain his curiosity no longer. He wanted to know more about this young beauty. Julie told him that she had been born on a plantation but her mother had died at birth. The house slaves raised her until she was old enough to go away to one of the most prestigious boarding schools in New Orleans. She had never been back to the plantation. Her father came to see her on his business trips to the city and on holidays. He would take her to buy the finest wardrobe that he could purchase. He would always take her to the operas and the fine restaurants for which New Orleans was famous. She said that she had always been told that she looked like her father. Buck could tell that she idolized her Papa as she called him.

She then told Buck that she was now an orphan. Her Papa had died two years earlier. This was when she had left the boarding school and took employment at a famous local seamstress's shop. This was where she had discovered that she had a talent for designing and making dresses.

Buck asked, "What happened to the plantation and the rest of your family?" She replied, "It is too painful for me to talk about! Please do not ask me any more questions." Buck, realizing that he had been too inquisitive, said, 'I am so sorry. I shouldn't have asked so many questions. I didn't mean to upset you. I will never bring this subject up again." Her mood changed immediately, and she laughed and laughed as Buck told her of some of his experiences after leaving South Carolina.

As everyone else had been, she was stunned when the carriage came out of the woods and she could get a clear view of Mount Hope. "My goodness, is this your home? Is this where I will be staying?" she asked.

"It's not so big when you get used to it," Buck said, cutting his eyes toward her. "All it needs is a lot of children running around to make it feel like a home."

"What a delightful place for children to grow up. Running free and swimming in the lake. I wish that I could have grown up somewhere like this. As I said, I lived at the boarding school. I wasn't allowed to go to our plantation. The only thing I was exposed to was life in the city," Julie said wistfully. Buck sure was glad that she liked the house and lake. He was also pleased that it didn't seem like she would mind living at Mount Hope. Strange thoughts were running through his mind!

When the carriage pulled up to the front of the house, two of the stable boys ran out and unloaded the trunks on the front porch. They then took the carriage and Prince to the barn. Buck was greeted by a male house servant as he pulled up. Birdie was right behind him. They were trying to figure out who this girl was. Buck said," Rufus, go and tell the ladies that we have a guest. Then on the way back, bring some more help to carry these trunks to one of the upstairs guest bedrooms."

While they were waiting in the front parlor for the ladies, Birdie got a chance to question Buck alone. "Dat's about the purtiest lady I ever seen, Mr. Buck. Where in de world did you find her?" she asked. "It's a long story, Birdie. I'll tell you about it when I have more time. She really is a pretty thing, isn't she?" Buck replied.

At this time, Mistress and the girls arrived at the front. Buck introduced Josephine Juliette Jourdain to his family and told them that he had invited her to be their guest for a few days. Although Mistress was puzzled, she said, "What a pretty name. We are so glad to have you."

"Please call me Julie. I know this is a surprise and I hope I won't be too much trouble." The sisters spoke up and told her that she would be no trouble. They said that, in fact, they would be happy to have someone close to their own age to talk to. They then told Julie how much they admired the dress that she had on. Julie told them that she had designed and made the dress herself. They couldn't believe it. Buck broke in and said that they could discuss all of this at supper that night.

Birdie, who had been standing to one side listening, spoke up and said," I best git back to the kitchen fore dem girls burns up ya'lls supper. I'll have it ready in about thirty minutes if ya'll are ready to eat." She could hardly wait to listen in while Buck was telling his family about this strange girl!

Over the meal, Buck told how he had met Julie and her plight. He didn't go into any details about her past. He felt that Julie had told him her story in confidence. He did take this opportunity to tell them about his plans to have Julie make new dresses for them. He told them that he hoped that they would agree. He explained that Julie didn't want charity, but wanted to earn enough money to continue her trip north.

Mistress spoke up and said, "If she can make us any dresses that compare to hers, I will be thrilled. I would love to show off one at church." Buck's sisters told Julie how excited they would be to have her make their clothes. They asked if they could assist her. Julie said, "Certainly."

Buck thought, "This is going better than I hoped."

When the three girls left to get Julie settled in her room, Mistress finally had a chance to question Buck about Julie. Buck told her all he knew, which was very little. He did tell Mistress that he hoped everyone would honor Julie's request not to question her about her family. He told Mistress that he just could not leave the young lady crying on the dock. Satisfied, Mistress said, "You did the Christian thing. It was as if you were the good Samaritan of the Bible." Buck said, "I sure wanted to help her. However I will admit that her being so pretty made my decision easier!"

The following weeks were busy times for the Inman family. Buck was still trying to get Mount Hope finished. He had added two wings. Over one wing were more guest rooms. Below them was Birdie's room. Birdie loved it. She was across from her beloved kitchen. In the wings were the kitchen, the dairy room, a dark potato room, and a two story smoke house. There was also a room for the butler. The upstairs of the other wing contained more guest rooms.

Man and his crews were still working hard completing the cabins, planting gardens and getting in a crop of corn and sorghum. They were all conscious that they would have to get a lot of food put up for the winter. Buck wanted them to be as self-sufficient as possible. They would forgo planting the cash crop of cotton this first year.

Buck became more smitten with Julie as the weeks went by. In addition to her looks, her kind, sweet character was making an impression on him. It seemed as if they had known each other forever. After breakfast each day, they would take their coffee out on one of the porches and just talk.

One morning while they were having their coffee, Julie was disturbed by a low moaning sound coming from the back of the place. She said, "What in the world is that sound?" Buck laughed and said, "I can tell you weren't raised on a plantation. That is the field hands singing as they chop the weeds out of the corn. They do this to break the monotony. This singing consists of a lead singer singing a line and everyone else repeating it. They do it in a cadence that from a distance sounds like moaning. I have always liked to hear them. I don't know why they choose songs that sound so sad. They never seem to sing happy tunes."

"I don't expect there's too much for the slaves to be happy about when they're working in those fields from sun up to sun down," Julie said.

"I really hadn't thought about that," Buck replied. "I will tell you one thing if you can keep a secret. All of the Nigras on this place are free. I freed them about a year ago. We have worked out a plan for them to work here at Mount Hope for a share of the crops' proceeds. Right now, I am just paying them to work since we aren't planting a cash crop this year. Next year, they will all have their own acreage to take care of."

"I thought they had just passed a law making it illegal to free slaves," Julie said.

"They did. That is why I told you that this a secret that we are keeping," Buck replied.

It was late summer and Buck realized that Julie was accumulating enough money to continue her trip. Not only did she have the money from the Inmans, but when the ladies at the church saw the dresses that Julie had designed and made, they were envious. They had pleaded with Julie to also make dresses for them The results were that Julie had quite a business by the end of the summer. Buck really didn't want her working so hard but he had to admire her determination.

One night, Buck and Julie decided to take a walk on the trail that ran besides the lake. It was a beautiful night with a bright yellow moon. The moon was so bright that it lit the path. They didn't have to carry a lantern. As they walked along, Julie was exuberant as usual. She was skipping ahead of Buck when all of a sudden, her foot slipped in the sand. She ended up sitting in the lake. Fortunately, the water was not very deep. Buck couldn't help but laugh. Julie soon joined in. She just sat on the edge of the bank and giggled and giggled. Buck reached down and pulled her up. As she stood up, she tripped and fell into his arms. Then it happened! All of the pent-up emotion that they both had been trying to restrain came out. For the first time, Buck took her in his arms and kissed her longingly. She returned the kiss passionately. Buck knew instantly that he was in love! He told her so. Julie told him that she had loved him from the time that he had helped her on the dock, but hadn't dared to hope that he felt the same way. They spent hours sitting on the bank expressing their feelings for each other and discussing what the future would hold.

Finally, Buck said, "I am not going to let you leave me. If you will agree, I want us to get married and live here at Mount Hope the rest of our lives." Julie replied, "I never want to leave you. I will live here at your home or I will follow you wherever you go. I just want to be with you!"

When Buck and Julie returned to the house, he sent for Mistress, Rachel and Becky. When the ladies came into the parlor, they were astounded. There stood Buck and Julie covered with mud and water.

Mistress said, "What in the world happened to you two? You look like you fell in the lake!" Buck replied, "That's exactly what happened. Julie slipped and fell in the lake, and I got wet and muddy pulling her out!"

"Don't you two want to go dry off and change clothes? I know you must be miserable."

Buck said, "Not yet. We have something to tell you. It is going to come as a surprise, but I have asked Julie to marry me!" . . . "and I have accepted," Julie added.

"A surprise!" Becky exclaimed. "We have known ya'll were in love for months. We just didn't know when you two were going to figure it out!"

"Yea, Buck Inman. You have been following Julie all moon struck ever since she got here! Everybody on the plantation could see that ya'll were in love. I guess you were the last to know!" added Rachel.

Embarrassed, Buck said, "Anyway, we want to get married as soon as possible!"

"Buchanan Inman! We are not going to have a jumped up wedding! It takes time to prepare for a large wedding; It must be done properly. You are my only son and I hope this is your only wedding! This will be a wedding ceremony that everyone will remember!" Then thinking, Mistress said, " That is if that's what Julie wants."

Julie agreed, "I would love a large wedding and reception. Maybe we could have a dance, too! I also want Rachel and Becky to be bridesmaids."

"Oh, yes," Rachel replied. "It is going to be so much fun!"

Becky said, "Julie, do you think you think you could make matching dresses for us?"

"We'll need to order the material at once. I want to make my dress, also. I have had in mind what I wanted my wedding dress to look like for years. Mistress, I'll make you a dress, too, if you will allow me."

Buck, realizing that he was out numbered four to one, gave up. He said, "When ya'll get all of the plans made, let me know. Just tell me when to show up and what to do. In the meantime, while ya'll are making plans, I think I'll go and tell Big Man the news."

Back in the next room, Birdie was listening to all of the conversations. She said to herself, "Knowing Mistress, this is going to turn into a lot of work and I know who's going to be doing most of it!"

When Buck got back to the quarters, he found Man sitting in a rocker on the porch of his original cabin. After Birdie moved to her new quarters, he had the cabin to himself. When Buck walked up, Man said, "Congratulations, Mr. Buck, I hear you is about to be married!" The plantation grapevine was still working well. By now, just about everyone on the plantation knew of Buck's engagement.

Man rocked and smoked his pipe as he and Buck discussed the upcoming event. "We been thinking for months you and Miss Julie wuz going to get hitched up. Us just didn't know when ya'll wuz going to figure out you wuz in love. Seems like you wuz a tat slow, Mr. Buck."

Buck laughed and said, "I guess everyone knew but us, and I will admit I was a little slow catching on." He then asked Man something that he had been wondering about. "Man, how come you have never married? I know you have had a lot of opportunities." Man answered kind of sadly, "I never wanted to have kids that would be raised as slaves. Slavery ain't fit for nobody, much less my children! Maybe now I might consider it."

While the ladies worked on the wedding plans, Buck had a dilemma of his own. When he was making plans to free the slaves, he also made plans to pay them for their labor until they could get the land cleared for sharecropping. The problem that he had not thought of was, where would they spend their money? Five hundred free slaves could not show up in Leota with money to spend! He decided that the only solution would be to build a store there on the place.

Julie became excited when Buck told her about his plans for a plantation store. She wanted to go with him to purchase the stock for the store. She told him that this would be a great opportunity for her to buy all of the material to make the wedding dresses. She said that she would purchase her material with the money she had earned sewing. Buck took her in his arms and gave her a hug. He said, "This is what I love about you. You try so hard to be independent.

However, you don't have to worry about money. I am going to pay for this wedding. All you have to do is pick out what you want."

The next day, Buck made one of his usual trips to town. While he was coming out of the telegraph office, he ran into Mr. Harden. He asked Buck if he had time for a cup of coffee at Miss Jane's. Buck said he would take time. While enjoying each other's company, Mr. Harden inquired as to how the house was coming along. Buck said it would probably be Spring before the finishing touches were complete, but everyone in his family was comfortable. Then Buck told him that he was going to have to turn his attention to another matter. He told Mr. Harden about his engagement to Julie. This surprised Mr. Harden and also disappointed him. He was hoping that Buck might choose Linda for his bride. He didn't mention that; though, and congratulated Buck.

Buck then told Mr. Harden about the plans to buy a large amount of supplies and also about Julie's desire to purchase material to make the wedding dresses. Buck said he dreaded the trip to New Orleans. Mr. Harden suggested that they go to Memphis. It was a large city with up-scale stores. He thought they could find what they needed and it would be closer. He also suggested a hotel for them to spend their nights. It was the Gayoso House Hotel. Buck thanked him for the information and took his leave. He was anxious to get back home and share this with Julie.

When Buck arrived home, the ladies could tell that he was excited. He explained to them that he was excited because he didn't have to go all of the way to New Orleans. Memphis was only 150 miles north. He then told Julie, Rachel and Becky to make plans to travel. The sisters were glad that it was improper for Buck and Julie to travel together without a chaperone. This meant that they were invited to make the trip. Buck asked his mother if she wanted to go. She said, "No thank you. I would just be in the way. You young people go and have a good time."

Buck told the girls that he would like to leave the next day. He had checked and the *Delta Queen* would be leaving Leota for Memphis about eleven o'clock. He asked if they could be ready early in the morning. They all replied that if they started packing immediately, they could be ready to leave whenever he wanted the next day. Buck said, "Let's try to leave about eight in the morning. That should give us plenty of time. We will probably spend a week in Memphis, so pack accordingly."

The next morning, Buck had the large carriage pulled around. The house servants loaded the luggage and the four young people climbed aboard. Buck had decided not to carry a driver. He would drive himself. He would leave the carriage and horses with Sam where they would be waiting when they returned.

As the Delta Queen approached the riverbank at Memphis, the young people were treated to a view of the imposing Gayoso House Hotel. It was a magnificent structure of some 300 rooms. They could see people standing on the balconies of their rooms watching the paddle-wheeler pull up to the dock. Buck and the ladies could hardly wait to see their accommodations. They hired someone to bring their luggage up and made the steep walk up to the hotel's entrance. They were shown to their rooms. The hotel was rated as one of the best in the south and they could see why. It had wrought iron balconies, marble tubs in the bathrooms, with silver faucets and flushing toilets and its own sewage system. It had every modern convenience that was available at that time.

Julie and the Inmans spent the next week shopping for wedding supplies and supplies for the plantation store. As the girls shopped, Buck took the opportunity to make purchases for the plantation store. He tried to put himself in the place of the freed nigras. He attempted to stock the store with what he thought they would be interested in buying and what he thought they needed. He was satisfied with the contacts that he made. He was able to secure a line of credit for the future. Everyone assured him that they would be glad to ship future orders to Mount Hope Commissary. This was the name that Julie and Buck had given their new business.

After spending a satisfying and profitable week in Memphis, they boarded the Delta Queen back to Leota. Buck was glad that Mr. Harden had recommended Memphis as a shopping center.

When they landed at Leota, Buck pulled Sam aside and told him that there would be a steady stream of goods arriving from Memphis. Sam told Buck that he would take care of everything. Again, he surely was glad that Buchanan Inman had come to town.

After going in the house and greeting his mother, Buck headed to the back to see how Man was coming along with the construction of the new store. He could tell that there had been a lot of progress while he was gone. Man told him that John and Jim were being a lot of help on the construction. Their previous experience building cabins was coming in handy.

While they were talking, Birdie came around the corner. She said, "Man and I need to talk to you about something. We folks on the place need a favor out of you. I guess I be the one to do the asking. We wuz wondering if you would allow us to build a church here on the place. We ain't had been to no church since we left Inman Place. We sho do miss it."

Buck replied, "Certainly! I don't know why I hadn't already thought of it. That just goes to show you want happens when you get all involved in the things of this world. I guess I have been neglecting the spiritual needs of all of us! Mine and yours. You just pick out a spot and we will build your church while we are building the store. The sawmill is going to be running anyway." "Do you know where you want to build?" Buck asked.

Birdie said, "We thought down by the edge of the woods. "We can use the lake to baptize," Man added, with a grin. "Besides, if the church is dat far from the big house, maybe we don't disturb ya'll when we go to sanging and hollering."

Buck laughed and said, "I guess ya'll are going to have to find a preacher." Man and Birdie quickly exchanged glances. Birdie said, "We thinks we already have one. His name is BIG MAN!" Somewhat surprised, Buck looked at Big Man. Man kind of ducked his head for a moment then he looked directly at Buck and said, "De Lawd been dealing with me for months 'bout preaching. It just seems dat is what I is supposed to do. I know I ain't worthy, so I been trying to get out of it, but the Lawd want let me go. In my prayers, I finally told God I would do whatever he wanted me to do! I know down deep, He wants me to bring the message of Christ to all de's folks."

Buck said, "I couldn't be more proud! I knew you had something on your mind these past few months. I had noticed that you were spending a lot of time sitting by yourself in the evenings on your porch."

"I wasn't by myself, Mr. Buck, me and de Lawd wuz having us some mighty deep conversations."

17

The Commisary

The fall flew by. Everyone was busy. Land was being cleared. Trees were being cut. Lumber was being sawed. Cabins, the store, and the church were under construction. The girls, with the help of two young freed slaves, were busy sewing and preparing for the wedding. Mount Hope was almost completed. Sidewalks were being built and shrubbery planted. Mistress was making sure that everything would be in order when the wedding day arrived. The purchases from Memphis had arrived. Buck and some of the hands were busy unpacking the goods for the store.

Buck had decided to hire a young man from Leota to run the store. This young gentleman had just graduated from Davidson in North Carolina. Tired from spending so much time in the academic world, he had decided to come to the frontier and visit his kin, the Knox's. He and Buck had met at the telegraph office. Striking up a conversation, they liked each other instantly. While having lunch at Miss Jane's, Buck approached him about running the commissary. Justin Knox said that he would be available for about two years; then he was going to study law. He said being involved in the start up of the store would be a change for him. He would look forward to it. Buck told Justin that he would pay him a salary and that he would attach living quarters to the back of the store. He also said that he could take his meals at the big house with the family.

Buck had an ulterior motive for this invitation. He thought that this good looking, well—educated young man who came from a prominent family might be a good catch for one of his sisters. There weren't that many eligible bachelors around Leota.

When Buck returned home he told the girls about Justin and his plans for the store. Mistress said that it would be nice to have someone with culture and education to converse with. This was something that she had missed since she left Inman Place. The sisters were more curious about his age and looks.

In one week, Buck returned to Leota and picked up Justin. He brought him home and introduced him to the family and to Big Man. He showed him to his new quarters that had just been completed. The ladies of the house had furnished and decorated his quarters. Justin was pleased and told Buck that he would be quite comfortable. With Justin in charge of stocking the commissary, Buck could turn his attention to the upcoming wedding.

They had decided to have a Christmas wedding and the time was fast approaching. They thought that having it one week before Christmas would be an appropriate time. The house would already be decorated for Christmas. This would also be a good time to allow people to see Mount Hope. Buck said some people would come for the wedding and others would probably come to see the house.

It was about two weeks before Christmas. As Buck rode around inspecting the buildings and crops, he was greeted by the freed slaves who were saying, "Christmas gift, Mr. Buck!" This was the customary request made to the slave owners just before Christmas. When they had been slaves, they had been dependent on the owner for any gifts, large or small. In most of their minds, they were still slaves. Buck decided it was time to keep his promise that he had made to them. He had a large table and a chair set up on the front porch of the commissary. He told Man that he wanted all of the former slaves there the next morning. He would have a surprise for them. The former slaves came expecting their usual small Christmas gifts. Buck had them form a long line.

Buck and Man had calculated each person's wages from the time that they had started working on the plantation. Buck first paid the families and then the individuals. As he paid them, he told them that they were free to spend their money on anything they wanted in the commissary. He did advise them not to it spend it all at once. They were to save some for another day. As he told them this, he realized that most of them would probably spend everything at once. He couldn't blame them. This was the first time that they had ever had any money and the first time they could make the decision of what they wanted. In the past, everything had always been handed to them. Buck thought, "They will have to learn sometime. It might as well start now."

Excitement spread through the crowd as word got out as to how much money everyone was getting. The ones at the front of the line were allowed to go in and make their selections. Man restricted entry to ten individuals at a time. Although the ladies had volunteered to help, this was all that Justin could handle at a time. It took all day and part of the night before everyone was paid and waited on. Buck and his family agreed that this had been one of the best experiences of their lives. It was touching to see people being able to make their own decisions for the first times in their lives!

18

The Wedding

It was the week before Christmas and the wedding date had arrived. The house was decorated for Christmas and for the wedding. Big wreaths and ribbons decorated the front door. Small branches of greenery, entwined with ribbons, wound their way around the stair banisters. There were ribbons and greenery draped over the interior doors and windows. Candles had been placed in each window. Mistress had brought out all of her silver services, silver punch bowls, silver goblets and silver trays. The floors had been polished to a high shine. There were hurricane lanterns lining the driveway. They had decided on a late evening wedding.

There would only be room for the immediate family and friends at the wedding itself since it was being held in the upstairs ballroom. The actual ceremony would be held on the ballroom balcony overlooking the lake. The almanac had forecast a warmer than usual December. Buck and Julie had decided to take a chance and have the wedding on the balcony. Family and close friends could view the ceremony from the ballroom, and the other guests and freed slaves could observe from the front lawn.

The weather cooperated. Although the ceremony was held at dusk, it was a warm December evening. Everyone had a good view of Buck and Julie as they said their vows. Julie, Mistress, Rachel, and Becky were resplendent in the dresses they had created. Buck and the groomsmen looked handsome in their tuxedos.

The guests had come from miles around. They almost filled the lawn between the house and the lake. All of the former slaves, who had not been assigned a job, stood to one side observing. They had never seen anything like this.

After the ceremony was over, the fun began. The reception started! Mistress had planned it all. She had made arrangements with Mr. Worthington of Wayside Plantation to use his slave orchestra. They had been trained by northern musicians that Mr. Worthington had hired several years earlier. They were immaculate in their black tuxes and white shirts.

Food had been placed all over the house. Tables were brought out and placed strategically all over the front lawn. They were laden with food and punch. The plantation workers had killed enough steers and hogs to feed everyone. Birdie and her help had worked all week baking and making deserts. Everybody was in a festive mood. Buck had opened up Mount Hope to his guests. He just smiled as everyone admired what had been created out on the lake.

Buck and Julie led off the first waltz in the ballroom. Others soon followed. The dance lasted almost to midnight.

After dancing a short time, Buck and Julie mingled with the guests. Some they knew and a lot they didn't. Everyone that was anybody had taken advantage of the opportunity to attend the largest social event of they had ever seen. Many also wanted an opportunity to see this house that they had heard so much about.

Julie and Buck had discussed going to Europe on their honeymoon. Buck was reluctant to be away from Mount Hope for that period of time. He told Julie that he would take her the next year, after he got the affairs of the plantation in order. Julie, good natured as usual, told him that she understood. She did request that they go to New Orleans. She wanted to show Buck her school and all of the places that she had frequented while she was living there. Although

Buck had now visited New Orleans a few times, he had never spent enough time to take everything in. Therefore, he readily agreed to make New Orleans their honeymoon destination. Julie particularly wanted to stay at the CORNSTALK HOTEL on Royal Street in the French Quarter. She told him that the hotel took its name from the cast iron fence in front of it. The fence had simulated ears of corn along the top. Cast iron pumpkins formed the base of the fence columns. Pumpkin vines and leaves entwined the top of the fence. She told Buck that she really liked the yellow metal butterfly that adorned the front gate. She had passed by it often while she was in boarding school, but she had never thought that she might spend her honeymoon there.

When Buck and Julie left Mount Hope to catch the paddle wheeler to New Orleans, they were driven by John and Jim in the carriage. Big Man drove the second carriage containing Mistress, Rachel and Becky, who wanted to see them off.

Many of the people at the reception were having such a good time that they were in no hurry to leave. Buck had booked passage on the Delta Queen. He had been able to secure a night passage, but he had to be on time. He asked Justin to look after the guests once the family was gone. Justin told him not worry; he would take care of things.

As the boat slowly backed into the river and turned south, the figures waving on the bank became smaller and smaller. For the first time, Buck and Julie fully realized that they were man and wife and that they were alone. As they stood there with their arms wrapped around each other, a cool breeze started blowing. The weather had cooperated just long enough for the wedding to take place. With these cold blasts of air, Buck was reminded that winter was on its way. The Captain found them and escorted them to their suite. On the way, he kept glancing at Julie as if he had seen her before. Julie never changed expressions.

After entering their stateroom, they decided to go and get something to eat before retiring. When they entered the large dining area, all of the passengers stood and started clapping. The Captain had alerted everyone that they had a newly married couple on board.

The boat's band struck up a tune and everyone insisted that Buck and Julie have the first dance. Although they were tired, they thought it would be impolite not to comply. Eating would have to wait.

After spending a festive evening in the dining room, Buck and Julie returned to their stateroom. Buck opened the door, swept Julie into his arms and carried her over the threshold. Alone with the love of his life at last!

When they reached New Orleans, they made their way to the Corn Stalk Hotel. Buck could see why Julie was infatuated with the hotel. He couldn't believe the details of the cast iron fence. The interior was just as impressive. They both were so glad that they had made this their honeymoon destination.

Julie was anxious to show Buck her boarding school. They took one of the carriages on Jackson Square and rode down St. Charles Street. There were beautiful houses lining both sides of the street. After a short ride, they reached Julie's school. It sat on the right behind a large wrought iron fence. The carriage stopped and Julie and Buck got out. Julie told Buck that although she missed her father, the years she had spent here had been happy ones. Buck asked if she wanted to go in. She replied, "No. Everyone will be in class or studying for exams. I wouldn't want to cause a disruption. Besides, coming here has kind of made me nostalgic. This part of my life is gone forever." Buck was quiet for a few moments and then said, "Yes, that part is gone, but life moves on. Let's think about the life that we are going to have together." Changing her mood, Julie said, "You are right. This is a happy time. Let's go and I will take you to one of the best restaurants in the French Quarters."

The week was spent visiting the Mays, the shop where Julie had learned to sew, and the theaters of New Orleans. Julie also added to her wardrobe.

The theaters were decorated for Christmas and the Mays had used their influence to get the Inmans the best box seats. It was an idyllic and happy time for them and for the others in their social circles. They could not imagine the troubles that lay in their future.

After this fun filled week, they boarded the Delta Queen for the trip back to the plantation. The weather turned extremely cold and the freezing wind coming off of the water made it impossible to spend any time on the deck, so Buck and Julie spent their time in the dining room or their quarters. They were glad when they reached Leota.

Buck engaged Tom to transport them and their luggage to Mount Hope. Tom was glad to do so. Again, he was thankful that Buchanan Inman had come to town.

When they arrived at the plantation, it was Christmas Eve. Buck unloaded all of the gifts that he and Julie had purchased in New Orleans and placed them under the twelve foot high tree that was set up in the entry hall. He had made sure that they returned home in time to hear Mistress read the Christmas story. This had been a tradition ever since he could remember. He had not wanted to miss it.

After a large Christmas Eve meal, everyone gathered around the piano to sing Christmas carols. Buck couldn't help but notice that Justin always managed to stand by Becky. With the large fires blazing, and the gasoliers burning, it was a warm festive time for all at Mount Hope.

Winter set in out on the lake and time stood still. There was hardly anything going on. A light snow had come and the ground was frozen. Some of the freedmen spent their time chasing rabbits.

Others just hunkered down in their quarters and tried to stay warm. The only other mandatory activity was cutting and hauling wood to the fireplaces in the cabins and in the big house.

It was the first of February and Buck was passing time reading in the library when Birdie appeared, all out of breath and flustered. "Mr. Buck, Mr. Buck, you better come quick. De law is at yo front door!"

"Who!" Buck exclaimed.

'It's de law. He got a badge and a big ole pistol. He got some more men with him, too!"

"Just relax!" Buck said. "I'll go see what he wants."

When Buck opened the front door and stepped out, a strange sight greeted him. There was indeed a lawman, who was accompanied by two other men. Behind them was a fine rented carriage. It was driven by a finely dressed slave. Its occupant was a large portly gentleman bundled up against the cold in a big fur coat. He reeked of importance. He appeared to be about thirty-five years old.

Buck said, "What can I do for ya'll?"

The officer replied, "I am Federal Marshal Joe Temple. These two men are deputized slave trackers." He didn't introduce the man in the carriage.

Puzzled, Buck asked again how he could help them.

Marshal Temple replied, "These trackers have traced a slave to your plantation."

"Uh oh," Buck thought, "they must be looking for John and Jim." He then said, "I do have two young nigras here. I don't know where they came from, but I will be glad to pay for them if the gentleman will name his price."

The man in the carriage spoke up and shouted, "I ain't looking for no two nigra boys. I am looking for a young female slave. You know who I am looking for! You are harboring a run-a-way slave!"

Stunned, Buck replied, "I don't know what ya'll are talking about! We don't have a female fugitive slave!"

One of the trackers spoke up and said, "Let me describe her. She could pass for white. She has long black hair, a dark complexion, and a fine figure. She is twenty-two years old. She is one of the prettiest women you will ever see. We tracked her to Leota where she got off of the Delta Queen. We have been told that she is here!"

It dawned on Buck that they were talking about Julie. "Wait a minute. There has to be some mistake. You are talking about my wife."

The Marshall said, "Mr. Buchanan, it doesn't pleasure me, but I will have to take her and return her to Mr. Jourdain. I am sure you are familiar with the "COMPROMISE OF 1850, and the Fugitive Slave Act. I have no choice in the matter. I must take her!"

Buck said, "No one is taking her! Didn't you hear me? This is my wife you are talking about! You had better leave my property. I have two hundred men at my disposal! I will not allow you to take her!"

The Marshal calmly said, "Sir, you cannot defy the law. You know that the Fugitive Slave Act says that anyone who helps an escaped slave is to be fined and imprisoned. I don't want to have to return with a regiment of soldiers, but I will if you persist in being defiant!"

Buck, trying to collect his thoughts, said, "Would you allow me a moment to go talk to my wife?"

"Certainly. There is no hurry. I just wish I didn't have to do this."

Buck walked back into the house calling Julie. She came running with the rest of the family.

"There is some big mistake going on here!" Buck said. He related to everyone the conversations that he just had outside.

Julie said, "This has to be a case of mistaken identity. I am certainly no slave!! Let's go outside and let me tell them who I am."

They all walked out on the porch. Julie almost fainted when she saw who was in the carriage. She regained her composure and shouted at the gentleman, "I might have known it was you! I knew that you were jealous of me but I didn't think you hated me enough to start a rumor like this! You go ahead and tell them who I am and that I am not a SLAVE!"

The gentleman introduced himself for the first time. "I am Je'rome Jourdain. Her half brother! And, yes, she is a slave! Although my father was her father, her mother was an Octoroon, which makes her a Quintroon. Under Louisiana law, she is a SLAVE! I have all of the documentation to prove it."

Julie now understood everything. She understood why her father never took her back to the plantation and why she was never introduced to any of his friends. She understood why Jerome had refused to pay for her boarding school after her father's death and why she was forced to work in the seamstress shop. Julie understood why she HAD to run away.

Buck was trying to think fast and he said, "This my wife! I will pay you any amount that will satisfy you. Just name your price!"

Je'rome Jourdain replied, "I don't want your money! I want my slave. My wife and I have three young children. One of them is sickly. We need a governess. Keep your money and give me my PROPERTY! Marshal do your duty!"

The last time Buck saw Julie, she was in the carriage looking back at him and crying. This scene would be imprinted in his mind forever. He just didn't know what to do or what else he could have done!

Buck was so distraught that he couldn't sleep and he wouldn't eat. His family tried to console him to no avail.

A few days later, Buck was in the offices of the Honorable Robert Montgomery located in Vicksburg. Mr. Montgomery had a reputation as one of the best lawyers in Mississippi. Buck told him about what had happened to Julie and her situation. He faulted himself for not doing more.

Mr. Montgomery said, "My dear man, there was absolutely nothing that you could have done. Mr. Je'rome Jordain had the law on his side and the Marshall was bound to enforce it. The Fugitive Slave Act was passed as part of the Compromise of 1850. The Act makes Federal Marshals responsible for returning fugitive slaves to their owners. The local law enforcement was sometimes negligent in enforcing the slave laws. It also requires citizens to help in the recovery of fugitive slaves. Persons who help escaped slaves can be fined and imprisoned. The Act does not even provide for a jury trial to learn the facts. So you see, there was nothing you could have done besides go to prison yourself. Even though your wife is only a Quintroon, which is one-sixteenth Nigra, under the law she might as well be full-blooded. I am sorry but that is the way it is. One drop of Nigra blood and you are a Nigra!"

After paying Mr. Montgomery for his time, he returned home even more despondent. Again, he couldn't eat and he couldn't sleep. At night he walked the lake bank by himself until late in the night. He lost so much weight that he didn't even look like himself. He stopped shaving and his hair grew long. He stopped going to town and he wouldn't talk to anyone, not even Man. His family was afraid that he was having a mental breakdown.

It had been over a year since Julie went away. As the old saying goes "time heals". Buck began to function again. He was still morass— but he had started eating. He still did not sleep well at night. He woke all during the night wondering about Julie.

It was the Spring of 1861 when Buck made his first trip into Leota. He decided to go get something to eat at Miss Jane's before he went to the telegraph office. Miss Jane could not believe her eyes, "Is that you Buck Inman? I don't hardly recognize you! You know it's been over a year since I saw you. I heard about the tragedy with your wife. I sure am sorry. Are you alright?"

Buck didn't want to go into any details, so he only replied, "I am better."

Miss Jane then said, "Well come on over here and let me fatten you up." She then added, "Have you heard the news? The CSA has fired on Fort Sumter. It looks like the war is on. South Carolina is seceding and Mississippi is right behind them."

Buck had been a recluse so long that this was all news to him.

19

Off to War

After dining with Miss Jane, Buck starting walking toward the telegraph office. On the way, he met Mr. Knox. Mr. Knox said, "I guess you heard about the war breaking out. I told you us Southerners were not going to stand for the federal government telling us what to do. All of the men around here are already signing up to go fight! Are you going to join the Calvary or the infantry?"

"Neither! If you will remember our conversation when I first arrived here, I told you then that I didn't believe in slavery. I am certainly not going to fight for it!" Buck replied.

"Man, this isn't about slavery! This is about the rights of sovereign states! Our federal constitution does not give the Feds the right to tell us what we can do and not do. Anyway, this is strange talk coming from a man that owns more slaves than anyone around here!

"It really isn't any of your business what I own and what I don't own! Good day!"

Moving away from Mr. Knox, Buck made his way to the telegraph office. The telegraph operator greeted him with more war news. "I guess you heard about the STAR OF THE WEST firing on Fort Sumter. Men all over the south are raising up armies to fight! This war will soon be over with. Any southern boy can whip any ten Yankees!"

Knowing that the North had ten times the population of the South and knowing that most of the munitions factories were in the North, Buck didn't want to get in a discussion about who would win a protracted war. He said, "Maybe they can work out a compromise before too much blood is shed!"

Having enough of war talk, Buck mounted Prince and headed back to the solitude of the lake.

A few weeks later the butler knocked on the library door and told Buck that Justin Knox wished to see him. Buck told him to send him in. The nervous young man entered and apologized for interrupting Buck. Buck said that it was no problem and asked what he wanted. Justin told him that he felt compelled to join the forces of the Confederacy. All of his friends from back home were joining up and he was going back to join up too. He said that he sure hated to leave the plantation without someone to run the commissary, but he hoped Buck would understand. He also asked Buck if it would be possible for him to call on Becky before he left.

Buck told him that he would hate to lose him and complimented him on a job well done. He also gave him permission to call on his sister. He had seen this coming.

After meeting with Becky and telling her about his deep feelings for her, Justin promised to return just as soon as possible. Becky cried but told him she understood. The next morning he was on his way to fight in the war!

It had been several months since Buck had gone to town. He still did not feel like talking to people. He had not recovered from the loss of Julie. He also did not like the stares and whispers of the town people. He had heard what everyone was calling him. Coward! Traitor! Scalawag! He did not leave the plantation unless he just had to.

It was a hot summer day and Buck decided he must go to the telegraph office to take care of some business. He rode down the main street feeling the stares of the people of Leota. The onlookers were mostly women, children and old men. He tied Prince up and walked into the telegraph office. He was greeted with the question, "Have you heard the news? The Union invaded Virginia with 38,000 men!! Our boys gave them a good whipping at Manassas and chased them Yankees back to Washington. Maybe that will change their mind about invading the South. I told everybody that one Southerner could whip ten Yanks. We got them scared all right! Lincoln is calling for 500,000 more men to enlist. You know what else they did? They shelled an eighty five year old woman's house and killed her! That's the kind of folks we are fighting!"

Buck took all of this in, turned without a word, mounted Prince and headed for the lake. On the way he had plenty of time to think. Although he didn't agree with secession and slavery, he had not thought that the Federal government would actually invade the South with such a massive force. He had thought that after a few skirmishes, the Northerners and the Southerners in congress would sit down and work things out. Never did he think that it would come to Lincoln raising 500,000 more troops. He could see now that the North was intent on crushing the South!

The next year brought heavy losses to both the Union and the Rebels as the federal troops moved relentlessly south. Although the Rebels won many of the early battles, the numbers of men were not in their favor. The Yankees had fresh troops to replace their losses; the South did not. The best the South could hope for would be for England to come in on their side. They thought this was a probability since they felt that England needed the South's cotton.

It was the next spring before Buck returned to town. He had almost become a recluse at the plantation. He had decided that he needed seeds and supplies to start his cotton crop. He had retained enough seed corn. He rode to the livery stable first. He hadn't seen Sam in almost a year. Sam couldn't believe how much Buck had aged and how much weight he had lost. Not wanting to talk about Buck's appearance, Sam said, "Have you heard the latest war news? Johnston took 40,000 men and marched from Corinth to attack the Union at Shiloh in Tennessee. They drove the Yankees all of the way to the Tennessee River, but darkness stopped them. The next day the Yankees received re-enforcements and pushed the Rebels back to Corinth. Thousands were killed on both sides."

Buck could not believe how many men were being killed. He decided to return home.

When he arrived home, he called a meeting with his family. He told them what had happened at Shiloh. Then he broke the news to them. He had decided to offer his services to the Confederacy. The ladies were shocked and scared. They just hoped that the Yankees could be stopped before they reached Mount Hope! Buck told them that he was going to go back to town the next day to get information about enlisting, and would return to make preparations for his absence.

Buck had decided during a sleepless night that the person he needed to talk to was Mr. Knox. Although he did not particularly care for him, Mr. Knox was now in charge of the home guard. He should be able to give Buck advice on enlistment.

When Buck walked into Mr. Knox's office he was greeted, disdainfully. "What do you want?" growled Mr. Knox.

"I have come to get information about enlisting in the Confederacy."

Surprised, Mr. Knox said, "I thought you said you didn't believe in slavery and that you were going to sit the war out!"

"I don't believe in slavery! However, when an army is invading and coming to burn you out, I think almost any man WILL FIGHT!"

Mr. Knox's attitude changed. "Well Boy, maybe you ain't a coward after all! Are you wanting to join the infantry or the cavalry?

"If possible, the cavalry. I believe I will be more useful with my horse. I would really hate to leave him behind anyway."

Mr. Knox said, "I just might have the right situation for you. Look here. I have a copy of the MEMPHIS APPEAL. A drummer left it with me when he came through last week. He was calling on the mercantile store. This is an ad placed by Nathan Bedford Forrest. He is credited with being the toughest cavalryman in the Confederacy! Have you heard of him?"

Buck said, "I don't think so."

"'Let me tell you who he is. He has become quite famous since the beginning of the war. He is a millionaire slave trader from Memphis. He also has a lot of acreage below Helena in Mississippi. It is said that his cavalry whips union forces many times their size. He does it by moving fast and by surprise. The other thing is that he always leads the charge. Unlike many officers, he doesn't remain behind and watch his men fight. He is always out front. This is what got him in trouble at Corinth. He charged a bunch of Yankees and got himself cut off from his men. One of the Yankees shot him in the hip but he managed to get away. I heard he had to have two operations. He is in Memphis now, and it looks like he is well and trying to enlist more men. Look at what the ad says!"

'Come on boys if you want a heap of fun and
a chance to kill some Yankees!'

Buck returned home to start preparing for his absence. He started sending wagons everyday to get supplies and more seed. They planted the cotton and corn crops. He then turned his attention to the gardens. He had Man call a meeting of all of the former slaves. They all gathered in front of the commissary. Mistress, the girls, and Big Man sat behind Buck as he spoke.

He said, "Ya'll have done everything that I have asked of you. Ya'll made the hard trip from South Carolina. Ya'll have worked hard clearing the land and building homes. I had hoped that this would be the year that things would get a lot easier for all of us. I am sorry to have to tell you that it is not to be. War has broken out between everybody up North (he pointed towards Wayside) and all of the white people down here. The white people up North have crossed into the South. People are getting killed everywhere. The Yankees are burning everything in their path. They are also freeing the slaves as they come. Now, you know I have already freed you! You can leave and go north at any time. However, for those that choose to stay, we have to make plans. You see, I will be leaving to go fight. We must stop the Yankees before they rob and burn the whole South."

Big Man stood up and said, "We is free now and we got a good place to live. It don't make no sense to me to jump up and leave for the North. I don't know nothing bout dem folks up there. Besides, Mount Hope is my home and de Inmans are my family. Me and Birdie are staying. Mr. Buck has put me in charge while he is gone, so I needs to know who going to be leaving and who going to stay." He then stuck out his arm and said, "Everybody that is staying move over here. Dem that wants to go, move over there."

To Man's amazement, everyone moved over to the side that was staying. They figured that they already had as good a situation as they were ever going to get.

Buck stood back up and said, "If this is your decision, then you are going to have to get busy. I am expecting our supplies to be cut off in the future. You are going to have to make and grow everything that you are going to need. I want you to plant big gardens and put up as much food as possible. I figure that it will take about six months to a year for the Yanks to get here if we are not able to stop them. When they get here, they will take everything we have to eat, all of the live stock, and they will probably burn the Big House. Big Man and I will be meeting to try to make plans to save what we can."

Buck and Big Man went into the commissary to devise their plans. Buck said, "If the Yankees come, all that I know that you can do is drive the stock back into the woods and hide them. You will have to do this in secret because some of these Nigras like Fannie will tell the Yanks where they are for sure. If you hear the Yankees are getting close, drive the stock out in the middle of the night so no one here will know where they are. Use John, Jim and any others that you trust. You will have to hide your canned goods and everything else where ever you can."

Big Man said, "I has another good idea. If I hear they is coming, why don't I hide our valuables in the garden? I could bury all of the watches and all of ya'll's silverware and then plant on top of them. I 'spect the Yankees will be too busy stealing our vegetables to think about digging." Buck said, "That sounds good. Also, I have another plan. This will be just between us. I want us to load the bell onto one of the wagons. We will fill it with most of our gold coins. Next, we will seal the bottom with concrete. Then, in the middle of the night we will drive down to the lake bank and push the bell off into the water, I don't think the Yanks will ever find it there."

On the first really dark night, Buck and Man successfully put the bell into the lake.

20

Buck Joins Forrest

When the paddle wheeler landed in Memphis, Buck mounted Prince and road to the front of the Gayoso Hotel. He was a different man than the one who spent the night there with his sisters and Julie. He tied Prince at the front and started up the steps. He was greeted by a man sitting on the porch who said, "That's a mighty fine animal you have there!" Buck looked around and said, "Thank you. He's a good one all right." He then added, "Do you know where I could find Colonel Nathan Bedford Forrest?"

"I 'spect I could," was the reply, as the man stood up. "You are looking at him!"

Buck then took a closer look. The general was a large hulking man with coal black hair and a full mustache and beard. He was an intimidating figure. What intrigued Buck the most were his piercing eyes. It seemed that they were looking right through him. He had an air about him that said, "Don't mess with me!" Buck could see why the Yankees were scared of him. In fact, he felt a little intimidated himself.

He introduced himself, "I am Buchanan Inman. I am here to inquire about your newspaper notice asking for Calvary recruits. I would like to offer my services. I know nothing about war but I would like to help the Confederates if I can."

"You don't have to know anything about the Calvary to join up. You will learn in a hurry. I see you've got a good horse! My men must be willing to ride hard, fight hard and not retreat. I don't believe in giving up! I didn't know anything about battle when I signed up either, but I learned fast. I've been able to teach those West Point Yankees a thing or two. The most important thing is to always be on the attack! These professional soldiers on both sides want to sit around and plan and plan. I don't have time for that! When we meet the enemy, we charge! The Yankees aren't used to that! So if you think you can keep up, we'll be glad to have you. I am up here getting over a gunshot wound, but I'll be ready to ride in a couple of weeks. Here, I'll give you a note and you can ride out east of town where the rest of the fellars are. One of my captains will sign you up and tell you what to do."

Just like that, Buck was in the Calvary!

He rode east of town where Forrest's men were camped. They were a mixture of veterans and new recruits. Buck couldn't help notice the difference. Although most were young, the vets had a strange look about them like someone who had faced death many times. He also noticed that they looked hard and tough. There was not an ounce of fat on them. He figured out quickly that the new recruits were going to have to put out a lot of effort to keep up with these boys.

He was directed to one of the Captains who signed him up. The Captain told Buck that they had been understaffed since the battle of Shilo. They had lost a lot of good men during that battle. They were glad to get new recruits. He outfitted Buck and informed him that Forrest was a millionaire who furnished most of the equipment and uniforms. He took Buck over to a group of men sitting around a camp fire and introduced him. They showed him the tent that he would be sharing. He was now Private Buck Inman of the Confederate States of America!

Colonel Forrest was soon pronounced fit to return to service. He was ordered to Chattanooga to help General Bragg in central Tennessee. Fortunately for Buck and the other new recruits, this trek gave themselves a chance to acclimate to Calvary life. This trip was relatively slow with a chance to rest along the way. The vets told the recruits that they had better enjoy the ride while they could. This wasn't the way they usually rode. Normally, Forrest would be pushing them to get somewhere quickly for a battle.

This also gave Buck a chance to see how Prince was to handle the long rides. He had noticed most of the Vets were riding small wiry horses that might ride rough but had great stamina. After several days on the trail he decided Prince was going to be able to keep up just fine. He figured out the reason that there was not many bloodied stock in the Calvary. The men had to furnish their own mounts. Since most of the riders came from small hill farms, they rode what they had.

After arriving in Chattanooga and joining the rest of the cavalry there, they set up camp. They had no clue that they would soon be riding and fighting hard all over central Tennessee. There were about 1500 troops camped there. They came from all over the South. Next to Buck's camp was a group from Georgia. On the other side were some Texas boys. Buck thought that they all looked like they could take care of business.

After a few days of rest, rumors started flying around the camp. The word was that Forrest had been given new orders. They were fixing to be on the move!

The rumors were true. Forrest had been ordered north to disrupt the supply line of Union General Buell who was moving slowly toward Chattanooga. Forrest's plan was to attack and capture the Union Garrison at Murfreesboro, Tennessee. The Nashville and Chattanooga Railroad ran through the middle of town. The orders were to destroy this railroad which the Yankees were using to supply Buell.

It was shortly after July 4, 1862 when Forrest's troops broke camp and headed north. Buck and the new recruits were both excited and apprehensive. Most of them had not been in battle before. They didn't know that they were on a raid that would carry them over a hundred miles in three days.

After everyone fell into place, the caravan moved steadily southeast. As they moved, they started alternating between a canter and a walk. They did this for hours at a time.

When they finally took a break after riding five hours, Buck and the new recruits dismounted stiffly. The vets laughed at them. "We told you that the Colonel rode hard! We is just getting started. We will probably ride way into the night." They were right. Except for a few breaks along the way and a short nap each night, the troops pushed on.

At the beginning of the third day, the pace quickened. Col Forrest wanted to get within striking distance of Murfreesboro before night fall. Buck knew now why Forrest was called the toughest man in the South. He was relentless. Just before dark, a halt was called so that the men and their horses could rest. A night attack was planned!

The Calvary was spread out, resting and waiting for dark. Forrest had sent scouts to check out the Union troops. They returned and told the Colonel that they estimated that there was over two thousand Union troops in and around Murfreesboro. Forrest realized that was too many troops to take head on. He would have to use surprise and subterfuge. They also told Forrest that they had talked to a civilian that was loyal to the Confederacy. The civilian had told them that there were two Confederates being held in the county jail. They were supposed to be executed the next day. Forrest said, "We'll see about that!"

Forrest split his troops into three groups. One would attack from the east and one from the west. The third led by Forrest would attack the center of the town. As soon as it came completely dark, the Rebels attacked. Intimidating Rebel Yells could be heard everywhere. The Union soldiers were taken by surprise but put up a valiant fight. They were well fortified.

Buck's company was assigned the task of freeing the prisoners. They rode straight toward the jail as the others surrounded the town. At first the going was easy for the Rebels since the Yankees were caught off guard. This did not last. The Yankee Calvary mounted and charged Buck's company. They met head-on with sabers swinging. The horses were neighing and raring. The men were trying to maintain their balance and swing their sabers at the same time. This was the first time that Buck had been in actual battle. Like Forrest had told him, he learned fast. Swinging and dodging, he managed to kill one Union solider who attacked him from the side. Another He shot in the face. With some of his comrades, he broke through the Union line and headed for the jail. He could hear gunfire going off in the jail. He surmised that the Yankees were firing at the prisoners. A few seconds later they were at the prison. The Yankee guards came running out. Flames were licking up behind them. They had set fire to the jail in an attempt to kill the prisoners. The Rebels shot them dead on the spot. One of the Georgia Calvary men grabbed a rope and ran into the prison. He tied the rope to the iron prison door. He ran back out and handed the end to Buck. Buck tied the rope to his saddle horn and urged Prince forward. The weight of the big stallion snatched the door out of the building. Following right behind the door were the prisoners, coughing and sneezing from the smoke! All they could say was, "Thank you, boys."

As Buck was untying the rope, he looked down the road into the shadows. He saw a large hulking Rebel battling for his life. The man's horse was wheeling and kicking. He was swinging his saber and slashing in every direction.

Buck took off at full gallop to help him. As he got closer, he recognized Colonel Forrest. Just as he had done at Shiloh, Forrest had out run his men. He now had Union Infantry men trying to pull him off of his horse. Buck did not hesitate. He rode Prince straight into the melee. Prince knocked Yankees in every direction. Buck wheeled and charged again. He decapitated one of the Yankees as he went by. With both Forrest and Buck charging and slashing, the Yankee foot soldiers had enough. They scattered in every direction. Buck and Forrest did not have time to converse. Forrest gave Buck a little salute and rode off to resume his command. Buck turned back to help his comrades with the prisoners that they captured.

After a night of fighting, the Rebels managed to capture the city. The next day was spent securing the prisoners and tending to the wounded and dead on both sides.

Buck was busy helping with the inventory of all of the captured supplies when he was approached by one of Colonel Forrest's aides. He was told that Forrest wanted him to report to headquarters at once. When he arrived at Forrest's tent, he was greeted by the Colonel who was sitting in a folding chair. Buck came to attention and saluted. He said, "Private Buck Inman reporting, Sir". Forrest said, "At ease! Are you the soldier who helped me when I was having a little tussle with some Yanks last night?"

"Yes Sir! But it looked like it was more than a little tussle."

A smile played across Forrest's face. "Well, I guess I did need a little help. I am glad you showed up. By the way aren't you the fellow from Mississippi that joined up with me at the Gayoso Hotel in Memphis?

"Yes Sir! I am the same one. You told me that I would learn how to fight in a hurry. You were sure right."

"I thought so. I recognized that big stallion you were riding last night. I tell you what. You are the kind of Calvary man that I like. Not afraid of anything! If I had more like you, we would run them

Yanks back to where they came from." Forrest said. He then turned to his aid. "I want you to make Private Inman here, a lieutenant. Find him an officer's uniform and place him in charge of one of the companies. I don't care if he doesn't have a lot of experience. He has a lot of fight in him. That's what I am looking for."

Buck replied. "Thank you, Sir! I will do the best that I can. However, I want to correct one thing. I don't want you to think that I wasn't scared. I was just fighting for my life!"

"That's all right. Sometimes it helps to be a little bit scared. A man ain't got good sense if this war don't scare him. It's what you do when you are scared that counts! Now you go back and get yourself and your company organized. We got a lot of train track to tear up in the morning. We are then going to make a little sweep through middle Tennessee. We are going to make Buell's army sorry they came to this part of the country. I have been ordered to cut off their supply lines. We'll see how they like marching on an empty stomach!"

Buck walked into headquarters a Private and walked out an officer.

True to his word, Forrest spent the next few weeks raiding the county side where he burned bridges and tore down telegraph lines. Buck and his men were given the task of destroying the railroads. They would pry up the rails and pile up the cross ties. After setting the cross ties on fire, they would then place the metal rails across the flames. When the rails were heated, they were able to bend them around a tree. This prevented the union from using the rails again.

Forrest's raids and tactics were so successful that Buell had to divert two divisions to try and protect his supply lines. This allowed General Bragg's Army of Tennessee which contained 40,000 men to advance against Buell.

Having completed his assignment at Murfreesboro, Tennessee, Forrest was given a new assignment. The Yankees were desperate to capture Vicksburg, Mississippi. The city sat upon high bluffs alongside the Mississippi River. The Rebels had placed cannons all along the high points of the bluffs. From this vantage point they could control the river traffic. They prevented the mid-western farmers from shipping their grain south. The Union had captured Memphis in June of 1862. They also controlled New Orleans. The only place preventing them from controlling the whole river was Vicksburg.

Grant decided to take Vicksburg by attacking the city from the east. He wanted to go directly south from Memphis but couldn't cross the swampy delta. He decided instead to go through Holly Springs and Grenada. He had a long supply line stretched out behind him.

The supply line became Forrest's mission. General Pemberton, who commanded the confederates around Vicksburg, asked General Bragg for help. Bragg sent help, Colonel Forrest! His mission was to destroy the railroads and the railroad bridges that Grant was using to supply his troops.

It was a cold December rain in which the 2000 Rebels rode as they headed toward the Tennessee River. Buck and his command had been sent ahead to construct flatboats that would be used to carry the troops across. When they got there they began cutting trees, trimming the limbs and lashing the logs together. It was miserable work in the rain. Everyone was wet from the rain and the river water. Trying to ward off the cold, they built huge bonfires to back up against. By the time Forrest arrived, they had two flatboats constructed. The Colonel said that they didn't have time to construct more. They would just have to make do and make a lot of trips.

Buck had never ridden so fast or fought so hard as he did the next few days. After crossing the Tennessee, they routed the 800 troops at Lexington, Tennessee. They then continued on to Jackson which was controlled by ten thousand Yankee troops. Although this was too strong a contingent to attack head on, Forrest sent raiding parties in every direction while the balance of the Calvary men kept the Union contained. Again Buck's Company was assigned the task of destroying all of the bridges of the Mobile and Ohio Railroad. They managed to successfully complete their mission in spite of being attacked by the small garrisons in the outlying areas.

After destroying the railroad, the Calvary continued their raid. They decimated the small garrisons around the country side. Swinging back toward the Tennessee River, they destroyed the Nashville and Northwestern Railroad. They were about fifty miles from the river crossing when the Union organized a force to try to capture the Colonel and his men. The Yankees were moving on him from three different directions but Forrest managed to out run them back to the river. The federal gun boats had destroyed all of the boats and ferries up and down the river so they thought that the rebel Cavalry was trapped. What they didn't know was that Forrest had had Buck and his company of men, sink the flatboats they had built. When the rebels reached the, river, they raised the boats, and started ferrying the men and the horses across the Tennessee River.

It was Buck's Company's duty to load everyone onto the flatboats and send them across. With the river swollen from the winter rains, this was no easy task. The going was slow but the boats made trip after trip. Buck was glad when the last of the men and horses were loaded for the last trip. He was to be the last person to board.

Then the unthinkable happened! Buck was going to jump on the boat by stepping on a large rock lying on the bank. When he stepped on the rock so that he could jump to the back of the raft, the rock turned and slid out into the river, dumping Buck into the swift current. The men on the boat saw what happened but were unable to do anything about it. The current was too fast and Buck was gone!

When they got to the other side, Forrest was sitting on his horse watching everyone disembark. When the last men got off he asked, "Where is Lt. Inman?" One of the men replied, "We don't know.

Probably drowned! When he tried to jump on the back of the boat he slipped and fell into the river. The last time we saw him, he was in a fast current heading downstream." Forrest said "I sure hope he makes it! He's a good'un! I wish we could go back and see about him but we can't! We've got to get out of here before them blue bellies bring up their cannons and start shelling us!"

He then said, "You men cut them logs apart! We don't want them Yankees using them. Send them on down the river. We'll let them Yanks try to figure out how we got across this river." The Calvary was soon riding hard as usual!

The cold water almost took Buck's breath. He started kicking and paddling. He could not make much progress because of the heavy clothes he had on. "So this is the way I am going to die!" He thought. Just as he was going down for the second time, he felt his hand strike something. It was a big log still covered with branches that was floating down the river. Buck grabbed one of the branches and pulled himself over to the large limb. "Thank you, Lord! I thought I was a goner!" He exclaimed.

Buck could do nothing but hold on. Where ever the log went, he went. He was worried about drowning, but now he was worried about freezing to death! Just as he was about to pass out from the cold, he heard a scraping noise. The front of the limb had hung up on the bank. Buck was too weak to wade out. He then heard talking.

He yelled, "Help! Help!"

Out of the brush along the bank came four young men dressed in the butternut colored uniforms of the Confederate infantry. "Hold on, we'll git you out!" they hollered.

Two of them braved the cold water and waded out to Buck. With the other two helping, they managed to pull him onto the bank. Buck was so cold he couldn't talk. All he could do was sit there and shiver.

The young men took hold of him and carried him back to the campfire they had built. They laid Buck on a blanket by the fire and covered him with another. It took a little while but Buck began to thaw out.

Feeling better he sat up and said, "I sure appreciate your help! Who are you?"

One of the young men spoke up and introduced everyone. He told Buck that they were part of the 30th regiment out of Mississippi. They belonged to the Confederate force that was withdrawing south after the Battle Of Stone's Mountain near Murfreesboro. The Army was camped out along the Duck River. The young soldiers had been sent on a scouting patrol. They had walked southwest while the army had moved close to Shelbyville. They were camping out for the night. They hoped to catch up with their unit the next week.

One of the other soldiers asked, "Feller, what in the world was you doing in that river? Don't you know it's too cold to be taking a bath?"

Buck laughed and said, "I agree." He then started telling them his story.

21

On the Infantry

The next morning the group set out to find the main force. After walking for several days, they could hear the noise of the camp. When they arrived, they took Buck to their Company Commander, Major Drane. He was very interested in Buck's story, especially the part about Forrest's attack on Murfreesboro a few months earlier. He then said, "There is no way that you can catch up with Forrest's Calvary. The best that I can offer you is a position with our infantry. We are going to winter here along the Duck River. Then this spring when weather permits, we are going to go east and re-enforce General Bragg's Army of Tennessee. He is expecting an attack from Union Major General Rosecrans' army coming up from Georgia."

Buck replied, "I am a Calvary man, but I sure would rather be in ya'll's infantry than in one of the Yankees prisons."

"Good", Major Drane said. "However, you sure can't march in those boots you are wearing and you sure can't wear that uniform. It looks like it has shrunk about 3 sizes."

He told one of the rescuers to take Buck over to the supply wagon and get him an infantry uniform and some shoes. After searching, Buck finally found some things that fit him.

He thought, "Yesterday I was a Calvary man. Today, I am in the infantry!"

Since the weather was so bad, the army camped there by the Duck River all winter. Then in the spring after the weather broke, they moved out. Despite a few skirmishes along the way, the Confederate force moved slowly southeast. Buck had a hard time adjusting to the slow pace of the infantry. He was used to riding hard and fast. It was nothing for the Calvary to cover 100 miles in three days while fighting as they traveled. He sure did miss Prince.

Since Buck had lost his rifle in the river, they issued him a new one. During the skirmishes that the army had with Union raiders, he had proved to be quite a good shot. In fact, he was so good that they made him one of the sharpshooters. With this new responsibility, he walked out front with the scouts. This was a lot better than walking with the other troops in the churned up mud. Day after day, the army moved slowly southeast.

The forces that Buck was with didn't have to travel far before they made contact with the Army of Tennessee under the command of General Bragg. After the battle of Stone River, both the Union and the Rebels were licking their wounds. Bragg had pulled back about thirty miles. He had deployed picket lines along a seventy mile front. Before the Mississippians could join up with the Tennessee army, Rosecrans moved out of Murfreesboro and attacked. Bragg was forced to retreat back to Chattanooga. It was during this retreat that the Mississippians joined them.

While the officers were meeting and making plans, the foot soldiers made camp for the night. Buck's company bedded down next to a group of boys from Tennessee. It wasn't long before the two groups were telling war stories. Buck couldn't help but smile at the Tennessee boy's mountain twang. Both groups were trying to make their exploits rougher than the other. They didn't have to do too much exaggerating. There had been tremendous casualties in all of the battles, both Union and Confederate. These young men had seen their comrades blown up, shot and killed. They had seen legs and arms cut off by the surgeons without anesthesia. It was a bloody war!

The officer's decision was to retreat back to Chattanooga. With all of the mountains around the city, they thought this would be a good place to make a stand. While they were holed up there, the war was raging in Mississippi. Grant's numerically superior forces were slowly forcing the Confederates under the command of General Pemberton back to the Mississippi River.

Grant had finally been successful in reaching the east side of Vicksburg. Since his troops could not travel across the Yazoo Delta, he had tried everything else. He thought if he could just get to the Yazoo River North of Vicksburg, he could ferry his troops south to the city. He tried entering the Yazoo tributaries south of Memphis, but the rebels stopped him at Fort Pillow near Greenwood, Mississippi. He also tried to reach the east side by leaving the Mississippi and going up the Yazoo River. The Rebels stopped him with chains across the river and sharpshooters. He tried going north up the Steel Bayou to the intersection of Deer Creek and the Rolling Fork Creek. Boats had gone first with 10,000 troops following. The Rebels stopped the Union again by cutting trees that fell across the Creeks. He even tried to dig a by-pass around the Mississippi on the west side. The river flooded the pass before they could complete it. Grant was finally successful by floating his almost empty boats down the river. He marched his troops down the Louisiana side and ferried them across near Port Gibson, Mississippi. From there, he made a loop around to the capital city of Jackson. He then turned west to Vicksburg. General Pemberton's forces tried to hold at the battle of Champion Hill but Grant and Sherman had too many men. Pemberton had no choice but to retreat into Vicksburg. The Union assaulted several times but could not enter the stronghold. A siege was decided on by the Yankees. With the Union navy shelling from the river and Grant's troops encircling the city, the Rebels were trapped. They could not get food or supplies into the city. Their only hope was help from General Bragg's Army Of Tennessee. It was not to be.

After eating all of their supplies, all of their mules, all of the rats and finally boiling their leather apparel to make soup, the Rebel soldiers and the populace were starving. The Confederates surrendered on July 4, 1863.

Under pressure from the Union War Department and from President Lincoln, Rosecrans decided to try and force the Confederates out of Chattanooga. His Army of the Cumberland managed to encircle Bragg and force him out of the city and surrounding area, supposedly with "few casualties". Bragg was under pressure to re-take Chattanooga. It was a major railroad crossing and the Tennessee River could be controlled from there. Without the control of the city, neither side could move their needed supplies.

The Army of Tennessee and its reinforcements moved out September 17, 1863, with about 65,000 men. They were met by the Army of The Cumberland with 60,000 troops.

Buck had already seen as much fighting and death as he ever wanted to see. However, he and the other infantrymen had no choice. Fight or be killed. The Confederates charged the Union line. After running out of ammunition, both sides resorted to using bayonets in hand—to—hand combat. On both sides, men fell by the thousands.

Buck was fighting in the area of Snodgrass Hill. His unit attacked General Thomas's position there 25 times before taking the hill. During each attack, men on both sides were killed or wounded.

Finally, the Rebels were victorious, if one could call 18,000 Confederates and 16,000 Union men either killed, wounded, or missing—a victory for anyone!

Rosecran's troops were able to slip away and take refuge in Chattanooga. Bragg decided on the strategy of a siege. He positioned his men atop the mountains circling the city. He prepared to starve the Yankees out just as Grant had starved the Rebels out at Vicksburg. The 30th Mississippi, of which Buck was now a member, was one of the regiments stretched out along the top of Lookout Mountain.

During this standoff, the Union War Department made a major change. They relieved Rosecran and replaced him with General Grant. Grant was in good favor after his victory at Vicksburg.

After his appointment, Grant started north from Mississippi with a large contingent of troops. When Grant arrived with his troops, he was able to break the siege and supply the troops at Chattanooga. He then began making preparations for an attack on Bragg's' positions.

He first moved against Orchard Knob. Bragg reacted by sending a majority of the troops stationed on Look Out Mountain to Missionary Ridge which was located behind Orchard Knob. The 30th Mississippi along with the other troops stationed at Look Out Mountain were really stretched thin.

The men of the 29th, the 30th and 34th Mississippi were positioned for miles along the west side of the mountain.

On a cold windy November morning, Buck was stationed as a picket on one of the huge boulders located at the top of Lookout Mountain. From his vantage point, he could usually see for miles. This morning he could see nothing because of the heavy fog. He did not see the 10,000 Union troops that were leading the advance of Grant's army. As he stood there peering into the mist, the fog suddenly lifted and he was spun around and knocked to the ground! An enemy sharp shooter, making a long difficult shot, had hit the rifle Buck was holding in front of him. Although the bullet tore off two of his fingers and knocked the rifle down the mountain, Buck was fortunate that the weapon had shielded him from death. Holding his bleeding hand, Buck ran back to his unit to report on the Union advancement!

The 29th and 30th Mississippians tried to stop the Yankees on the west side, but they were heavily outnumbered and out—gunned. They were able to slow the advance for a short time, but the Union troops pushed them back. Cannon fire and rifle shots could be heard all across the mountain. Grant's army, under cover of the fog, was attacking all around the mountain. Whenever the fog lifted momentarily, the Rebels could see the massive force that they faced.

One of the surgeons had bandaged Buck's hand which helped stymie the bleeding. Grabbing another rifle, Buck was soon back in the fighting. He was glad the two fingers he lost were on his left hand.

He met the 30th as they were being forced to retreat. As Buck joined them, they were doing their best to hold off the Yankees as they retreated over the boulders and crevices back up the mountain. Then, their retreat was stopped! The Yankee cannon fire became effective. Since they couldn't hit the Mississippians directly because of the overhangs, the Yankees began firing over them to stop their retreat. Cannon balls started landing behind the Rebels and rolling back down on them. The cannon fire not only stopped the retreat, it kept the Mississippians from getting more ammunition. After firing their last volley, Buck and his company resorted to hand-to-hand combat. Some fought with bayonets and others started using their rifles as clubs. It was a fight to the death. Buck was at a disadvantage with one hand hurt but he hardly thought about his injury. He was too busy trying to survive!

Then the fight came to an end. Several hundred Union troops had cut them off at the back. With no ammunition and being completely surrounded, Buck and his company had to surrender. They were taken to a holding area with the many other Confederates that had surrendered. There they huddled together in the dark and freezing rain wondering what their fate would be.

After several days of fighting, Bragg decided that Lookout Mountain was lost. He ordered the remaining Confederate troop to retreat to Missionary Ridge.

22

Captured

After Buck and his company surrendered at the Battle of Lookout Mountain, they were at the mercy of the Union soldiers that they had been fighting. They were herded together with the other Confederate captives and marched to Chattanooga. Buck's hand was killing him as he plodded along down the mountain in the rain. When he looked around, he saw that he was a lot better off than some of the other wounded. Some had their heads bandaged where they had been shot. Others were dragging a leg that had been wounded by the shrapnel of the cannon balls. Then there were those that were missing an arm. There were very few that had not been injured during the conflict. Everyone was struggling down the road to Chattanooga. Some wouldn't make it. They died on the side of the road.

The Yankees could show the Rebels little mercy even if they were so inclined. They were tired from the battle and were having to also fight the elements. There was a mass of humanity streaming down the mountain. The victorious Yankees with their dead and wounded. The captured Confederates trying to help their casualties. At this point everyone was just trying to survive the march.

When they reached the city, the over—whelmed doctors did what they could for the Confederate prisoners, which was not much. They were then lined up for interrogation. The Union kept meticulous records. They registered each captive, noting name, rank and unit.

Buck was in the first five hundred prisoners placed on railroad cars to be shipped to Nashville. He had never been so cold! The only thing that kept him from freezing to death was the body heat from the other men crowded in the cars with him. The stench and moans of the wounded almost overcame him. Everyone was stinking.

The train carried the captives to Nashville, Tennessee, to Louisville, Kentucky and on to the prison at Rock Island, Illinois.

Rock Island prison, situated on an island by the Mississippi River, was just being completed. The island was three miles long and one half of a mile wide. The prison had 84 barracks. Each contained sixty double bunks. Each barrack was designed to hold 120 men. The total capacity of the camp when completed was over ten thousand captives. Buck and his fellow prisoners were the first to be incarcerated there. It was a cold damp December morning when the troop train pulled across the bridge to the island. It was just before Christmas. The temperature was below freezing. The locals had heard that the train was coming. They lined the street trying to get look at these Rebels. They got a look alright. The Rebels looked like hell. Their clothes were tattered. Their hair and beards were matted. No one had had a hair cut or bath in months. Many were cold and sick. Some had died along the way. When the prisoners disembarked, they just stepped over the dead.

Buck and the other prisoners were herded into the first five barracks. Buck's barrack was like all of the rest; 120 bunks, two coal heaters and a kitchen on the end. Since the camp was just opening, all of the supplies had not arrived. The prisoners were each allotted one blanket to ward off the cold. Even with the heaters operating at full capacity, the boys from the South were terribly cold. WELCOME TO ROCK ISLAND PRISON!

Buck did not get any sleep the first night he was imprisoned. He was cold; he was hungry: his hand ached. All during the night, he could hear the moaning of the sick and wounded. Small pox and pneumonia ran rampant through the camp. The Union doctors tried to contain the sickness, but again they were overwhelmed. Their problems were compounded by the steady stream of captives arriving. It wasn't until the doctors separated the infected from the general population were they able to get control. Despite the best efforts of the doctors, six hundred Confederates died in the first three months. A total of 2000 Rebels would eventually die.

In the bunks next to Buck were two prisoners that he had never met, even though they were also in the 30th Mississippi. One was fairly young, but the other was approaching middle age. Buck found out that they were father and son. These two were among the lucky ones. They weren't sick or wounded.

"I am Buck Inman. Who are ya'll?"

The younger spoke up, sticking his hand out, "I am Joseph Peacock, and this is my pa, Allan Peacock. We are from the central hills of Mississippi. Where you from?"

"I am originally from South Carolina, but my place is over next to the river south of Vicksburg. Mississippi. It's strange, but my mother was a Peacock in South Carolina before she married."

"Well, that is strange," the older Peacock said. "That is where all of our family originated. My family moved to Mississippi when I was a boy. They came right after the Choctaws gave up their land.

Buck said, "We might be kin."

"If that is true, you have got some mighty pore kinfolks," Joseph said. "We don't come from a big Delta Plantation. I heard everyone in the Delta is rich with lots of slaves. We are small hill farmers with no slaves."

"Why in the world are you fighting in this war if you don't have any slaves?"

"We put off enlisting for as long as we could, but when we heard them Yankees were fighting around Corinth, we decided that we better join up and try to stop them. We ain't been joined up but about ten months. We been catching hell every since. I never would have thought this many folks could get killed. I sho didn't think we would wind up in a Yankee prison. We just had to surrender. We always heard the saying, "One Rebel can whip ten Yankees!" That might be true, but I'll tell you something, one rebel can't whip twenty Yankees! That's what we wuz up aginst. But, we might have if we hadn't run out of ammunition. We wuz putting up a fight!"

Buck said, "My unit had the same problem. We ended up fighting with bayonets and throwing rocks. That's all we could do. The Yanks had us completely surrounded."

It was Christmas day, and Buck and the other prisoners were huddled around the barrack heaters trying to stay warm. Everyone had their blanket wrapped tightly around them. Since it was Christmas, Buck and the Peacocks from Mississippi held a little Christmas service. They didn't understand their situation, but as the elder Peacock said in his prayer, "We can't depend on ourselves; we are just going to have to trust in you, Lord, to get us out of this mess alive."

Buck's thoughts turned to his family and Julie. He wondered how they were faring. He couldn't believe what a change the last two years had brought.

23

Back Home

After Buck left, life on the plantation continued without much change. They did as Buck had instructed. They planted a small cotton crop, but planted large fields of corn. Families put in large gardens. Big Man had all of the single Nigras put in a communal garden. They tried to ration the meat so that they would have enough during the hard times that Buck had warned them about.

Mistress told Big Man that she and the girls wanted to plant their own turnip green patch. They just wanted Big Man to have it broken up for them. Man understood what she was planning immediately. He realized that she didn't want the rest of the Nigras knowing where she was hiding her valuables.

Big Man had a spot next to the house broke up. He plowed it real deep. He then told John and Jim that he wanted them to turn the soil over and over to break it up real good. After this was done, he knocked on the door and told Mistress that her green patch was ready to be planted. She told him that she and the girls would plant it the next day.

That night she and the girls arose about midnight. Everyone on the plantation was sleeping. The gold, silver and other valuables had already been wrapped in wax paper and placed in boxes. There was no moon that night so it was pitch black. The ladies took the shovels from the back porch and buried the valuables deep in the garden. They then took rakes and smoothed out the surface.

After sleeping the rest of the night the ladies went out and scattered seed all over the garden.. They then took their rakes and covered the seeds loosely. Big Man was watching from the commissary porch with amusement. Two things amused him. First he had never seen the ladiesof the house do any work. Secondly, he could just see the Yankees stealing those greens, not knowing what was under them.

The people at Mount Hope didn't feel threatened until January of 1863. The Northern blockade was starting to take effect. Just as Buck had predicted, supplies were no longer coming in. The goods in the commissary had long been gone. They were now totally dependent on the produce of the plantation. Still, it wasn't too bad. They had prepared well. Every night the ladies prayed for Buck and asked the Lord to bless and watch over him where ever he was.

The only contact they had with people off of the plantation was when they attended the Sunday services at the church. There was always a large attendance each Sunday. It was amazing how people turned to God in a crisis. People started showing up that had never darkened the door of a church.

After a February Sunday service, everyone stood around talking. People were anxious to hear the latest war news. Almost everyone had men serving somewhere.

Mr. Harden approached Mistress and said, "Have you heard the latest news? Grant is coming to attack Vicksburg. The Yankees say that if they can break the Confederates hold on Vicksburg, they will control the entire river."

"Oh my goodness! Do you think he will stop here?"

"I don't think so. There is little of value around here that the Union would want. I did hear that they stopped and burned Greenville a while back because some of the young fellas up there wouldn't stop taking pot shots at the boats as they went by. They probably wouldn't have bothered the town if those hot heads had stopped firing! They say the Captain of the boat stopped and gave a warning. He said he would burn the town if the shooting didn't stop. I guess they didn't believe him! Anyway, I don't think you have too much too worry about since you live back off of the river."

Life went on as usual on the plantation. They didn't plant any cotton that spring because there was no market for it. They concentrated on growing food, grain and hay for the animals. Big Man was pleased. Everyone worked hard with few complaints. It was if they knew their life depended on these crops. It did!

At the onset of the summer, they began to hear more and more about the fighting around Vicksburg. They couldn't imagine the thousands of troops that everyone was saying were fighting there. Although this conflict didn't affect them directly, they couldn't stifle the fear that they were feeling. Then it happened. Vicksburg fell! Mr. Hardin rode out to give them the news.

He warned them to expect raiders. Sherman had just declared a policy to bring the South to its knees. He would live off of the land. This meant that his troops were allowed to pillage the plantations for food. He also allowed them to strip the Southern civilians of any valuables. When this was completed, they were to burn the houses!

Since most of the plantations were void of men, Sherman had declared war on the women and children of the South!

After the surrender of Vicksburg, Grant soon moved north to re-enforce Rosecrans' troops at Chattanooga. Sherman began his relentless move east. Before leaving Vicksburg, a decision had to be made about the captured confederate soldiers. Grant decided to parole most of them on condition that they would not take up the fight again. This was not a problem with the Rebels. The fight was taken out of them by starvation. They could see that the North was going to win the war. They just wanted to return to their homes, grateful to be alive. About all that the remaining Confederate troops left in the area could do was snipe at the Union troops moving toward the east. These attacks slowed the advance, but there were not enough Rebels to deter them.

Now that they were in control of the river, the Yankees turned their attention to the plantations up and down the river. Raiding parties were sent out to confiscate food, cotton and valuables. They were following Sherman's plan to live off of the land. In other words, they were to take all of the civilian's food for the Union troops.

It was a hot August day when a young man rode up to Mount Hope. Miss Jane had sent him to warn Mistress and the girls about the recent Union raiders' activities up and down the river. The Yankees were moving further and further out from Vicksburg as they slowly confiscated all of the available food. Big Man met him when he rode up and told Birdie to go fetch Mistress.

The young man said, "Miss Jane sent me to warn ya'll that the raiders will probably be here pretty soon. Several hundred of them have already hit Belmont. They took all of the cotton, mules, horses and livestock even down to the chickens. The only good thing was they didn't burn everything like them other raiders did to Mr. Hardin's place."

"Oh my goodness! Are you saying Mr. Hardin has been burned out?" Mistress said.

"Yes, Ma'am. Mr. Harden let them have all of their food and live stock without a fuss, but when they started ransacking his house, he protested. He tried to stop them from taking his wife's wedding rings and that is when they decided to burn his place. They burned it to the ground!"

"Are they all right? Where are they staying? What happened to their slaves?"

"Most of the slaves run off to Vicksburg. The Union is feeding them there. Someone said the Hardens are making do by staying in one of the tenant houses that didn't get burned. I really don't know. We just heard about what happened. Miss Jane is expecting the Yanks to come and clean Leota out at any time. We are about the only place on the river that they haven't hit! That's why she sent me out here to warn ya'll to hide everything you can. Them damn Yankees are looting and taking everything. They especially like jewelry. They always take the women's and men's watches. They say they don't turn a lot of the plunder in. They keep most of the valuables for themselves!"

Mistress immediately turned to Big Man and said, "Go get John and Jim! Ya'll hitch up the buggy and the wagons. Go get the Harden family as fast as you can. Bring them and everything they have left back here. Tell them that I won't take "No" for an answer. They are going to stay with us! Be careful and look out for the Yankees. If you run into them, they probably won't bother ya'll. Just be polite."

It was dark by the time the three men reached the Harden place. There were just a few slaves remaining. They were the house servants that were still loyal to the Harden family. The place was a sad sight. The big house and the store houses were burned to the ground. All of the livestock and chickens were gone. The Yankees had taken everything they could find that was edible. They had ridden their horses all over Mrs. Harden's flower beds, and the vegetable gardens. There were holes all over the yard where they had dug looking for buried valuables. When leaving, some of them had spitefully broken the spokes on the carriage wheels. The Harden's were completely ruined!

After receiving Mistress's invitation, the Hardens accepted gratefully. It was no time to stand on pride!

There was very little to load on the wagons. Man, John and Jim helped the family pick up any family heirlooms that they could find. There were a few supplies they had hidden and the Yanks had missed. After everything was loaded, they assisted the Hardens into the carriage. They then helped the old slaves onto the wagons. It was dark but they headed back to Mount Hope.

It was after midnight when the carriage and wagons arrived at the plantation. Birdie, Ole Tom the butler, and the three ladies were waiting. They all rushed out to greet the people from the Harden Plantation.

Mistress said, "I am so sorry about your troubles. I just want you to know that you can stay here as long as you need to." Becky said, "Where is Linda?"

Mr. Harden replied, "We sent her to some relatives close to New Orleans a couple of months ago. We thought it would be safer there. It looks like we made the right decision."

Mistress turned to Man and said, "Why don't ya'll find a place for these old folks to stay. When you get that done, just pull the wagons up into the barn. We can get them unloaded in the morning. We'll be getting the family settled in."

Birdie and some of the other help had already prepared a room for the guest. They had a big tub of hot water waiting in it. There were also some fresh clothes for them. The Hardens were so grateful. They hadn't been really clean in over a week. After cleaning up and putting on fresh clothes, they came down to the dining room where Birdie had a meal waiting. After eating, they couldn't wait to get to bed.

On the way they paused to thank Mistress again.

Mistress replied, "I am only doing what a Christian is supposed to do! You would have done the same for us!"

After the burning of the Harden's place, Big Man brought a mattress and placed it in the entry hall of Mount Hope. This is where he slept. He remembered what he had promised Buck. He meant to take care of the Inman ladies if at all possible. He didn't want anyone slipping in during the night.

For the next few weeks, Big Man made preparations to save as much of the Mount Hope livestock as possible. He did as Buck had suggested. He and the men drove most of the hogs, mules, cows and horses deep into the woods at the back of the plantation. They strung barbed wire to contain them. The chickens were put in homemade cages and hid. They took most of the grain and supplies and put them in the wagons. They covered each wagon with cotton. The wagons were also hid deep in the woods. They left a little stock and grain for the Yankees to steal so that they would be satisfied. Big Man had already instructed all of the slaves to wrap their meat in wax paper and sacks. They buried it and their canned goods in their gardens. Each family planted vegetables to cover the ground. This was about all that Big Man knew to do to keep the Yankees from stealing everything.

It was only two weeks after Man had finished the preparations that John and Jim came running up the driveway. They were all out of breath. 'Big Man! Big Man!" they were yelling. "De Yankees is coming!

The boys had been fishing at the end of the lake when they spotted the long line of Union troops. Taking a path through the woods, they ran for home. This gave Man a little time to warn everyone. He told John and Jim to go tell all of the former slaves to go inside of their houses and to not come out! He then went to confer with Mistress. They decided that everyone inside the Big House with the exception of Mistress would remain indoors with the doors locked. Mistress would sit in one of the rockers on the front porch and wait. Big Man sat on the steps, not knowing what would happen.

In a few minutes the Yankees came into view. When they turned off of the road, Man and Mistress could see two officers on horseback with a column of infantry following. Bringing up the rear were several wagons to be used to haul everything they would confiscate.

When the soldiers arrived, the young officer got off of his horse and introduced himself. "I am Ralph Pendergrass of the 24th Illinois Infantry. My orders are to go to every plantation north of Vicksburg and confiscate all valuables, food, and livestock that we can find. General Sherman has given orders that our troops must live off of the land. To that regard, I will give you and yours fifteen minutes to get everyone out of the house. My officers will search it while my troops gather up the live stock and grain.

Big Man stood up and said, "Sir, whut is we supposed to do for food?"

The Officer replied, "I really don't care. I guess you will be hunting and fishing. I am only worried about my comrades back in Vicksburg! By the way, what are you Nigras doing here? Don't you know that President Lincoln has freed all of the slaves?"

"He didn't have to free us. Our Master freed us a few years ago. Mister Buck don't believe in slavery."

"Where is this Mister Buck?"

"He be gone to fight in de war"

"If he doesn't believe in slavery, why is he fighting?"

'He say he is fighting to try and stop you Yankees from stealing and burning everything in de South!"

The officer taken aback said, "I thought all of the Nigras in the South were slaves and mistreated!"

"Most is slaves but they is not all mistreated. It depends on de master. De is some more free slaves down here but most of dem live in towns."

Having listened to this conversation, Mistress stood up, looked the young officer in the eye and said, "Let me tell you something Lt. PenderASS or whatever your name is. This is my home. You and your uncouth men will not enter it unless I invite you!"

The Yankee officer replied, "Look lady, we can do this easy or do this hard. The easy way is for you and your nigras to move out of the way and we will search your house! The hard way is for my UNCOUTH men to go in, ransack the place, and then burn it to the ground!"

Mistress said, "I am Mrs. John Inman, formally of Inman, South Carolina! My first cousin just happens to be married to General Sherman! He has spent many nights in my house! I don't believe he would think very kindly of you if you burned his wife's cousin's place. I suggest that you line up your thieving troops and march them back to where ever ya'll came from!"

Not wanting Mistress to think he was intimidated by her claim to kinship with General Sherman, the officer said, "The name is PENDERGRASS! Since all of these Nigras have been set free by your folks, I am going to spare this place. I know they all need something to live on since they won't be leaving for the Union lines like all of the rest of the freed slaves. There are plenty more plantations up and down the river that we can raid. Count yourselves lucky!"

After that exchange of words, the lieutenant called his men to attention and they headed out of the driveway just like they came in.

"You sho told him!" Big Man said.

Mistress almost collapsed as she returned to her chair. "I have never been so scared in my life! I am so glad he believed me about my relationship with General Sherman. You know what I told him was the truth. The General is married to one of my Yankee cousins. This is the first time I have been proud of the fact!"

The war years continued but Mount Hope was never invaded again.

24

Prison Life

During the early months of 1864, the winter brought a penetrating cold that Buck and the other Southerners were not used to. Although the two stoves in the barracks were kept going continually, it was never warm. The sickly Rebels were dying every day. Buck and the other able-bodied men dreaded waking up in the mornings. They knew that someone would have died during the night. They also knew that they would be assigned the task of carrying the dead out and burying them. This task and having to brave the weather to go to the latrines was what they dreaded the most.

By the time the weather finally broke in May, Buck had lost twenty pounds of his normal two hundred. Other prisoners that were not as healthy as Buck lost even more. Everyone was always hungry. The Union camp was simply not prepared for this many captives. Matters got even worse when the news of the starving Union prisoners in Andersonville, Georgia reached the North. In retaliation to the treatment of the Union prisoners, the ration of the rebels was cut even more at Rock Island Prison. The weak, sickly men continued to die.

With the arrival of the warmer weather of spring, the surviving prisoners started to recuperate. This is when the boredom set in. Buck was no different from the rest of the prisoners. Being confined with nothing to do was extremely depressing. Buck tried desperately to stop himself from succumbing to this feeling. The only way he found to fight this was to think of his family and Julie. He let his mind think about the good times that he had back home. He also wanted to be well when he did get out of prison. He wondered everyday where and what Julie was doing. The hope of finding Julie after the war kept him going. He had no idea as to how the war was proceeding. Listening to the stories of the new prisoners being brought in made him think that things were not going too well for the South.

Time passed, oh so slow, but Buck and the Mississippians survived 1864. They were able to make it through the winter and into the first months of 1865. By this time Buck had lost another twenty pounds. The others had done the same. Everyone was emaciated and eaten up with lice. They were barely hanging on.

One early February morning, Buck was in his bed trying to stay warm when he was disturbed by a commotion at the front of the barracks. The camp commander and several guards had entered. They made every Rebel prisoner stand up so they could hear the announcement.

"Men! I have come to inform you that the men in this barrack have been selected to participate in a prisoner exchange! You will be paroled in the morning. To participate, you will have to sign a pledge not to take up arms against the United States again! If you agree to these terms, come forward and sign these pledges that my men have. The ones that sign will be on a train heading south in the morning!"

Every rebel signed. They would have pledged anything to get out of the "Hell Hole of the North"!

25

Going Home

It was the first of March, and the cold wind was howling when Buck and his fellow prisoners boarded the freight cars for the ride south. They were dressed in their tattered clothes but each man had been allowed to carry a blanket with them to help ward off the cold. The prisoners were crowded into the cars with standing room only. In just a few moments, the car gave a lurch and they were on their way. It seemed as if the Yankees were as glad to get rid of these wretched men as the men were ready to go.

The cold wind penetrated every crack. The men next to the walls suffered the most. There was no room to lie down. They either slept standing up or squatting. They had to wait for the occasional stops to relieve themselves. Those that had dysentery and could not wait for the stops had no choice but to soil themselves. Soon there was a terrible odor of sick men, unwashed bodies and the soiled clothes. The stench and moaning of the sick was almost unbearable. The train ran day and night. Buck had no idea where he was. The only chance he had to look around was when they were allowed off of the train to relieve themselves. It was at these stops that the prisoners were given a piece of bread and water. Then it was back on the train and heading south. As they rode, there became a little more room as the poor fellows that died along the way were taken off.

They finally came to a small town south of Nashville called Franklin. Here they were let off of the train and met by a Union General and a company of soldiers.

The General told them, "You are south of Nashville, Tennessee." Pointing with his finger, he continued, "That is south! You are free to go. However, if any of you turn your face back north again, we will pick you up and put you back in prison. On your way, stop by that table over there and pick up your passes."

"But General, we ain't got nothing to eat!", one of the young rebels whined.

"That's your problem! You should have thought about that when you took up arms against your country!" the General replied.

After that remark, the Yankees turned and boarded the train for the ride back to Nashville. The Southerners were on their own. Soon everyone was making plans. Some chose to make their way up to Knoxville and cross the Blue Ridge there. The ones from Alabama and Georgia chose to head to Chattanooga where they would cross the Smokies and head home. Buck and his friends from Mississippi decided that the closet way home would be down the Natchez Trace that ran from Nashville to Natchez.

In a couple of hours, everyone had said their goodbyes. In some ways, it was sad parting. These men had been confined together for a year and a half and had become very close. They realized that they probably would never see each other again.

As everyone was departing, Buck and the Peacocks stood and looked at each other. Joseph said, "I ain't got no idy where we are!"

His father replied, " I ain't never been in these parts. I'm lost as a goose. I don't know whichaway is home."

Buck spoke up. "I pretty well know where we are. When I was riding with General Forrest, we raided and fought all up in here. If I'm not mistaken, the Natchez Trace is west of here about ten or twelve miles. I think it runs by a place called Lippers or maybe Leapers.

Anyway, it's a small town close to the trace. Once we find the trace, all we have to do is follow it south to Mississippi."

The Southerners looked like three Mexicans as they plodded along. They had torn slits in the center of their blankets and were wearing them like ponchos.

It was getting dark when they reached Leipers Creek. They decided to spend the night there along the bank. They chose a place back in the woods hoping that the trees and brush would help block some of the wind. They also wanted to be hidden from any Yankees that might be traveling the road. After eating the bread that they had been given on the train ride, they settled down for a miserable night. Although it was cold, they counted themselves lucky that it was not raining.

Since the conditions made it almost impossible to get any sleep, the trio was up early the next morning. Since they had nothing to eat, they started walking again. They were hoping that the exercise might help combat the cold. As the sun came up, things got a little better. The wind died down and it got a little warmer, but they were still hungry.

Just as they crossed the creek, Allan jumped down to the edge of the water. He reached down and picked up a rock. "I thought I recognized this. This is a flint rock. Man! If I just had a knife I could start a fire after this rock dries out."

Buck answered, 'You'll be surprised at what I have." He then pulled out an old Barlow knife that he had hidden. "I been hiding this knife ever since I was captured. Them Yanks missed it when they searched me. I had it stuck up in my long hair! I must'a been saving it for this."

Allan said, "That'll do the trick. When we stop tonight, I'll show you youngsters how to start a fire by striking this rock with the knife."

They started walking again. Just as they topped a hill, Joseph said, "Fellows, we might be in luck! I believe those are pecan trees that I see over yonder."

They turned off of the road and walked to the grove. Sure enough, there were native pecan trees lining a ditch bank. They started searching the ground underneath the trees for any nuts that the squirrels might have missed. They were in luck. Not only were there nuts on the ground, but there were a few clinging to the branches of the trees. Throwing limbs, they soon knocked all of the nuts to the ground. Although the nuts were not too large, they were rich in oil. The men ate their fill and carried the rest with them.

"I guess we know how the animals feel having to depend on these nuts to stay alive!" Joseph said.

With the sun warming them and their bellies full of pecans, the men felt better. They were soon moving toward the Trace again. Everything was going well until nightfall. The wind picked back up and it started to rain. The men were getting soaked. Allan said, "I don't guess we will be lighting a fire in this rain." Buck replied, "I think we ought to turn around and go back to that old barn we saw back up the road. At least we can get out of the wind and rain."

By this time, it was pitch black dark. They hurried back up the road and found the barn. When they got in it, they found some piles of hay scattered around. They lay on the hay and pulled some over them to help stay warm. Tired, they were soon sound asleep.

They woke the next morning to the sound of a screeching door. It was still a little dark but they could make out the figure of an old woman standing in the doorway pointing a shotgun at them.

"Ya'll put yo hands up! Who is You'uns?"

Buck getting up slowly said, "We don't mean any harm. We were just trying to find a place to get out of the weather. We didn't know there was anyone living around here."

"Where ya'll from? You look terrible."

Buck, not knowing which side of the war she was on, was hesitant to answer. He decided to tell the truth.

"Ma'am. We are some Southern men a long way from home. For the last year and a half we were locked up in Rock Island Prison in Illinois. We were captured in the battle of Lookout Mountain. The Yanks paroled us and put us out at Franklin. We've got to get home the best way we can."

"You poor fellows! No wonder you look a mess. I feel for you. My two boys were killed at Missionary Ridge. I don't know where they are buried. I just know that they ain't coming home. I guess ya'll are hungry. Come on up to the house and I will try to find you something to eat. Those thieving soldiers ain't left me much. 'Bout the best I can do is to make you some soup and corn pone. That's what I been making out on until I can put my garden in. I had my canned vegetables and taters hid up in the corn crib. The Yankees didn't find them but they took about everything else."

Allan said, "It sure will be a blessing to get something to eat. All they gave us when we got off of the train was a chunk of bread. We'll try not to eat too much. We don't want to run you out."

The old woman laughed as she said, "You won't run me out. The good thing about soup is that you can always add a little more water!"

Joseph spoke and said, "Maybe we can repay you by working up your garden spot so that you can plant it when it gets warmer."

"That sure would be a big help. I been dreading using that shovel. I just ain't as strong as I was when I was in my sixties!"

After eating and being full for the first time in over a year, the men started doing some chores for the old lady. The Peacocks took shovels and turned over the soil in her garden. They were lucky that the rain had stopped the previous night before the soil became saturated. While they worked, Buck spent his time chopping and splitting wood. After completing these tasks, the men were ready to head south again. The lady gave them directions to the Trace, which was quite near.

As they started to leave, the old lady brought out two sacks and a tin bucket. The flour sack was stuffed with men's clothes. The bucket was full of corn pones. The smaller sack contained a fish hook, a line of string and two bars of homemade lye soap. She told them that she wouldn't be needing the men's clothes. They had belonged to her sons. She said that they might be able to use the twine and hook to catch fish on their way. She said that they could use one bar of soap to bathe with and that they could cut up the other bar to use for bait. Allan agreed that lye soap made mighty fine bait. Buck thanked the lady profusely because he appreciated the fact that, although she didn't have much, she had shared with them.

"Will you be alright here by yourself?" asked Buck.

She replied with a grin, "Sure I'll be all right. Won't nobody bother me. I'm too poor to be robbed and too old to be raped!"

The men followed the directions given to them, and were soon on the Trace. The going was pretty difficult due to all of the rain over the past few weeks. They were surprised at the amount of traffic on the road. Wagons, carriages, horses and walkers-there were a lot of people traveling. Since the three men didn't know if the people they were meeting were friend or foe, they would try to ease off into the woods and let everyone pass. The fact that they didn't have any weapons gave them an uneasy feeling.

They slogged south for days. Along the way they became proficient at catching fish and building fires. They had even had one meal of rabbit. Joseph had spotted the rabbit easing down the ditch by the road.

He said, "Ya'll be still and I will try to hit that rabbit with a rock." He picked up several stones, and slowly tried to get closer. Just as he threw, the rabbit turned and headed for the woods. Joseph chased after him. He couldn't catch him, but he did see him go into a hole in a hollow tree. When his father got there, Joseph said, "Well, he got away. He went in that hole in that old tree."

Allan said, "We ain't going to give up that easy."

He told Buck to cut him a small limb and to split in on the end. The young men didn't know what he was up to. Allan took the limb and pushed it up into the hole until the split end touched the rabbit. He began to twist the stick round and round. The rabbit's hair, which was caught in the split, was soon wrapped tight. Allan slowly pulled the rabbit out. As soon as the back end of the rabbit appeared, Joseph grabbed it and Buck slit it's throat. They then roasted the rabbit over a small fire. They all agreed that this was the best meal they had eaten since they were captured.

As these proud men of the South trekked homeward, they were reduced to virtual beggars. One would not know by looking at them that they had marched bravely off to war with the sound of bands in their ears as they carried their fluttering flags. They didn't even think of how the Southern ladies had waved their handkerchiefs at them and clapped as they left for battle. They were now starving, defeated men. Although they had exchanged the prison garb for the clothes that the old lady gave them, they still looked like tramps in their ill-fitting garments.

They were able to catch a few fish and field mice as they walked. This was not enough to sustain them. They had to swallow their pride and ask for food from the residents along the road. They always offered to work in exchange of food. This helped assuage their pride. Since they were getting farther south, most people wanted to help them. The problem was that almost all of the farms had been raided during the battles. The locals didn't have much to share.

After weeks of travel, they ran into a larger obstacle. The Tennessee River! When they saw it in the distance, they did not know how they were going to get across. They just knew that they had to cross it. There was no way around.

They hesitated to go down to the bank. They could see a company of Federal troops stopped next to the ferry. Having no other choice, they walked down to the soldiers.

The captain, who had been talking to the ferryman, turned to meet them. "Halt and tell me who you are!" he demanded.

Buck speaking for the three said, "We are paroled prisoners from the Rock Island prison in Illinois. We are on our way home."

"And where is home?

"They are from the hill country next to the Tombigbee River. I am from the delta country north of Vicksburg.

The Captain said, "I thought you 'uns looked mighty funny. Where in the world did you get those clothes?"

"A kind old lady gave them to us. I know they don't fit, but if you had seen what we left prison wearing, you could understand why we were glad to get them.

"You are supposed to have papers if you are paroled!"

247

Buck said, "We got them right here.", and handed the Captain the parole papers.

After looking over the papers intently, the Captain said, "Everything seems to be in order. Just don't let me catch you doubling back. You just keep heading south."

All of the time this conversation was going on, the ferryman was standing by listening. He was a light-skinned Indian with both Scottish and Chickasaw blood running through his veins.

This mixed breed was a Colbert, a descendant of the Scotch trader, James Logan Colbert who had taken many Chickasaw wives. His father was the son of the Scotchman. He was also a Chickasaw chief and his family had controlled this ferry crossing since the early 1700s.

Buck, swallowing his pride, walked over to him and said, "I guess you heard our conversation. We are paroled prisoners, and we have no money. We don't want anything for nothing. Can we do some work for you to secure passage across the river?"

Colbert looked at Buck and said quietly, 'I really don't like them blue coats with their high and mighty attitudes. I tell you what. I'll just charge them a little extra to pay for your passage." Then, with a grin he added, "That is if you don't mind the Yankees paying your way."

Buck replied, "Anything you want to do will be fine with us. We just want to head home and get away from these Union soldiers."

"I know how you feel. The Union has never treated my people very well," Colbert replied.

After collecting the Yankees fare with a little extra for the Rebels, Colbert soon had them on the other side. As the troops rode off, the Captain said, "Remember what I told you. Don't turn back north!"

"He ain't got to worry about that. I've seen enough Yanks to last me a life time!" Joseph said.

The trio kept moving south. The weather began to change in their favor. They were starting to have a few warm days along the way. This was a welcome respite from the cold. The soles of their shoes were wearing out, so they stuffed leaves in the bottom to try to make them last longer. As the weather warmed, they had a chance to bathe every once in a while. They thought that they would never get really clean again.

After walking for days, they went by the edge of Tupelo, Mississippi. The Peacocks started to recognize where they were.

"Buck, we are in Mississippi!" Allan Peacock said. "Our company fought all around here. We are not too far from Corinth and Shiloh. I sure don't want to stop anywhere around here. I've seen too many good men lose their lives in this area. If we have to walk day and night, let's move on away from here!

Buck said, "I didn't sign up until after the Battle of Shiloh, so this area isn't too familiar to me. I heard that thousands lost their lives at the battles of Corinth and Shiloh."

Joseph said, "I don't even like to think about it. Thousands of men lined up charging each other. There were cannon balls ripping all through our lines. Rebels and Yankees were falling everywhere. As we charged, we had to jump and step on bodies. Some were dead, others were just wounded. I can hear their moans and cries for help every night when I try to sleep. I was so scared that I would have probably turned and run but I knew the officers in the rear would shoot anyone who retreated without orders!"

With the weather moderating, the men made better time. Since the Peacocks knew they were getting close to home, they were walking as fast as they could. Buck was just trying to keep up. The last night the men spent together was in the vicinity of Greensborough. While camping out that night, Allan told Buck, "I guess we will be leaving you in the morning. We live about ten or fifteen miles from here out on Ebenezer Creek. From here on out, we'll be all right. We are bout kin to everyone around here."

Buck said, "I wish I was that close. Do you have any idea how far it is to the town of Kosciusko? That's where I will be turning west."

"I would guess about fifty or sixty miles. You'll pass by French Camp first. Then just keep on going. You'll run right into the town."

The men got up early the next morning. It was a beautiful Spring day. After an emotional goodbye and with promises to come visit each other, the men parted ways.

It felt strange to Buck to be by himself. He had been in the company of the Peacocks ever since being captured nearly two years ago. The faith of those two men had helped sustain him during the trying times of the past two years. They had never wavered in their belief that God was going to deliver them safely back home. Buck had admired Allan when he said, "I believe that God is going to sustain us and return us home. However, if He doesn't, I am willing to accept His will."

As Buck plodded along, he was overtaken by a man traveling by himself in a surrey. Pulling his horse to a stop, he asked Buck who he was and where he was going. Buck told him his usual story about how he had been captured and imprisoned at Rock Island. He added that he was trying to make it home.

The gentleman introduced himself. He was Colonel Drane. He told Buck that he lived close to French Camp and was returning home from Greensborough where he had gone on business. He related that he, too, had been captured near Nashville. He had been paroled about two months earlier. He invited Buck to ride with him. Buck sure was glad to have a ride. It seemed that he had been walking forever.

As they rode along and talked, they found that they had fought over the same parts of Mississippi and Tennessee. Colonel Drane took an instant liking to Buck. He was particularly interested in the stories about General Forrest.

When the surrey reached French Camp, Colonel Drane told Buck that he lived west of the hamlet. He was planning on turning off there but had decided to carry Buck on to Kosciusko. He said that was the least he could do for a fellow soldier that had suffered so much. He added that he had a brother living there that would be glad to lend Buck a horse so that he could complete the rest of the journey on horseback.

Upon arriving at Kosciusko, Colonel Drane introduced Buck to his brother, Captain Robert Drane. Being a parolee from Vicksburg himself, Captain Drane was sympathetic to Buck's plight. He and his family took Buck in for the night. The first thing they made available was a good hot bath. After the bath, Buck felt really clean for the first time in years. They then sat him down to a good meal. Buck tried to be polite and not eat too much, but he couldn't help himself. He ate and ate. His host knew how he felt. He had come home starving from the siege of Vicksburg.

Colonel Drane had decided to spend the night with his brother. After supper, the three men gathered in front of the fireplace with the Dranes smoking their pipes. The two brothers quizzed Buck about Rock Island Prison. Everyone had heard about how many Rebels had died there, many of them Mississippians.

Buck entered into the conversation as long as he could, but drowsiness soon overcame him. Watching the flames flicker in the fireplace made him so sleepy that he could hardly stay awake. He asked if he could be excused to go to bed. The captain told him that he certainly could and showed him to a small bedroom off to the side of the house. Buck slid in between sheets for the first time in over two years. The weary young man tried to say his prayers as he lay there, but he was unable to complete them. He went sound to sleep!

The next morning Buck sat down with the Dranes' for breakfast. Mrs. Drane had used her limited resources to cook her guests a large country breakfast. Colonel Drane told Buck that since this area of Mississippi was made up of mostly small farms, the Yankees hadn't raided here very much. The only serious raid was when they came down from Pontotoc to burn the tanning plant at Bankston.

Captain Drane said to Buck, "I understand that you need a horse to get home on. I have one that you can use." Buck replied, "I sure would appreciate it. I will be glad to pay you for the use when I return it."

"That's not going to be necessary. The horse that I am going to let you have is old and not worth anything, but she'll beat walking. You won't have to worry about returning her."

Buck stood up wearing the clean clothes that the Dranes' had given him. "If it is all right, I would like to be on my way. I am kinda anxious to get home."

After Buck thanked the ladies, the three men walked back to the barn. The Captain brought out an old gray saddle mare. "She was a good'un in her day, but she is kinda like me, getting old!"

After shaking the hands of his benefactors and thanking them, Buck mounted up and headed home.

The old mare was not real fast, but she had an easy gait. The Captain had sure been right, Buck thought. Riding sure beat walking.

As he traveled west, the way started looking familiar. He followed the road through the hilly country until he reached the small town of Lexington. He thought about the time that he had brought Big Man and the wagon train past here. It seemed so long ago.

After going around Lexington, the old mare kept a steady pace. Buck could tell that she had been a good horse in her younger days. He let her take her time. Although he was in a hurry to get home, he didn't want to push her too hard. Moving steadily, they finally reached the Delta. Buck gazed out over the vast stretch of flatland while he rested the mare. After the rest, he mounted up and headed down the long hill toward the Delta. He was hoping to make it to The Barr's. He was hoping to spend the night there. As he traveled, he noticed that everything had changed since his last trip. The immaculate fields now lay fallow. As he passed the plantations, the slave quarters were empty. Some of the barns, homes and storage houses stood empty. Others had been burned. Without the slave labor, many of the plantations were desolate. He thought about how the field hands had joked with the wagon train Nigras as they passed by long ago.

He realized that he wasn't going to make it to the Barrs' by nightfall. He turned the mare into a driveway that led to an old plantation home. The whole place was empty. Some of the windows were broken out and the front door swung on one hinge. Buck could tell that vandals had pilfered the place. There was broken furniture and torn books scattered everywhere. The house had the pervasive smell of mildew that old houses have when left empty-with the roof leaking. He decided that he had rather sleep outdoors.

He bedded down under a large magnolia tree. He could tell that it was over a hundred years old. It's massive branches reached out until they touched the ground and then curved back up again. He was glad that he had made this choice. The smell of the tree and the fresh air was a whole lot better than the air in the house. He hobbled the mare so that she could eat her fill. She had consumed plenty of water at the bayou before they got there. Buck ate some of the provisions that Captain Drane's wife had so kindly provided and went fast to sleep.

After a small meal the next morning, he saddled up and was on his way. Although everything was desolate, it was a beautiful morning. Spring was in the air. He could hear the mocking birds singing and the rat-a-tat-tat of the Redheaded Woodpeckers. He even thought that he had caught a glimpse of the orange breast of the male Blue Bird as he looked for a nesting spot for his mate. He started looking for Hummingbirds. He thought that there might be some early ones about the budding fruit trees. He decided to dismount under a large oak tree and pray to God, thanking him for his being alive on this beautiful morning. He could see God's handy-work everywhere he looked.

Remounting, he started for the Barr's again. He was looking forward to visiting with them for a short time while the mare rested. He was also hoping they might have a little something for him to eat.

It was not to be! When he reached The Barr plantation, it was just as desolate as the one where he spent the night.

The difference was that the Barr house was gone. Burned to the ground! The lawn was grown up and the fences torn down. Buck decided to look around to see if he could find anything to eat. His first stop was the corn crib. Someone had emptied it. Buck suspected it had been the Yankee raiders. Searching under some corn stalks, he did come upon a few nubbins to feed the mare. He then made his way to the potato cellar. He pulled up the door and then jumped back! There were two sets of eyes peering at him out of the darkness. After flinging the door all the way open, he was able to make out two old Nigras hiding in the corner.

"Come on out of there; I ain't going to hurt you!"

The old slaves slowly emerged, looking Buck over as they came out.

"Who are ya'll and what are ya'll doing hiding in the cellar? Where is Mr. and Mrs. Barr?"

Realizing that this white man knew the Barr's, the old slaves relaxed.

"We wuz hiding in de cellar cause we thought you might be another one of dem Yankees. You know de killed Mr. Robert. He tried to stop dem from stealin" he belongings and dem bad Yanks shot him tween de eyes! Then de stole everything and burned up de house!"

'Where are the rest of the slaves and Mrs. Barr?"

"Mrs. Barr wern't here. She be gone to visit her sister over in Atlanta. De rest of dem sorry Nigras followed de soldiers when de rode off. De was hollering, "We is free!" We stayed to bury Mr. Barr. We wuzn't able to make no long walk anyway. We been about the only ones here on de place for over a year. We been staying out yonder in dat old barn."

"How ya'll been eating?"

"We been making out. We plants a garden every year and I be pretty good at trapping rabbits and squirrels. Is you hongry?"

" I sure am. Have you got anything to spare?

"We sho does. Old woman, why don't you cook dis white man a mess of dem poke salad greens? I'll skin dat rabbit I caught dis morning in the trap and we will have us a meal. You'll have to drank just water. We ain't got nothing else. We is glad that ole well is still working."

"That sure sounds good to me. While ya'll are getting that ready, I'll go over to the well and draw up some water for us and the mare," Buck said.

After sharing a meal with the two old nigras, Buck made his bed under a huge oak tree. It wasn't like sleeping in his bed at home, but it was a lot better than sleeping in the stinking prison. As he was going to sleep, he thought about how life for him had changed in the past few years. Who would have thought that one of the richest men in the South would be sharing a meal with two old slaves in a barn and be glad to get it. Times had changed!

Before Buck left the next morning, he asked the two old slaves what their plans were. The old man replied, "We don't really knows. We ain't got nowhere to go so I 'spect we'll stay around here until someone comes and runs us off. You knows dis have been our home all our lives. We ain't never been off dis place."

Buck answered, "I would take you with me but I know you can't walk very far. However, I'll tell you what . . . if you want me to, when I get home and if I have anything left, I'll send a wagon back for you and you can live on my plantation. But you got to remember this might not be possible. Like I said, I don't know what I am going to find at my home."

"Yas, Suh. If you could send for us, we'd be mighty obliged. We'd work for you as best we could. You wouldn't be sorry."

"We won't worry about the work. I am going to repay you for sharing what little you have with me. If I can, when I reach my plantation, I promise that I'll send for you!"

Riding toward home, Bucked looked back at the old slaves standing under the tree. He was reminded again why he had never liked slavery.

Buck knew that he was going to have to rest the old mare along the way, but he was determined to reach Mount Hope even if he had to ride all day and all night. As he rode, he couldn't believe the changes in the countryside. Some of the plantations that hadn't been raided were still limping along. The slaves on these plantations had no idea that Lincoln's Emancipation Proclamation had freed them. Unless the South lost the war, they never would be free. Even if the plantation slaves had heard that they were free, they wouldn't know what to do or where to go. That was the reason so many slaves remained on the plantations after the war was over.

This is what greeted Buck at Wayside. The ladies there told him that the Yankees had raided their plantation with hundreds of soldiers. They confiscated thousands of bales of cotton that the Worthington men had stored before going off to war. The Union soldiers had loaded everything they could find onto river boats. Although this raid had left them destitute, at least their homes were not burned.

Buck decided that it must have been left to the officers of the raiders to decide whether to burn homes or not. That must be why some places were burned, but others were not. Some officers were kind enough to leave the southern ladies somewhere to live. Others burned with a vengeance!

It was almost dark when Buck reached the upper end of Lake Yazoo. He knew that he had only a few more miles to go to reach home. Although he was in a hurry to get there, he knew better than to push the old mare. He had to be patient and let her amble along.

26

Buck Arrives Home

"Big Man! Big Man! De is a ole man on an ole gray hoss coming up de road. He looks like one of dem tramps!"

As usual Jim had been fishing on the lake north of the plantation. Big Man had told him and the other nigras to come get him if any strangers showed up. When Jim spotted the stranger, he had " hightailed" it home.

Big Man and Jim walked to the front of the house and waited. In about fifteen minutes they could make out in the dusk, a man on an old horse moving slowly toward them. Jim said, "I wonder who dat ole man is?"

Big Man answered, "Probably some ole white man dat's lost his plantation and be looking for something to eat!"

Buck was unrecognizable to the two nigras. The ill-fitting clothes that he had been given barely covered his skinny frame. His hair hung below his shoulders. He had a foot long beard. His eyes peered out at the two men from a gaunt face.

When the horse stopped, the rider said, "Hello, Big Man!"

Big Man didn't recognize the man but he recognized the voice.

"Is dat you, Mr. Buck?"

"Sometimes I wonder myself, but it is me," Buck replied.

"Praise de Lord. We bout give you up for dead," Man said as he reached out to Buck. 'Jim, go get Mistress. Tell her Mr. Buck has made it home!"

In a few minutes pandemonium broke out on the plantation. Mistress, the girls, Justin and the house servants came pouring out of the big house. Word spread like wildfire across the plantation!

MR. BUCK IS HOME!

Everyone coming out of the Big House had questions for Buck. Mistress grabbed him and hugged and hugged him. In her mind, he was still her baby boy!

"Where have you been? What happened to your fingers? What prison were you in? How'd you get home?" The questions were thrown at him faster than he could answer. He said, "Wait, wait. If you will just let me go get me a bath and something to eat, I'll tell you everything you want to know."

Mistress said, "I am so sorry. Of course you must be tired and hungry. Birdie, ya'll go heat up Mr. Buck a big tub of hot water. Lay him out some of his clean clothes. Ya'll can burn the ones he has on. When you are through doing that, go to the kitchen and start supper. Buck you just go and enjoy your bath. Take your time. Supper will be ready when you come out."

"Birdie, see if you can round up me a razor and a pair of scissors. I can't wait to get some of this hair off of me."

"Cut off what you can and I will give you a shave and haircut in the morning. I have become good at cutting Justin's hair," Becky said. Buck didn't reply, but looked at her quizzically. What was she doing cutting Justin's hair?

While Buck was soaking months and months of grime away, Mistress and Birdie planned the menu. Jim had brought over the fish that he had caught. They were all catfish, about a foot long. The lake teemed with them in the spring. He brought enough fish to feed twice the number of people in the house. Birdie knew what he wanted. He was hoping to get the leftover fish. He loved Birdie's fried catfish. Birdie told him, "You go and get Big Man. Ya'll can skin these fish for me. When ya'll get through, just set here at the table. After I serve the folks up front, ya'll can eat all you want."

After Buck got through bathing, shaving and cutting his hair, he resembled more of his old self. He went to the dining room to meet with the rest of the household.

Birdie and her help had prepared a meal of catfish, corn pone and mustard greens. As the members of the household sat down, she said, "Mr. Buck I is ashamed of dis meal. I know it ain't nothing like what I use to cook for you. I is got you some cold milk though. I knows how you use to love it. We been kinda' making do since you been gone."

Buck got up and went over and put his arm around her and said, "Birdie, Birdie! You don't have anything to be ashamed of. This is a meal fit for a King. It is so much better than what I have been eating for the last three years. All the way home I've been thinking about your cooking."

Birdie beamed. She said, "Just you wait. I is going to put some meat back on yo bones!" "I sure do need some," Buck said with a laugh.

Before they ate, Mistress asked everyone to join hands and thank the Lord for answering their prayers for Buck. They had been praying for his safe return.

The household sat around and talked and talked. Buck told them all about his experiences of the last three years. Birdie, Big Man, Jim and the household help listened spellbound in the kitchen. The only thing that Buck didn't go into detail about was his time in prison. He was trying to put those painful memories out of his mind.

Buck then turned the subject to Justin. He asked where he had served and where he was paroled from. Justin told him that his service had not been nearly as exciting or as hard as Buck's. He had been assigned to a unit on the Gulf coast. He was stationed at the fort on Ship Island. He said his unit was supposed to protect the port of Gulfport from Yankee ships. He said they saw very little action until Admiral Farragut arrived. He said that the Union outnumbered them so badly that they had to surrender. He and the rest of the Southerners were held as prisoners on the Island. He said that prison life wasn't too bad. There just wasn't much to do but sit there and look at the water. They were allowed to go swimming in the Gulf on occasion. He said that this and the gulf weather allowed the prisoners to stay clean and healthy. The Union had paroled all of the prisoners on Ship Island about six months earlier. He had been allowed to go home.

Justin could see that Buck was getting tired. He said, "Come on Becky, it is about time for us to go to bed."

Buck 's head snapped around and he looked intently at Justin. Mistress said, "Don't get upset, Son. Becky and Justin were married right after he returned home."

Buck relaxed and said, "I am surprised, but I am glad to know that they are married if they are sleeping in the same bed! I know things have changed but I didn't think they had changed that much!" Becky and the rest of the family laughed and laughed. After a few minutes, Buck joined in. He then said to Becky, "Tell me about your marriage."

Becky said that her wedding was not anything like Buck and Julie's. It had been a nice simple affair at the church in Leota. There hadn't been too many people there with all the men absent and so many women gone to live with relatives. She added, "It really didn't matter if the wedding was small, the most important thing is that we love each other and we are married."

Mistress joined in, "As soon as this horrible war is over, I am going to give them the nicest reception that has been held in this area." She could afford to. All of her money was in the banks up north and not tied up in the worthless Confederate currency.

Buck was tired. He excused himself so that he could retire to his room. Even though he was tired and glad to be in his own bed, he couldn't go to sleep immediately. This room and bed held so many memories. His thoughts turned to Julie. He wondered where she was and how she was doing. He promised himself that as soon as the war was over, he was going to go find her no matter what. He had killed many a man these last three years, and if he had to, he could do it again. He was going to bring Julie home!

The next morning after breakfast Buck walked over and sat down with Man on his front porch. The two old friends sat and talked as if Buck had only been gone a few weeks instead of years.

"How have ya'll been making it? Why aren't we burnt out like so many other plantations that I passed on the way home?"

"Well, Mr. Buck, we sho been blessed. I did everything jest like you told me. I put the stock over on the other side of de woods. They been making out mighty fine. In fact dem pigs is producing like crazy. De love eating and rooting around in dem woods. We been having plenty to eat cause I did like you say and hid all dem seeds. We been planting corn and gardens every spring. Along with the fish, turtles, alligator tails and a few rabbits, we been making out mighty fine. We ain't been planting any cotton cause there ain't nothing to do with it even if you have a good crop.

"You mean to tell me that there haven't been any Yankee raiders out here!"

"No Suh! I didn't say that. They come out here about a year after you left. Dem Yankee officers come riding up the driveway just like de owned de place. De had a mess of foot soldiers following them. Mistress met them at the door. De say de was going to search de house. You should have seen yo mama. She got right in front of dat white soldier and told him dat none of dem was coming in HER house! When she got through telling him bout how her cousin wuz married to General Sherman, he left just like he come. Ain't none of dem Yankees ever been back!"

"That's my mama. She's never been scared of anybody or anything. In fact, she scares most folks. What else went on?"

"Well Suh, not too much. Mr. and Mrs. Harden stayed with us for a spell after de got burned out. After a couple of months, de left for some of de kinfolk's house. Since then it be mighty quiet except for the weddings. Miss Becky married Mr. Justin bout five months ago and Jim and Fanny got hitched last month."

"They told me about my sister's wedding, but are you telling me that Jim and Fannie are married?"

"De sho is. I married dem myself. I reckon Fannie was about ready to settle down. Jim been begging her to marry him forever."

"How are they getting along?"

"Mighty fine. Fannie tells Jim what to do and he do it. Dat makes Fannie happy and if Fannie happy, Jim happy!"

Buck said, "You'll never know how much I appreciate the way you took care of my family while I was gone."

"You know Mister Buck, I promised you that I would take care of everything. We IS family!"

Buck then told Man about the two old slave that he had met. He instructed Man to send a wagon after them. He wanted to keep his promise.

27

Life Goes On

Although life on the plantation wasn't like it was, it was a lot better than other places. The weather had broken and spring was in the air. The fruit trees were blooming and the trees were starting to leaf out. Everywhere you looked you could see that the birds had returned. Over in the woods, there were new calves and pigs being born. You could hear the wailing of new babies born by some of the young Nigras. Everyone was preparing the soil for their crops and gardens.

With his hair and beard trimmed and more weight, Buck was starting to look more like the owner of Mount Hope. Birdie had done what she had promised, she was fattening him up. With improved health Bucks spirits improved also. After several weeks, he told his family that he would like to attend church in town the next Sunday. He had been slipping in the back of the church that Big Man founded each Sunday. He was surprised at the depth and passion of Man's sermons. He could see the fruit of the Pastor's labor. Many of the former slaves had become committed Christians.

It was a beautiful spring Sunday morning when Buck had the carriages brought around. He had asked John and Jim to drive the family to church in Leota. It was a gay trip as they rode through the countryside.

When they arrived at the church, they were greeted warmly by the now small congregation and the elderly pastor. Buck was surprised at how few males were in attendance. He then realized that, with the exception of a few parolees like himself, there were no men.

The rest of the men between twelve and sixty had been impressed into Confederate service. Now, he understood the significance of all the battle deaths. So many of the men that had left so bravely to fight for the South would not be returning home. They had died by the thousands all across the South. It was a strange feeling standing around with mostly women. Buck was impressed again with how blessed he was to have made it home.

After the service the family decided to go and eat at Miss Jane's. On the way, Buck told them to let him off at the livery stable. He wanted to visit old Tom. He got out of the carriage and walked around the stables to Tom's house. Tom almost fell out when he saw him.

"Is that you, Buck Inman? I heard you wuz dead!"

"I came close to dying several times, but I made it!"

They talked for a little while and then Tom said, "Come out here to the stable. I got something to show you." When they walked into the stable, they heard the neighing of a horse. As Buck's eyes adjusted, he could make out the head of a large horse protruding over one of the stall gates. Could it be? It was! Prince was staring at Buck and whinnying. The big stallion knew exactly who Buck was.

Almost speechless, Buck said, "How in the world did Prince get here? I lost him in battle way up in Tennessee. I thought I would never see him again!"

Tom explained, "There was a Yankee Captain riding him when he came through here. Said he found him after a battle in Tennessee. I recognized Prince at once. I traded two horses for him. He didn't want to give him up, but when I added several gallons of moonshine to the deal; he traded."

"I'll pay you for your trouble the next time I come to town," Buck said.

"Don't you worry 'bout that. I just appreciate all of the business you gave through the years. Before you came to town, I was barely making it. You just go ahead and take your horse. I been saving him for you. I was hoping that you would make it back."

"I sure am grateful. However I'm still going to pay you. I'm just glad you out—traded that Yankee like you used to do to me! "

Tom just grinned.

Buck saddled up and rode Prince up to Miss Jane's. As he rode up the street, he saw that many of the stores were boarded up. The others didn't look too prosperous.

He tied Prince up and walked into the cafe. The ladies had prepared Miss Jane for Buck's appearance so she didn't start her usual talk about how good looking he was. She just told him how glad she was to see him.

Miss Jane told them that she didn't have a very large menu but she was glad to have their business. Times had been hard for her since so many people had left. In fact, she said she was doing her own cooking. Almost all of her help had left. The war was affecting everyone in the South.

Over a modest meal Buck told them about finding Prince. Everyone was pleased. They knew how much that stallion meant to Buck. They were thankful that old cantankerous Tom had thought enough of Buck to go to that much trouble.

After eating, the family headed back to the Lake. Buck led the way, riding Prince. The big stallion had already recovered from his ordeals of war. Tom had taken real good care of him. Although corn was scarce, Spring had brought an abundance of grass. Prince was fat and frisky. He eagerly carried Buck toward home.

28

The War Ends

It was the second week of April, 1865, and Buck had decided to ride into town. He was craving a chocolate cake like Birdie used to make for him when he was a boy. He was hoping one of the river boats might stop and have flour on board. He had hidden away both Confederate and Union currency. He carried some of both. He didn't know which the trading boats would accept.

When he got close to town, he could hear the church bell ringing. He thought that maybe something was on fire. He kicked Prince up into a canter and headed for Leota. When he got there, he found the townspeople milling around in the street. He spotted Tom and rode over to him.

"What's going on, Tom?"

"Haven't you heard? Lee just surrendered in Virginia! THE WAR IS OVER!"

The citizens of Leota were so excited by the news. Many thought that everything would return to normal. They hadn't realized how the South was devastated. Homes were burned. Fields were grown up. Many of the slaves were gone. Bridges were destroyed. Factories were burned. Railroads were torn up. Public buildings were gone. The greatest loss to the South had been the thousands and thousands of men who would not be returning! The South had lost much of her manpower.

They didn't know that they would be living in a military district presided over by Federal troops. They wouldn't have believed that they would be living in an era where former slaves with the help of the Yankees would be in charge of the political system-a time when no veteran or supporter of secession would be allowed to vote. A time when former slaves, scalawags and carpetbaggers held all of the elected offices. A time when their property would be auctioned off to the carpetbaggers because they couldn't pay their taxes. Their way of life was gone. The South went from being one of the wealthiest areas of the nation to one of the poorest. States like Mississippi and cities like Natchez, who had more millionaires per capita than any place in the United States before the war, would never recover.

Buck and his family were one of the fortunate ones. He had seen the war and its effect coming. Although he bought some Confederate bonds and currencies to support the war effort, he had transferred a lot of his money abroad. Mistress's kin had placed her funds in banks up North. Buck still had his gold buried in the lake. Again, he would be one of the wealthiest men in the state.

Buck rushed back home to tell everyone the news. THE WAR WAS OVER!

The next few weeks were spent getting things back to normal on the plantation. They brought the stock back from the woods. Their canned goods and preserved meat came out of hiding. Buck and Big Man had a good laugh when Mistress told them to dig up her garden so that she could recover her silver and valuables. They couldn't believe the women had secretly buried everything by themselves.

The big project was retrieving the heavy bell filled with gold out of the lake. Over the years, it had broken through the hardpan of sand and was held firmly by the mud of the lake. They tried digging and pulling to no avail. Buck then had an idea. He sent for a large pole, a large chain and four mules. They secured the chain around the bell, and leaned the pole against the chain in the direction of the bell. The mules were hooked to the chain. As the mules began to pull, the pole began to slowly stand up. The result was that the bell came out of the lake with a sucking sound. The mud didn't want to let go.

Big Man said, "I sho thought we was going to have to get two more mules."

Buck replied, "I was afraid that the pole would break. If it hadn't been oak, I believe it would have!"

They rolled the bell up on a slide and pulled it into the blacksmith shop. The rest of the Nigras were wondering how that bell got in the lake. The next morning, when everyone had gone to the fields, Buck walked down to the shop. He and Man went inside and shut the door. Taking chisels and mauls, they soon had the concrete off the bottom of the bell. There was Buck's gold. Man, with Buck's assistance, loaded the gold into a large trunk and then loaded it onto a wheelbarrow. Man rolled it up to the Big House. When they got the wheelbarrow into the entry hall, Buck told Man that he could handle everything from there. After Man left, it took him several trips but he got the gold to his hiding place.

They spent the next day building a stand and mounting the bell. The big bell tolled over the plantation once more. It got everyone's attention when the clappers struck. Everything was returning to normal on the plantation.

29

The Return

Buck had decided that he needed to go to the telegraph office to see if he had any correspondence. He told his family he would be back before night. They were used to him riding off alone. When he thought of Julie, he still had bouts of depression. During those times, he wanted to be alone.

The May weather was beautiful. There was still a feel of Spring in the air. Buck dreaded the hot weather that he knew would arrive in June. As he rode, his thoughts turned to Julie as usual. He thought about her every day. He kept trying to formulate a plan to go get her. He assumed that since the war was over, she would no longer be under control of her brother. This was the purpose of his trip. He had telegraphed his lawyer to find out the status of slaves. He was hoping that he would have a reply at the telegraph office.

When he arrived in town he was hungry. He decided to have lunch at the Southern Inn. As he ate, Miss Jane brought him up on all of the local news. People were returning home to try and rebuild their lives. She told Buck that she felt so sorry for them. Buck told her that since he had so many hands on his place, maybe he could be of help. He told her that he would bring that up when his family attended church the next Sunday.

Feeling full, Buck decided to walk down to the telegraph office. Just as he got there and stepped up on the porch, he heard the sound of a steam whistle. The Delta King was pulling to the dock. He decided that he would go down and see what provisions the boat might be carrying.

Buck was surprised. Stepping off the boat was the most beautiful lady that Buck had ever seen. She was about twenty-four years old. She had a slim waist with long curly hair hanging down her back. Her light olive complexion shined in the noon sun. Her dress, shoes and parasol matched perfectly.

Walking faster, Buck started in that direction.

COULD IT BE? Buck's mind could hardly comprehend that thought! It was! It was Julie! With the war over, she was FREE!

When she spotted Buck, she started running toward him. Buck began running to her. When they met, not a word was said. Buck swept her into his arms and kissed her lovingly. As he was holding her, he looked over her shoulder to find himself looking into the eyes of a beautiful little girl who was hiding in the folds of her mother's dress. In Buck's excitement in seeing Julie; he hadn't noticed the little four year old girl. With the exception of her long hair, she was a carbon copy of Buck.

Buck stepped back as Julie said, "Buck, I want you to meet your daughter, Georgia Susanna Inman!"

The End

ABOUT THE AUTHOR

TROY CRAWFORD WOODS, JR.Businessman and Educator

BS, Business Administration; M ED, Secondary Supervision

The author grew up in the small delta town of Cleveland, Mississippi. Although a business major at Delta State University in Cleveland, his interest in history caused him to minor in the subject. He later received his Masters in Education ;Secondary Supervision. While serving as an administrator, he always found time to teach his passion, Southern History.

The author married his high school sweetheart, Ann Inman while in college. They are the parents of four children and fourteen grandchildren. They lived in Cleveland and were in business there until they bought and restored an antebellum home named Mount Holly. (another story) This fourteen thousand square foot house is located on Lake Washington in the Mississippi Delta. It is listed on the National Register of Historic Homes. The family lived there for twenty years until they sold it. They now reside in Flowood, Mississippi.

The author's early interest in history and genealogy caused him to converse with many older people through the years, both black and white. Some of their stories are included in this historical novel. Some of the war experiences are based upon the actual experiences of his ancestors.

It is hoped that the reader will come to understand what a complex society that the people of the South lived in before and during the Civil war.